TRIAD BLOOD

Praise for *Light*

"What's stunning about this debut is its assurance. In terms of character, plot, voice, and narrative skill, Burgoine knocks it out of the park as if this was his tenth book instead of his first. He, along with Tom Cardamone, has the considerable gift of being able to ground the extraordinary in the ordinary so that it becomes just an extension of everyday life."—*Out in Print*

"Burgoine's initial novel is a marvelously intricate story, stretching the boundaries of science and paranormal phenomena, with a cast of delightfully diverse characters, all fully nuanced and relatable to the reader. I honestly could not put the book down, and recommend it highly, as I look forward to his next novel."—Bob Lind, *Echo Magazine*

"*Light* manages to balance a playful sense of humour, hot sex scenes, and provocative thinking about the meanings of individuality, acceptance, pride, and love. Burgoine takes some known gay archetypes—the gay-pride junkie, the leather SM top—and unpacks them in knowing and nuanced ways that move beyond stereotypes or predictability. With such a dazzling novelistic debut, Burgoine's future looks bright."
—*Chelsea Station Magazine*

"*Light* by 'Nathan Burgoine is part mystery, part romance, and part superhero novel. Which is not to say that *Light* emulates such 'edgy' angst-filled comic book heroes as the X-Men; if you'll pardon the pun, it is much lighter in tone."
—*Lambda Literary*

By the Author

Light

Triad Blood

TRIAD BLOOD

by

'Nathan Burgoine

A Division of Bold Strokes Books

2016

TRIAD BLOOD

ISBN 13: 978-1-62639-587-9

This Trade Paperback Original Is Published By
Bold Strokes Books, Inc.
P.O. Box 249
Valley Falls, NY 12185

First Edition: May 2016

CREDITS
Editor: Jerry Wheeler
Production Design: Stacia Seaman
Cover Design by Jeanine Henning

Acknowledgments

This book came very much from all the people who contacted me saying how much they enjoyed the characters of Luc, Curtis, and Anders (especially Anders), and so to everyone who took the time to do so, a hearty thank you. You gave me the courage to leave my comfortable short-fiction cocoon and delve back into the realm of novels a second time. I hope you enjoy your time with them as much as I have. The sharp-eyed of you will notice there are some familiar character names in the book. Each of those is meant as a truly heartfelt thank-you. Tuckerization: it's the new fruit basket.

As always, major thanks to all the editors I've ever worked with. Every single time I work with an editor, I learn something valuable. I wouldn't be where I am without each and every editor I've been lucky enough to work with. Extra thank-yous to Jerry and Stacia and Cindy this time around. You rock.

Now last time, my acknowledgments changed my life.

No, really. I've always been a cat person. My husband has always been a dog person. So when I tucked in an agreement to get a dog at the end of the acknowledgments in *Light*, I wasn't sure what would come of it.

I'd honestly not really thought many people read the acknowledgments. Given how many emails I got about the acknowledgments from *Light* after it was released, however, I no longer have that illusion. Many of you asked if my husband had seen the agreement. Trust me, everyone told him to check them out. Poor guy was inundated with demands he drop everything and read my acknowledgments.

To answer the most common question I've received since: Yes. We rescued a dog (a husky named Coach) in April of 2014. My life is completely different now, and I have completely fallen for His Fuzzy

Lordship. It's true what they say: You don't only rescue them. They rescue you.

But, getting back to the reality that these are my acknowledgments? I'm feeling a little bit of pressure here. I have no grand gesture to offer my husband Dan this time.

Well, I mean beyond reminding him how much I love him and how I could not be living this amazing creative life without him.

There's still that.

Always that.

For my fellow booksellers,
be you coworkers from the last couple of decades or not.
You guys were my family when I had none.

PROLOGUE

A vampire, a demon, and a wizard walk into a bar," Anders said. "If that's a joke," Curtis said, "please tell me the punch line is 'and they lived happily ever after,' okay?"

"That wouldn't be very funny," Anders said.

Luc barely fought off an affected sigh. "Anders," he said. "We can't stand out here all night." Anders looked menacing in his plain black sleeveless shirt. He crossed his arms, and Luc paused to admire the play of muscle below the tanned skin.

"Sure we can," Curtis said. Though he was smiling, a false note was in his cheerful voice. "It's a nice sidewalk. Lovely night, too."

"Come," Luc said. He put a hand on the young man's shoulder. "We need to test if what you've done—what *we've* done—will work." *And if it doesn't, at least inside there will be too many witnesses for us to be attacked.*

Curtis exhaled. "Okay." He slid on a pair of thick black-framed glasses. They had no prescription, Luc knew. The wizard had enchanted the lenses to help him see the true natures of others. Curtis claimed the glasses were how he'd realized Anders was a demon and Luc a vampire.

Given everything else Curtis had managed to do so far, Luc saw no reason to doubt him. He was very new to the world that moved in the darkness around him, but he was talented.

But talented enough? Luc squeezed the young man's shoulder again, then let go. *Let's find out.*

❖

"Two gin and tonics," Luc said.

The bartender turned, met the vampire's gaze, and shivered. The bartender was shirtless, and Luc remembered him well from a previous encounter. In fact, this was the same bartender who'd been serving drinks the night Luc had met the other two. Luc released his glamour, feeling it dance between them like a cool autumn breeze. The bartender nodded. Swallowed. "Two G and T's." It took him a moment to move, then he seemed to come back to himself and poured the two drinks. Luc smiled as he realized the bartender was sneaking glances at him while he poured. The bartender was not a gay man, Luc knew, and his confusion over the attraction he felt was palpable. The scent was a delight.

Luc took the drinks and paid with a generous tip. The bartender swallowed again, sliding the toonies into the front pocket of his tight jeans.

Luc left the bartender there, enjoying the lingering trace of his scent. Aroused prey, with a heady mix of sweat and sex, was always better. The vampire looked for the other two and saw they had taken the same seats they'd had the night they'd all met, weeks earlier. He joined them, sliding the two glasses in front of them.

"You're not having anything?" Anders asked.

"I think he's having the bartender," Curtis said. Luc winked at him.

They waited, tense. It was not a full moon. In the past month, they'd done everything they'd needed to do, according to Curtis's research. Luc had shared blood with them. Curtis had woven a magical rite as complex as it was beautiful. They'd also had a very athletic evening "bonding" with Anders as well—it was no surprise that the incubus joined with sex. *If Curtis is right, we'll know soon enough*, Luc thought. *If he's wrong…*

Well.

"One of your kind," Curtis said, glancing over Luc's shoulder at the entrance. The lenses of his enchanted glasses glinted in the dim lights of the bar.

Luc turned. He knew the lean, tall vampire, a member of the largest coterie in the city. The blond curled his lip in distaste, and he walked confidently to the table, smiling in a way that seemed less amused and more cruel. Luc tried to remember his name, but couldn't. It wasn't surprising, since he'd had to hide from the other vampires since he was alone.

No longer, Luc thought, just as the newcomer arrived at their table.

"This place is mine," the blond said without preamble. "Leave. Now." Luc felt the will born of the vampire's coterie swarm against his skin, demanding his obeisance...

...and dissipate.

"*Non,*" Luc breathed. He smiled and let his fangs show. "We're staying right here." Then, feeling a rush of pure freedom, Luc added, "You leave."

Something happened. Curtis gasped, Anders grunted, and Luc slammed his own will into the blond vampire. The blond stumbled back a single step, a stunned look on his once haughty face. He opened his mouth, shivering, but said nothing. Luc met the blond vampire's gaze again, and this time, actively called upon his will. It gathered quickly, snapping into place with a force he couldn't believe. This was not just vampire. Nor was it demonic, or magical.

It was *more*.

Luc leaned forward, building his will until the pressure between his eyes was almost painful, and then he repeated himself. "Leave." His will struck out like a thing alive.

The blond vampire nearly tripped over himself scrambling back and didn't stop once he'd reached the other end of the bar. He was nearly running by the time he pushed through the doors and into the street.

Curtis stared at the door, his mouth open.

"I'd call that a success," Luc offered.

Curtis turned to him, his mouth still slack. Anders grinned and raised his glass.

"To not being alone," the demon said.

Curtis, still looking dazed, laughed and raised his own glass.

"If you'll excuse me, gentlemen," Luc said, looking back at the bar. The bartender blushed and looked away. "I need to go see about my drink." The words were spoken plainly, though with amusement. Luc had had more years than he cared to admit to perfect his disaffected tones. Inwardly, though, there was a word he wanted to scream as loud as he could, propriety be damned.

The word was *freedom*.

CHAPTER ONE

I am awake, Luc thought. *And that is sunlight.*

Luc stood at the top of the stairs, the threshold of the kitchen, content to watch the last of the red-orange glow that bathed the room creep along the floor. For a brief time he simply waited. The light of a sunset was no better to his kind than that of the highest point of noon, but he enjoyed seeing this moment in time and knowing it belonged to him.

Then the demon showed up.

"Lurking again?" Anders asked. He tossed a small pile of papers Luc assumed was the mail onto the kitchen table. Then he turned one of the kitchen chairs around backward and sat, crossing his arms and resting them against the back of the chair. Anders wore his usual plain sleeveless shirt, faded jeans, and a cocky smile that bordered on a smirk. Luc imagined the demon would be heading out soon to leech off the soul of some young, lustful trash.

"There are a few more minutes of daylight left," Luc said, though he knew Anders knew this well enough.

"Aww." Anders's smile was far from sincere. "Poor vampire."

"Hardly," Luc said.

The demon opened his mouth to say more, but then their third came in from the hall and stifled a yawn on the way.

"I take it we've begun the bickering part of the evening?" Curtis said. He rolled his shoulders and turned his head to the left and right. He had obviously gone for a run after his classes. Luc pulled air into his lungs and caught the scent of sweat just below the plain soap Curtis must have showered with at the university.

"How were your lessons?" Luc asked. Despite feigning nonchalance to Anders, he did feel a little foolish lurking at the top of the basement stairs, waiting for the last of the sunlight to fade.

Curtis passed by Anders, stopping to touch the demon's shoulder and kiss him on the top of his head, and then met Luc at the top of the stairs. Curtis leaned past the last few moments of the day's light into the shadow and kissed him on the lips.

"They were great," Curtis said.

Allowing the tip of one fang to show, Luc smiled. "You taste like magic, *lapin*."

"I get that a lot," Curtis said. He returned to the table and sat beside Anders. He looked at the table. "This the mail?"

Anders grunted. It wasn't an eloquent sound, Luc thought, but then again, nothing about the demon ever seemed cultured to him.

Curtis looked at him. "What's wrong?"

"He gets a kiss, I get a peck on the head?"

Luc didn't bother trying to hide a smug smile.

"Seriously? You two are worse than Mal and Jayne sometimes," Curtis said.

Anders stared at Curtis blankly. Curtis leaned back.

"Malcolm Reynolds? Jayne Cobb?" Curtis stared. "You don't know the hero of Canton? Captain Tight Pants? *Firefly*?"

Anders shrugged. Curtis looked at Luc, but the vampire could only shake his head.

"Wow. I can't believe I kissed you guys."

"You didn't kiss me," Anders said.

"You are such a big baby," Curtis said, but he leaned forward and when they kissed, Anders grabbed the back of Curtis's head and made it last longer than the kiss Curtis had shared with Luc.

Luc felt the last moment of sunlight pass. He knew the night truly began when a shiver of coolness spread through his body, so he joined them at the table.

Curtis leaned back, obviously having enjoyed the demon's kiss, and picked up the first letter. His expression soured. "Ugh."

"What's wrong?" Luc asked.

"It's the Realtors again. You'd think they'd get the hint." Curtis tore the letter in half without opening it.

"Realtors?" Anders asked.

"It started right after my parents died. Vultures. I get letters asking me if I'd like to sell. I assume they watch the obituaries. I guess a lot of people sell when their folks die." Curtis picked up the next envelope and handed it to Anders. "Yours."

"Payday." Anders folded the unopened envelope in half and slid it into the pocket of his jeans.

"You have a job?" Curtis said. He paused, holding the next piece of mail.

Anders shrugged.

"Really?" Curtis pressed. "Like a real job? For grownups? What is it?"

Luc waited for the demon to answer, but Anders just shrugged again.

Curtis shook his head. "Huh." He looked at Luc. "He has a job. Did you know that?"

"I didn't," Luc said. "I assumed he pilfered the wallets of his street trash."

Anders rolled his eyes. "You're both fucking hilarious." He reached out and grabbed the envelope Curtis was holding. "Occupant. I'm an occupant."

He slid his finger under the flap, and the letter burst into pale yellow-white flames. They flared out from the envelope and up Anders's wrists before the demon had time to react. Drawing on his vampire grace, Luc threw himself back from the table and leapt for the sink. Flame, like sunlight, was something better kept from a vampire's skin and invoked an instinctual fear. The world seemed to slow to a crawl around him. Still, the flames were moving quickly, even as he opened the cupboard beneath the sink and tugged out the fire extinguisher.

Sounds caught up to him, distorted by the blood-fueled speed. Anders yelling. Curtis speaking—loud, and with fear, but also with purpose.

Luc turned back to the table. He tugged out the orange plastic ring, aimed the small canister, and fired. He felt the limits of his grace being reached, the world winding back up again as his body slowed back down to mortal speed.

He sprayed directly into the pale flames clinging to the demon's arms, but it barely had any effect. The flames crawled their way up his skin, twisting ropes of thin flame lashing higher with tiny clawlike swipes, pulsing and hissing against the stream of foam.

The scent of burning flesh filled the air.

"Dantibus aere!"

Luc glanced to Curtis. The young man had pulled back from the table when the envelope had erupted, and now he was holding out one hand and casting. He met Luc's gaze and nodded fiercely.

Luc kept the spray on Anders and the flames slowly reduced. They'd climbed up to Anders's forearms, but between the white foam and the effect of the words Curtis was chanting, the strangely bright fire was dying now.

"Dantibus aere," Curtis repeated, clenching his fingers inward, arm outstretched. Snaps and sparks of static electricity danced between his fingers, and the air in the room began to whirl. To Luc's keen hearing, it seemed almost like the flame cried out—a keening whimper. Anders growled and snarled as twists of the yellow-white fire flared in a last rush toward his biceps, but held his hands still. *"Ignem extinctum, dantibus aere,"* Curtis said again, triumphant. He closed his fist. The room echoed with a small thunderclap loud enough to make Luc's ears ring, and he saw the fire struggle valiantly once before being pulled violently away from the demon's arms in all directions.

The flames snuffed out.

Anders closed his eyes. "Fuck."

Luc stepped forward. "Your hands?" He couldn't tell how damaged they were underneath the white foam.

"Hurts like a fucking sonofabitch, but..." Anders hissed. He rose slowly. "Can you turn on the sink?"

"That...That..." Curtis was panting. "That was balefire."

Luc turned on the taps. Anders took a deep breath, then put his hands under the water. The foam washed away, and both his hands were covered in bloody red burns that glistened sickly, but Luc knew at a glance that the demon would be okay despite the pain. Fire was no real threat to a demon, and demons healed fast.

"That was balefire," Curtis said again.

"What the fuck is balefire?" Anders asked, gritting his teeth as the cool water ran over his skin.

"It's..." Curtis shook his head. "How did they get that into the house?"

"Curtis?" Luc asked. The young man was wide-eyed and pale. This wasn't the first time they'd been attacked, and Luc knew the young man had worked hard on the wards he'd put in place on this home. It had belonged to Curtis's parents. Curtis had inherited it, but the home had been theirs for less than five years before they'd died. It didn't have a strong aura of residency, and this breach had obviously shaken the wizard.

"If that had been you or me..." Curtis said. Luc nodded.

"Wasn't that much fucking fun for me either," Anders said. "In case you wondered." He turned his arms under the water and swore again. "Do you know how fucking hot something has to be to burn me?"

"Are you okay?" Curtis asked. He stepped up to the sink and sucked in a breath at the sight of Anders's burned hands. Luc saw the extent of the damage. Already the demon's forearms and hands were covered in white, weeping blisters. Anders was right. Whatever balefire was, it was beyond hot if it burned the demon.

"I'll be—*Fuck!* That stings. I'll be okay," Anders said. "It'll heal fast enough. Fuck!" He exhaled and moved his hands under the cool water. More of the blisters burst.

Curtis gagged.

Luc put a hand on Curtis's shoulder. "What did you do?"

"Fire needs oxygen," Curtis said. "Even balefire. I pulled all the air away from his arms."

"Clever." Luc smiled. "But you always are. Now, what's balefire?"

Curtis met his gaze. As Luc had hoped, turning the topic to magic calmed him down. "It's a kind of lesser elemental—not sentient, exactly, but...instinctual. Like a predatory plant, but made of flame. It only burns flesh and bone. I've never seen one before, but I'd read about it. It takes some serious fire magic to bring balefire about, to make a seed. And I have no idea how you'd turn it into a..." Curtis gestured at the kitchen table, where not even the faintest of scorch marks were visible.

"Letter bomb?" Anders offered. He flinched as he twisted his forearms under the spray again, but already Luc could see the crimson flesh was losing the sickly, burned shine. Where the many blisters had already burst, the burned skin was sloughing off.

The demon would use a lot of power to heal from this, Luc thought. Luckily, their triad meant Anders had the reserves to do so.

"Right," Curtis said. He laughed, but Luc heard no mirth in it. "A magic letter bomb."

"What did the envelope say?" Luc asked.

"It just said 'Occupant,'" Curtis said. "I figured it was junk mail." He eyed the rest of the pile, now spread across the table from the burst of wind he'd conjured. Curtis went back to the table, reached out a hand, and spread his fingers apart over the scattered flyers and envelopes.

"Nothing else feels off," he said. He brushed the small pile, spreading them more evenly across the table top, though he avoided the swath of foam from the extinguisher. "It was a plain envelope. These aren't much different, but none of them match. Oh, hey. One for Luc," Curtis said, and slid one envelope, cream and addressed with handwriting, to the side of the table.

Luc joined him and picked up the letter.

"No, no, I'm good," Anders said. "Really. You guys do your thing."

The other two ignored him. Curtis glanced around and even checked under the table. "There's nothing left of the envelope it came in. That's even more magic. Balefire shouldn't have burned the paper. That was a seriously clever piece of work. That amount of fire magic… that's demon-level stuff, but with the finesse of a major wizard."

"Really. I'm okay," Anders said. "Already healing."

Luc looked at the letter again, turning it over carefully. Beyond his name and the address, it offered no clue.

"You feel no danger?" Luc asked.

Curtis squinted again, muttering under his breath and concentrating. A moment later, he shook his head. "Nothing magical about that at all. It's safe." He looked at the foam all over the chair, tabletop, and floor, and exhaled. "I guess I'll get a sponge."

Luc nodded. He readied another burst of vampire grace just in case, but nothing happened when he opened the envelope. He pulled out a single sheet of richly crafted paper, folded in thirds. He opened it up, and as he started to read, he realized Curtis hadn't been entirely right. It wasn't magical, no. But it was anything but safe.

"We've been invited to a *séance*," Luc said, and all his decades of practice failed him. His voice shook.

❖

Once Anders's hands had healed, they sat around the table again, foam mopped up, the invitation lying open in the space between them.

"So. A *séance*," Curtis said.

Luc stared at the open piece of paper. "Yes."

Anders leaned forward. "Like with a ouija board?"

Luc blinked. "Pardon?"

"Earth to Luc. Do we have a problem, Houston?" Curtis said. Luc regarded him blankly. "Right, if you don't know *Firefly*, probably NASA references aren't going to fly, eh?"

"I remember that," Luc said. "I saw it on the television." With an effort, he gathered his thoughts. "A *séance* is a meeting. There are no ouija boards." He paused. "I've only ever been to one, and it was..." He smiled. "A while ago."

"A vampire meeting?" Curtis asked.

Luc nodded. "Yes. Whenever a new coterie forms, or a new coterie moves into a new territory, the ruler calls for a *séance* and the order of dominance is established."

Anders smiled. "Sounds good to me."

"Not that kind of dominance," Luc said, and a trace of his frustration snuck through.

Curtis said, "Like that other vampire at the bar, back when we first made the triad?"

Luc nodded. "It's similar. Each coterie leader brings their two most powerful subordinates with them, and if they desire, they attempt to influence each other to make a kind of..." Luc raised a hand, looking for the right term. "Pecking order, I suppose. It's all part of maintaining the *lignage*."

"Okay," Curtis said. He didn't seem to have made the connection, Luc saw. The wizard must be tired. He was normally quite insightful.

It was Anders who got it. "Oh shit."

"Indeed."

"What?" Curtis asked.

"His two most powerful subordinates." Anders repeated the term in a mocking version of Luc's French Canadian accent. Then the demon turned to Curtis. "Guess who gets to be the two lesser flunkies?"

"Oh." Curtis swallowed. "But we're not vampires." He looked at Luc. "Are we invited?"

"A *séance*—like so many other things—requires three."

"Great," Anders said, his voice heavy with sarcasm. "Can't think of anything better than chatting with a bunch of bloodsuckers all night."

Luc cleared his throat. "That's something else. I would prefer it if you didn't speak at all." He caught Anders's gaze, and added, "At the *séance*, I mean. Either of you."

"Well, that doesn't sound ominous at all. Why?" Curtis said.

"We'll be speaking as one," Luc said. "It's a tradition. Small talk, of course, would be permitted—"

"Gosh, thanks," Anders muttered.

"But anything more than that could be dangerous. Anything you offer, agree to, or request would all be the same as if I had spoken the words. That's one of the reasons picking the right second and third for a *séance* is such an art."

"Except you've only got us," Anders said. "Which means you've already got the best."

Luc didn't dignify the demon with a reply.

Curtis rubbed his eyes. "When is it?"

"Two nights hence."

Curtis groaned. "Of course. Right before I have a paper due. That's it. I'm going to bed. No more disasters until morning, okay?" He got up from the table.

"Good night, *lapin*."

Curtis gave him a brief smile for the nickname and leaned down to kiss his head. He did the same to Anders, and then left, yawning.

Anders held out his hands. The flesh was still pink, but his tan and the dark hair on his forearms was already recovering. He lifted one palm, and golden white flames crackled into being.

Luc watched the fire dance a moment. "A demon at a *séance*," he said.

Anders smirked. "Burn, baby, burn."

"There will be no babies. And I've had quite my fill of fire tonight." Luc rose. He had a lot to organize and little time to do it. Also, he needed to feed. The vampire graces took effort, and it took blood to restore the speed he'd used. "But yes, vampires are quite flammable."

Anders closed his fingers, snuffing the flame. "Lucky I opened that bomb."

Luc nodded. "Yes."

Anders stretched. "Well, if I'm going to hobnob with a bunch of bloodsuckers, I guess I need to go find me some willing meat. Better be in top shape." He winked.

Luc smiled at him, and it had the desired effect. Anders stopped talking.

"For once, we agree," Luc said. "Go fuck anything that moves. I want you as strong as you can be."

As he left the kitchen, Luc took a little bit of pleasure in the silence that remained behind him. A speechless Anders was always to be treasured, even if it was small consolation in the face of what they'd be facing two nights from then.

CHAPTER TWO

L uc was at the top of the kitchen steps again, waiting for the last of the sunlight to fade. The deep red light was molten across the floor in front of him, and he made a conscious effort to remain still. Some part of him he'd thought was long gone wanted to see that light play on his skin, even just for a moment. But his flesh would scald quickly, and he could not afford to be healing a wound tonight.

So lost in thought was he that he didn't hear Curtis until the young man came in through the door that led to the backyard. Curtis wore a pair of navy running shorts and a T-shirt proclaiming he had "bent his wookiee." Luc had no idea what that meant, but the shirt was stuck to Curtis with sweat. Curtis was breathing heavily, and his skin gleamed in the last rays of the day. Luc watched him, noticing his frown and how much he'd obviously pushed himself on this evening run. Through the bond he shared with Curtis, Luc could also feel the wizard's preoccupied worry at the back of his mind, a sensation a little like the cool autumn breeze no doubt rustling the trees outside. Curtis poured himself a glass of water, gulping it down. He shivered.

"Late in the year for shorts, *lapin*," Luc said.

Curtis jumped, then smiled. "You're up," he said. He glanced at Luc, then looked back outside. The sun was setting, but the last of the light in the sky sent long beams across the kitchen floor. The same light played across Curtis's skin.

"*C'est magnifique*," Luc said.

Curtis's shifted his gaze out the window again. "It's very red. Sailor's delight."

"Yes." Luc smiled at him. "The sunset is also nice."

Curtis blushed. He put the glass in the sink and leaned back against the counter. Curtis moved with a restrained grace that Luc thought rare in youth—a fallout of his wizardly ability, Luc knew—but it was Curtis's smooth skin, tempered by the sun on his long runs, that made him beautiful. His legs, especially.

"You were running a long time?" Luc asked, looking down to Curtis's calves, which were firm.

"Yeah," Curtis said. "Helps me focus." He shivered again. "It's not summer anymore, that's for sure."

Gooseflesh sprang up across Curtis's arms. His face was calm, but Luc could still feel the young man's worry. Since forming the triad, sensing these glimmers of emotion from Curtis and Anders was almost second nature to him. Understanding where the emotion came from, however, wasn't always as obvious. Though Luc could guess.

"Are you prepared for tonight?" Luc asked.

Curtis nodded. "Anders and I went to the tailors first thing. The clothes you ordered were all ready. I've been reading and preparing as best I could all day."

"I'd prefer you well rested for this."

"I napped before the run." He refilled the glass. He took a big gulp of water, then looked down, avoiding Luc's gaze. "Which reminds me. At this meeting, the *séance*. I read that sometimes at the older *séances* there were offerings—as in, someone for everyone to…uh, take from." He paused, looking back up at the vampire. "That wouldn't be me, right?"

"You think I'd let strangers take you?" Luc arched an eyebrow, and he smiled. Curtis's skin reddened. *He is such an easy blush.* Luc hardened, and knew it would be obvious in the simple cloth pajamas he was wearing. Sure enough, Curtis noticed.

"That's, uh…not quite what I meant." He glanced out the window again, and Curtis's smile was more than a little coy. "Huh. Looks like the sun went down."

Luc was on him in a blur, and Curtis jumped but smiled when Luc gripped his waist.

"Seriously, though—" Curtis said, but Luc silenced him with a kiss before tipping his head back and licking at his Adam's apple.

"Don't worry, *lapin*," Luc said. "It is the host who provides. Even so, it is only done for special occasions." Luc didn't explain that the "offerings" often didn't survive the night. Curtis had grown up quickly, owing to his magical background and rough entry into the true world around him, but he had a gentle soul. Luc wasn't going to be the one to disabuse him of any more illusions than he had to.

Curtis put his glass down on the counter and slid his hand down between them, cupping the vampire's obvious arousal.

"Someone woke up happy," he said.

Luc kissed his throat, and Curtis shivered. Luc slid his hands up the young man's side, pulling the T-shirt up and exposing Curtis's narrow waist.

"I need a shower. I'm all sweaty," Curtis said, but he didn't stop Luc's hands.

"Then there is nothing lost in getting all the messier beforehand," Luc said.

Curtis raised his arms, and Luc pulled the shirt over his head. Pressed chest to chest, Luc basked in the heat from the young man's body and lowered his lips to Curtis's neck, kissing him where his suntanned skin lightened near his shoulder. The taste of his sweat was a tease.

Curtis rolled his head back, exhaling. Luc flicked his tongue at Curtis's skin, and Curtis pressed against him. Curtis slid his hands down Luc's back, reaching beneath the loose cotton fabric of the pyjama bottoms and squeezing Luc's ass.

"You have the most amazing butt," Curtis said.

Luc lifted just enough to put his lips next to Curtis's ear. "Thank you, *lapin*." He wrapped both arms around the young man, cradling Curtis's ass in kind. "As do you."

Curtis laughed and then gasped as Luc lifted him bodily off the counter. Luc turned and carried the young man from the kitchen to the hall, then up the stairs and into Curtis's bedroom. He tipped Curtis back onto the bed and stood over him.

"Have I mentioned how awesome that whole vampire strength thing can be?" Curtis said, grinning up at him.

Luc hooked two fingers into Curtis's shorts and tugged. Curtis rolled onto his side enough to let them slide free, and Luc threw them carelessly behind him, enjoying the sight of the lean naked body in front of him. Luc took air into his lungs and caught the scent of Curtis's musk, which was light despite the young man's protestations earlier, but undeniably masculine. Curtis's cock, as lean and slender as the young man himself, was already hard, and the young man stroked it leisurely with one hand.

Luc stepped out of his pyjamas and smiled as Curtis's eyes traveled down his body and stopped at his half-erect dick. "What else do you like about vampires?" Luc asked him, teasing.

"I like sucking them," he said. His face blazed red.

Luc stepped forward, bending his knee and half climbing onto the bed. Curtis shifted, opened his mouth, and then Luc felt the warmth of the young man's lips against his shaft. He moaned in pleasure, watching as Curtis licked the base of his cock first, then groaning louder when the young man took him farther into his mouth and teased beneath Luc's foreskin with his tongue. On reflex, he couldn't help but buck a little against Curtis's mouth.

Curtis slid his free hand up between Luc's legs, gripping as much of Luc's ass as he could with his splayed fingers, and pulled him, letting him know it was welcome. The pleasure ran up through his body, and he felt his fangs ache in that delicious way, their sharp points sliding free.

Not for the first time, Luc allowed himself to enjoy Curtis's mouth. He'd once heard Anders tell Curtis that he was a born cocksucker, and Curtis had agreed—blushing furiously. It was true enough.

Curtis swallowed him deeply, and as Luc felt his entire length encased in the young man's warm, wet mouth, he exhaled sharply and ran one hand through Curtis's hair. *"Tu es magique."* Luc's fangs were extended now, and he had to fight the urge to bite his own lip as Curtis began bobbing faster on his dick.

"Curtis," he warned, but in answer, Curtis sucked all the more vigorously, the fingers of his splayed hand urgent and strong. Luc tipped over the edge, and he bucked forward as he filled Curtis's mouth. He felt the man's first swallow, and the sensation was such a welcome heat that he pushed forward, eager for more. Curtis didn't disappoint.

When Curtis had licked and swirled a little more, Luc pulled away. Curtis looked up at him, skin flushed and panting. He worked his own cock steadily, and the redness of his blush darkened and spread to his neck, a sign he was close.

Luc climbed over him and lay on the bed, then hooked the young man under his arms and pulled him until he lay over him. He wrapped his arms around Curtis and squeezed just enough to make the young man gasp, then held him from behind, sliding his hands up and down Curtis's smooth skin, teasing a nipple, tickling a thigh. The scent of his blood was overwhelming, and the urge to bite was all-consuming. A wizard tasted particularly rich to a vampire, the magic in their blood like something twice alive.

"Okay," Curtis said, and his breath was short and choppy.

Luc cupped Curtis's chin and tipped his head to one side. As he bit down into Curtis's exposed neck, the young man cried out a soft noise from the back of his throat, and as Luc swallowed a single mouthful of blood, he felt the heat of Curtis's come spray across the arms that held him.

❖

After, Luc licked the wound closed. They showered together, enjoying the warm water, and then Luc sat on a chair in a towel and watched Curtis dress. Curtis unzipped the tailor's bags and pulled out each piece carefully, stepping into the gray linen pants and raising his eyebrows as he zipped up.

"They're very light," he said.

"They suit you."

Curtis smiled and pulled on the shirt, buttoning it. The shirt fit perfectly. He rolled his shoulders and turned to the mirror after he did up the last button. As Curtis put on his tie, Luc thought of the kind of cultured life Curtis had grown up with. Curtis tied a double Windsor without the slightest struggle. He tugged the silver silk tie until the crease was balanced, then pulled on the jacket.

Luc nodded. *Parfait.* It was an elegant and understated look for an elegant and understated man. The dove gray jacket matched the linen pants, and the crisp whiteness of the shirt seemed all the brighter against his tanned skin and hazel eyes.

"I don't think I've ever worn gray shoes before," Curtis said, lacing up the dress shoes. "I feel like I belong in the deep South, sipping on a mint julep or something." He mugged a face in the mirror. "I have always relied on the comfort of vampires."

"Light colors flatter you," Luc said. "And the colors are as close to the dress robes of wizards gathering for a coven moot as I could come up with. I want to remind them of who you are."

Curtis did a double-take in the mirror. "You're right. It's the same color as my robes. I hadn't noticed."

"What jewelry are you planning to bring?"

"The oldest things I own are my great-grandfather's gold cufflinks, but I don't think gold would match this outfit. I might just go with my silver rings and my white leather and silver bracelet. They're not old, but I made all of them, which makes them unique."

Luc smiled. "You paid attention."

"Hey, when you said we had to go meet with a dozen vampires, I figured it behooved me to pay attention." His smile was wan. "Anders and I are going to be the only ones there with a pulse. You said elegance, antiquity, and uniqueness. I can do that."

"I fucking can't."

They both turned.

Where Luc had dressed Curtis in pale grays and whites, Anders was covered in darkness. The suit was black, as was his tie, and the shirt was the dark red of a rich wine. His large, muscular body filled the suit perfectly. His face and bearing, on the other hand, clashed with the expensive suit. Anders loomed in Curtis's bedroom door, looking more like a hired thug than a dinner guest. With his full jaw of stubble, the dent in his nose, the deep brow over his dark eyes, and the obvious awkwardness with which the tie had been crookedly knotted, he couldn't have looked less elegant had he tried. Even his hair displayed his complete lack of any grooming sense. Anders was attractive—as an incubus, there was no way he could be unappealing—but while this masculine look was definitely a draw in its own way, Anders appeared rougher around the edges than when Luc had first met him many years ago.

"I think you look hot," Curtis said.

Anders leveled a glare at him. "I look stupid," the demon said.

"You look refined," Luc said. It just didn't "fit" his form. He regarded the demon. "Perhaps this evening you could allure yourself differently."

Curtis looked up. Anders frowned at Luc.

"How much *can* you change yourself?" Curtis asked. Luc could tell this was not a question that had just occurred to their wizard. Their abilities fascinated him. He would ask them questions for hours, were they in the mood to answer. No doubt Anders was rarely in that mood. Anders shrugged. "It depends on who I pick." Then the incubus looked at Luc. He took a breath, closed his eyes, and *changed.*

It was subtle at first. Anders's nose straightened. His chin narrowed, and the stubble vanished as though time and his beard growth reversed. Anders ran a hand through his hair, and it became straighter and fell into a tidy style. When Anders opened his eyes, he appeared darker, his hair closer to black than brown, his eyes a deeper shade. His features remained masculine, but cleaner.

Classier.

Luc approved, of course, and wondered if the demon's allure spread to the taste of his blood. For a brief moment, he wondered if they had time for the three of them to explore this new version of Anders on Curtis's bed. Then he remembered what was in store for them all and shook his head. Anders's looks had caught his attention and distracted him. But that was an incubus's gift.

"Wow," Curtis said. "You clean up nice."

The new Anders rolled his eyes. It seemed out of place in such an elegant face. "It's just for one night." His voice hadn't changed at all, of course.

"I hope so," Curtis said. "I like you better the other way. Do you want to borrow my cufflinks?"

The demon smiled. "Sure." He looked back at Luc. "And are you going like that? Don't think I can't smell the sex on you two."

"We showered," Curtis said. "You can't smell sex on us."

"Incubus," Anders said. "We breathe sex."

Luc rose. Scent of sex notwithstanding, the rest of what the demon said was true. He needed to get dressed. As he headed down the stairs, he heard Curtis asking Anders to take off his tie so he could re-knot it. He smiled. Maybe this night wouldn't be a disaster after all.

❖

They took Anders's SUV, and at Luc's urging, the demon didn't speed down Riverside Drive. Curtis was quiet in the backseat, and every time Luc looked back at him, he was looking out the window at the canal.

Anders squeezed left onto Rideau on a yellow light and brought the car to a stop in front of the Château. He tossed the keys to the uniformed valet, who snatched them out of the air with a practiced swipe of one hand.

"You dent it, I dent you," Anders said.

"Anders," Curtis warned.

The valet swallowed and climbed into the SUV with obvious care. Luc looked up at the Château for a moment, enjoying the sense of history the building afforded. Built of limestone, blocks of granite, white marble, and finished with an elegant green copper roof, the Château was a beauty that spoke of the era of the elite rich who enjoyed cross-country train travel. It had been commissioned by that rarest of creatures, an American with taste. But he never saw it open, as the journey he had booked back from England to witness the Château's finished glory had been aboard the *Titanic*.

Luc led the other two through the heavy front doors, the sounds of the street cut off abruptly as the doors swung shut behind them. The opulent entrance boasted high ceilings, richly polished wood, and thick carpets that muffled every step they took. People moved with purpose, but no one rushed. Elegance, culture, and propriety seemed infused in the very air of the place. Luc led them down to the large ballroom the invitation had listed. The three of them entered a small antechamber, about ten minutes early, and Luc took in the style while he waited. The building, the decoration, the very feel of the Château were from another era—his time, really. It was a welcome sensation, and he knew why their host had chosen it. They waited in the small room, either end of which opened into what Luc knew would be the main ballroom. The entire set-up spoke not only of class, but of hierarchy. They were to wait for someone else's welcome. It was a less-than-subtle message that someone else was in control.

Luc reminded himself of their goal: disturb nothing, change nothing, be as unexceptional as they could given their unique makeup. As Curtis had put it, "fly under the radar."

"Lovely room," Curtis said, admiring one of the paintings. He didn't whisper, and Luc smiled at him. A vampire's hearing is excellent, and Curtis knew that. No doubt, vampires beyond this chamber were listening to them already. No point in trying to keep their voices quiet.

"Have you been here before?" Luc asked.

"Not to the ballrooms. I've had high tea a few times, upstairs."

"Pourrais-je prendre votre manteaux?"

Luc turned. The farthest door was now open, where a man waited for their reply. He was young and blond—and very much alive. The youth was dressed finely enough, but something in his bearing and manner, not to mention the offer, spoke of his position. No doubt he was a servant to one of the coteries, but Luc was surprised. It was tradition that at a *séance* only the invited vampires would attend, each with two members of their coterie. Bringing a servant broke tradition.

Then again, I've brought a demon and a wizard.

"Bien sûr," Luc said, shrugging off his greatcoat. Curtis and Anders followed suit. The servant nodded and slipped away with them, back out through the doors he'd just entered through.

Curtis glanced at Luc and mouthed the word "alive?" Luc nodded. To Luc's surprise, Curtis scowled. Luc shook his head, hoping to convey that the slim youth would not be an offering—not as a servant—but the vampire had no real way of knowing if Curtis understood the gesture. It didn't matter. It was too late. They were here, and the *séance* would be under way in moments.

"Shall we?" Luc suggested.

They entered the ballroom. Grand and old, the three chandeliers were intricate arrangements of teardrop crystals linked in tassels of silver chains and spotlessly clean. Painted in creams, golds, and greens, the room had hosted royalty before, though Luc supposed some of those present this evening might be considerably older than the building itself. The windows across one wall were curtained with heavy cream-colored brocade, in front of which dozens of candelabra had been set up in three rows, each one filled with unlit green tapers. The tables had been moved aside, and the piano lay untouched.

Three of the other four coteries had already arrived. Ottawa hosted four coteries—five, including his own—but Luc had only rare dealings with the other vampires of Ottawa in the past. He'd been alone, and thus vulnerable to their dominance. He wasn't surprised he didn't recognize any of the vampires present.

The opposite was not true.

"Vous devez être Luc." A tall, beautiful woman smiled at him with just the barest hint of fang. Her long chestnut tresses were elegantly braided all the way to the small of her back, but her eyes struck Luc.

They were the color of honey. Her deep green dress left her smooth, pale shoulders and gentle neck exposed. The woman's poise, her accent, everything in her bearing spoke of someone who had been born to the highest levels of society and had never left. *"Notre sang neuf."* As she spoke, a single emerald on a perfectly understated gold chain sparkled at her throat.

"Oui," he said as he tilted his head to her gently in respect.

Luc felt Anders shift beside him. Anders spoke no French, Luc remembered.

"These are my companions," Luc said in English, a gentle suggestion to switch languages. "Curtis and Anders." Both men nodded deeper than he had, and the vampire was relieved to see Anders was on his best behavior. If he didn't open his mouth, Anders might even pass for civilized.

The woman, however, seemed more interested in Curtis. "You are the wizard?"

"Yes."

Though Luc could feel a nervousness coming from the wizard through their bond, the young man was a portrait of calm.

"No doubt you've been told how lovely you smell before." Her smile was just shy of predatory. She offered a hand. "I am the Lady Markham, though, please, you must call me Catharine."

Curtis didn't miss a beat. He drew her hand to his lips for a brief kiss. When he released her fingers, she turned back to Luc.

"My companions are Anna and Rhona." Catharine's accent was a melodious French, very far removed from the usual accent from Gatineau, and even the names of her companions played like music to Luc's ears.

Rhona was compact, with elfin features and short hair. Anna was the tallest, though none of the three women would be considered tall. She had the palest blue eyes Luc had ever seen. Both were dressed in a deeper green than their mistress, and both dresses were tailored to suit their frames. They turned their eyes to the ground as they offered Luc a bow befitting the leader of a coterie. Luc couldn't help but feel a rush of satisfaction. Their bows were a reminder of just how much his life had changed.

"You seem to have arrived in interesting times," Catharine said. Luc offered his arm, and she took it. He walked her to the edge of the ballroom, where overstuffed seats had been arranged. Luc felt himself on the edge of a smile, but he resisted. It had been a very long time since he had been able to enjoy the company of other vampires. He'd forgotten the way his kind spoke in circles.

"As you say." He had no idea what "interesting times" she was talking about.

"I daresay none will oppose Renard. Alas." When she said this, Luc felt the eyes of the other coteries shift to him, though their quiet conversations continued.

"I have not had the pleasure of meeting him," Luc said.

Catharine closed her eyes for a moment. *"Pardon. J'ai oublié.* Renard may be more familiar to your wizard...Curtis, was it?"

Again Luc forced his expression to remain neutral. This Catharine was playing with him somehow, and he didn't know why. Luc was the only vampire Curtis knew, so her suggestion that Curtis would be familiar with this Renard made no sense. How in the world would Curtis...?

The only possible reason came to him. Something in his face must have given him away, as Catharine tipped her head. It was a gesture so slight, Luc wondered if anyone else might have seen it. Luc realized she wasn't playing with him. She was preparing him.

No, he thought. *She's warning me.*

"If you will excuse me now, I should say hello to Denis and Étienne," Catharine said. "It was lovely meeting you."

Luc let go of her arm, and they bowed to each other, then separated. Curtis and Anders were exchanging small talk with Catharine's second and third. When he returned, the two vampires tipped their heads politely and trailed off after their mistress.

"You may know one of the coming vampires," Luc said casually to Curtis. As inferences went, it was a weak one.

Curtis blinked. Keeping his back to the rest of the room, Curtis frowned at Luc. Luc could feel his confusion. Anders, too, looked at him, a small line between his eyebrows.

Merde. He had no easy way to warn them of what might be coming.

A moment later, the point became moot. Three new vampires strode into the room, led by one who all but radiated power. Luc could feel the newcomer's dominance. His will, amplified and bound through his coterie, filled the room. He was taller than Luc and kept his hair short. His clothes were very modern, and his shirt was open at the throat—his style bordered on casual. He was classically handsome, but his comportment bore no refinement. Instead of bowing to the other coteries as he passed, he ignored them. None seemed surprised by his utter lack of decorum, and Luc looked at Catharine, whose pale golden eyes met Luc's for the barest moment before returning to the newcomer.

This, then, was Renard. He walked straight to Luc and stopped in front of him. Behind him, his second and third stared at the ground, unmoving. Luc had enough time to notice that they were both dressed casually as well, and that the woman to Renard's left wore the same suit as the man who stood to his right—black suit jacket, black suit pants, and a white collared shirt, yes, but no tie. Again, just shy of the formality usually accorded a *séance*.

"Luc, I presume?" Renard's voice boomed. His voice was slightly accented, and it worried Luc that he'd greeted him in English. Had Renard been listening long?

"Indeed," Luc said, bowing. "May I present my *frères de sang*, Curtis and Anders."

Renard skimmed past Anders with the briefest of glances and settled on Curtis. Curtis shivered as the two men exchanged their more formal bows.

"A wizard in our midst," Renard said. Curtis looked up at him. Renard narrowed his eyes when he smiled. His fangs were visible. "Tell me, what is your element?"

Curtis didn't falter. "Air."

"Oh. A pity." Renard gestured to the many candles. "I'd hoped that the inviting of a wizard would be grander. My fellow vampires grow tired of my own diminished skills." His smile was anything but self-deprecating. He pointed, flicked his wrist, and one of the wicks lit itself.

Curtis stared at it, his mouth slightly open.

Renard turned to the room in general. "See, Catharine?" he said. "Not all wizards are cut from the same cloth as—"

"Ignus," Curtis said.

Renard turned back to face the three of them. Behind, all the candles in the candelabra burst into flame simultaneously. It was impressive.

And foolish.

"You misunderstand me," Curtis said. Luc felt a dull anger radiating from the wizard and tried to meet his gaze to warn him off. This was no time for pride and certainly not a moment for anger, but Curtis avoided Luc's gaze. "I have a facility with air." Curtis smiled with enough self-effacement for his words not to seem rude. "It's not exclusive."

Renard's grin didn't falter. "Wonderful." He turned and clapped his hands. "Do I not always provide a good show?"

Curtis finally looked at Luc. Luc shook his head slightly. Curtis took a deep breath. Anders put his hand on the wizard's shoulder, but even the demon's classier face radiated obvious annoyance.

What game is being played here? Luc wondered.

"Your invitation was unclear as to the purpose of this *séance*," Catharine said.

"To welcome a new coterie, for the most part." Renard said. "To determine our new vampire's...place."

That was his cue. With relief, Luc bowed. "I need no position," he said. "My coterie and I prefer to cause no disarray." It was as close to saying "Leave us out of your vampire politics" as he could say without sounding weak.

Renard's laugh was hollow. "Then the prize didn't need wrapping after all. *Dommage.*" He nodded to the vampire woman he'd entered with, and she left. Curtis leaned against Luc, and Luc brushed his side with one hand. The wizard's nervousness beat like a drum along their bond.

This is taking too long, Luc thought. *We've declared ourselves for the lowest position available. Why is he continuing?*

The vampire returned with the young man who'd taken their coats. Between the two, they marched in a man whose hands were bound behind his back. He was shirtless and fit, though some bruises and cuts marred his otherwise smooth skin. Dark lines of dried blood had been painted across his chest in an intricate pattern that resembled an eight-spoked wheel. The marks seemed to shimmer as the man was brought forward.

Magic.

Luc heard Curtis's muttered "crap." No doubt everyone else in the room did as well, though none reacted.

The captive wore jeans, which were dirty and torn at one knee, but his feet were bare. His dark hair was shorn almost to the scalp. When Luc noticed a tattoo—a blue square with a sideways white figure eight within it—his tension rose. He took a closer look at the captive, and now that he knew what to look for, the cast of his features was obvious enough. He had some Native in his blood, Ojibwe perhaps, or Cree. But the tattoo told Luc the truth. The carried man's gaze was unfocused and lethargic. The vampire and the servant were all but holding him upright.

Renard was watching for a reaction. Luc had no doubt this show was for them, but he didn't know why.

Don't react, he told himself. *Don't show anything.*

"As you all know," Renard said, "we have a new coterie in our midst, albeit an unusual one. If they so desire, they may test their will against ours and take their rightful place in the *lignage.*" He looked at Luc, who felt the strength of his will flex between them. Renard had been a wizard before he was turned into a vampire. Luc didn't know his capabilities. Even though his intent had always been to abstain from any dominance games, he was all the more relieved to decline.

"That is not necessary. As I said," Luc paused to smile, "we do not wish to create any unnecessary changes."

"Then my little treat will remain my little treat. It was a great trouble to garner him—his sort can prove so very troublesome," Renard said. He turned to the rest of the room. "But he will no doubt taste fine, as those with gifts usually do. Unless anyone else would care to challenge?"

No one spoke. Curtis leaned forward, but Anders squeezed his shoulder again. Luc was grateful to the demon.

"Hold him upright," Renard said, and the vampire and the slender young man shifted the weight of the captive between them, straightening his posture. Renard's young servant had turned his face away slightly, looking afraid.

Renard bent down over the captive and tilted the man's head back. When his fangs pierced the captive's skin and the sound of the vampire's first swallow filled the room, the captive moaned.

Luc didn't know if Renard planned on draining the man dry in front of them, but he was starting to think he knew what Renard was trying to accomplish. Luc only hoped Curtis would know better than to—

"Stop!" Curtis said.

Merde.

Renard pulled away from the man. "You've changed your mind?" He asked, wiping some blood from his lips with his thumb. He spoke to Luc, but Luc could feel Renard's attention on the wizard beside him. The trembling captive sagged, moaning again but still not regaining consciousness.

"We speak as one," Luc said, keeping his voice calm with an effort of will. It was the only answer he could give.

Renard smiled. "To kneel, then?" he asked. "Prepare."

"Yes," Luc said. A simple enough dominance battle. Each of them would attempt to make the other kneel in turn. As the current *Duc,* Renard would go first. Luc *gathered* his will, another thing that had become much stronger since forming his bond with Anders and Curtis. The pressure of it built painfully behind his eyes.

"Kneel," Renard said. His order battered at Luc's mind from all sides, and he felt even the incredible strength he gathered from Curtis and Anders start to crumble. His legs trembled. Around him the room grew dark at the edges.

"No," Curtis grunted. Anders made a noise more like a growl. Luc felt a surge of strength pour from them like a strong wind from one side and wild heat from the other, and his mental walls redoubled.

Whole minutes went by before Renard had to relent. When the assault lessened, then stopped, his voice was startling in the quiet room.

"Your turn," he said. His voice was mild, as if barely interested. He gestured to the female vampire, who stepped away from the captive and joined Renard's other companion. They stood in a small triangle, facing Luc. Renard's second and third looked at Luc with open hatred.

What have we done to anger him?

Luc was already fatigued from resisting Renard's command, but he gathered his will again. He could feel Curtis and Anders shoring him up, their strength bleeding into his, and he launched it at Renard.

"Kneel," Luc demanded.

Renard's mind was like a solid wall, but Luc's assault was obviously much stronger than Renard had expected. His single reflexive twitch betrayed him. Luc felt the vampire's defenses crack, and he maintained his dominance for as long as it seemed wise. There was another moment where Renard's stance faltered, but he recovered and maintained until at least as much time had passed as his own failed attempt to make Luc kneel. Luc felt his reserves fading.

There was only one thing to do.

"A draw," Luc said, breaking off the mental assault. Once again he schooled his voice, forcing himself to sound controlled and even.

"Take him," Renard snapped, his careless composure gone. Then he took the young human servant by the shoulder and shoved him. "Tyson, give him to them and then get our coats. The rest of you can decide what order you wish to serve in on your own. I have an appointment I must attend."

Luc looked at Curtis. He was staring at the ground, but his fists were clenched and his knuckles were white. He swallowed.

"Sir," Renard's young servant, Tyson, said. He was awkwardly holding the captive, struggling with the weight of the bound man, and he gave Luc a frightened look. Luc reassessed his age. He was likely even younger than he looked. Who was this boy, and why had Renard chosen him as a servant?

"I've got him," Anders said, taking the weight of the captive with ease. Curtis took the man's other shoulder. His hand hovered over the markings on the captive's chest, but he didn't touch them. They pulsed with a dull red light.

Renard turned and followed Tyson out of the ballroom, the two vampires from his coterie close on his heels. The sound of the doors closing behind them echoed dully in the room.

"That," said Catharine, in a low voice, "was unexpected. I daresay the rest of us will forfeit the nuisance of dominance games this evening." She flicked her eyes at the captive. "Enjoy your…treat." She approached Luc, and leaned forward, pressing her hand to his chest and rising on her toes to kiss his cheek. "And *bienvenue à Ottawa*, Luc."

"*Merci,*" Luc said.

Luc looked around. The other vampires were smiling, but none other than Catharine would meet his gaze. He put his hand over his heart and bowed to Catharine. Whatever she'd slipped into the small pocket of his shirt was fairly small. A note, likely.

The bow she gave in return was lower than his, ceding his position as higher than hers in the *lignage*. She didn't seem remotely upset by that. In fact, her smile was genuine and, unless Luc was mistaken, relieved. At least someone was happy with how this evening had gone.

"We need to go," Curtis said.

"Good evening to you all," Luc said.

It had not been a graceful exit, since Anders and Curtis were mostly supporting a shirtless and bloodied captive who was barely conscious. Their coats were hung in the anteroom, and Curtis pulled Luc's awkwardly onto the groaning man. Tied closed, the greatcoat did a good enough job at covering the blood that marked his skin, and the collar hid the wound Renard had left.

"Too much to drink," Anders said to the only people they saw on their way out of the Château, a wealthy looking couple obviously displeased to have their evening include anything so lowbrow as a drunk. Anders and Curtis propped up their charge between them while the valet fetched their car. Anders continued to talk about cutting down on drinking until the car arrived.

Not a single passerby on the street so much as batted an eye.

Anders drove once they managed to get their new guest into the backseat. Curtis slid in beside the man, who had stopped groaning and was now apparently unconscious. Luc took the passenger side. He felt no relief until the Château was no longer in sight. After a few moments, Luc turned in his seat.

"That was very foolish," he said. There was no need to be more specific.

"Renard was going to kill him." Curtis's voice was still angry.

"What was I supposed to do?" He looked away from Luc's gaze, and Luc knew the wizard didn't want to pursue the discussion. Instead, Curtis opened up the coat and lowered his hand tentatively toward the bloodstained skin of Renard's "prize." Less than an inch from the intricate lines of dried blood, Curtis flinched and drew back his hand as if shocked.

"Crap. This is like a Geas."

"What's a Geas?" Anders asked, glancing in the rearview. Luc noticed he'd changed his form back to his rougher, more typical look, and nearly smiled. Heaven forbid the demon remain cultured for more than the time required. Then he regarded their passenger again, and his amusement faded. What a mess.

"You were supposed to let him die and let us leave in peace," Luc said.

Curtis stared at the back of Anders's head. "A Geas is a binding and a dampener and can let you dominate the mind of the person you've whammied with it," Curtis said. He paused, finally looking at Luc again. "I couldn't just watch."

Luc drew air into his lungs and sighed. "Of course not." It was hard to be mad at him. Curtis was young. And he was not a monster.

Anders turned onto Colonel By Drive and tapped his thumb on the steering wheel. "How much shit did we just get into?"

Luc thought about that, remembering the note tucked into his pocket. "It depends. Catharine was almost friendly. I didn't have any time to speak with Denis or Étienne, but they didn't seem hostile. In fact, it's a good sign the other three coteries didn't seem to care to challenge us to determine who was more dominant than the others."

"Because we're stronger," Anders said.

Luc had to agree. "Because we're stronger, yes. We blend differently than a typical vampire coterie. But more than that, I think they were all pleased someone stood up to Renard."

"Renard seemed stronger than a typical fucking vampire," Anders said.

"That thing he said about his own 'diminished' skills. He was a wizard," Curtis said. "Wasn't he?"

"Yes," Luc said.

"So he's a vampire and a fucking wizard?" Anders rolled his eyes. "Great."

"Not really," Curtis said. "Magic requires life, or so I've always read. I thought the magic would turn its back on a vampire. The elements oppose the vampiric, don't they? Wooden stakes, holy words, fire, running water..." He sighed. "The list of what I don't know seems to get longer every day."

"I don't know a lot about warlocks," Luc said. "Vampires who retain the magic they had in life are rare but not unheard of. I know their magic is much weaker than what they could do before they were turned. Still, alongside the vampire graces, even diminished magics are not to be dismissed."

"Warlock," Curtis repeated. "An oath-breaker."

"Pardon?"

Curtis shook his head. "Nothing. I guess I have homework."

Their guest moaned feebly, and Curtis shifted back to check on him. "We really need to get this Geas off him." He rubbed his eyes. "Which means even more homework. Unless you're both hiding a whole lot of knowledge about binding rituals I don't know about?"

"I've got handcuffs," Anders said. "Will that help?"

Curtis laughed. "Nice."

They drove in silence for a while. Luc checked his pocket, pulling out a small *billet-doux*. He noticed Anders glance at him, but the demon remained quiet. Luc unfolded the small piece of paper.

It was an address, a date, and a time. Beneath, a curved uppercase "C."

Luc wasn't sure if he felt better or worse. *Vampire politics.* He put the note away.

"What did Renard mean, anyway? About this guy being trouble?" Curtis asked, breaking the silence.

"Did you see his tattoo?" Luc asked.

"The infinity symbol? Yeah."

"It's not an infinity symbol," Luc said. "Or, well, yes, it is. But it's a flag. It's one of the oldest flags still used in this country, I believe. He's Métis."

"That means half-Native, right?" Curtis asked.

"Yes, but that's not what I mean. The Métis are a tribe in their own right," Luc said. "I think he may have an ability with spirits."

Anders turned his head and grinned. "A vampire sniffer?"

"To put it crudely."

Anders smirked. "Someone has to."

Luc carried the unconscious man down into the last empty bedroom of Curtis's home and gently placed him on the bed. Curtis pulled off the greatcoat, and after a moment looking at the patterns, he held out his hand again.

When Curtis's palm was less than an inch from the captive's skin, there was a flash of light. Curtis yanked his hand back and hissed. Luc caught the faintest hint of the scent of a burned match.

"Will he wake?" Luc asked.

Curtis blew out a breath. "I have no idea. I don't think so. If I had to guess, I'd say the Geas will keep him mostly unconscious. It's pretty powerful. It would take real finesse..." He leaned in and peered at the bloody marks again, then leaned back, shaking his head. "I have no idea what to do. I think it meant to make him, uh..."

"Edible?" Anders offered from the door.

"I was going to say pliable, but yeah. Edible." Curtis rubbed his eyes. He hesitated. "The bite on his neck...I don't think I should try a healing spell. I don't know how my magic will interact with a Geas. It's stopped bleeding, but..."

Luc crouched low beside the bed and leaned in over the captive. He touched the man's forehead without incident. Whatever the Geas was, it was not alarmed by a vampire's touch. He turned the man's head gently, exposing the wound Renard had inflicted. Leaning in, he drew his tongue across the wound. The taste of the bound man was rich, and Luc felt his fangs extending despite himself. Those with gifts always tasted so much better. He maintained composure as he pulled away. The wound was closed, and Luc's tongue had cleaned a small swipe across the man's neck of the dried blood.

Curtis exhaled. "That's something, at least."

"Kinky," Anders said. Luc ignored him.

"Can you undo the Geas?" Luc asked.

"Not without research." He reached into his pocket and pulled out his phone. He held it up over the prone man's chest and tapped the screen, taking a picture. After looking at the result, Curtis nodded to himself and put the phone away. "I'll head to the university library tomorrow." He yawned. He looked exhausted.

"You should go to bed," Luc said. "It's been a long night."

"Yeah, I guess so." He frowned at the man lying on the bed. "Do you think you could force some water down his throat? We have no idea when he ate or drank last, and..."

"We'll deal with him," Luc said. "Go to bed."

Curtis nodded. "Okay. Right. Good night." He left.

Anders joined Luc beside the bed. "Okay, he's gone. Now tell me the truth. How much shit are we in?"

"I didn't lie. But this"—Luc gestured at the prone man lying on the bed—"complicates things."

Anders sighed. "Curtis isn't going to stop until he figures out how to free him."

Luc nodded. "I know."

"So what do we do when this guy wakes up and realizes he's in the house with a vampire and a demon?" Anders asked. "Because I'm pretty sure he won't be happy to see us. More's the pity. He's cute."

"Anders."

"What? He's fuckable. Under that blood, anyway. Though I guess that's like, what, chocolate frosting for you?"

Luc resisted the temptation to answer the comment. Anders would only feel victorious. Instead, looking at the man's ripped and dirty clothes, he said, "We should get those jeans off him."

Anders smiled. "You dirty bastard."

Luc forced air into his lungs and sighed.

CHAPTER THREE

Curtis had a favorite hideaway on the top floor of the library. Seated in the carrels beyond the farthest corner of the stacks, he looked at the pile of books he'd gathered and sighed. The university library wasn't exactly the prime place to find books on actual magical application, but he didn't have a lot of other options. Third Eye Books, an occult shop tucked a few streets off the Market, wasn't open on Sundays. Even then, Curtis wasn't entirely sure the owner or staff had any real ability of their own.

He needed to spend more time building up his own private library. He had the money, but he was never quite sure where to start. Magic came naturally to him. Intent and words were often all he needed to let it out. But when it came to the magic of others, like, say, a wizard who'd since become a vampire and was using blood to somehow keep a strange "soul-sniffer" barely conscious, he was seriously lacking an education.

Curtis glanced down at the titles he'd gathered: *The Sternglantz Encyclopedia of Symbology. The Khātim Sulaymāni. Goetic Mysteries. Calling the Circle.* He ran his finger across the spines of the books, wondering where exactly to begin. He pulled out the sketch he'd made—he didn't want someone looking over his shoulder at his phone and seeing a picture of a man's torso marked with dried blood—and studied it.

The geometry of the design was simple enough: four crossed lines making eight equal branches, like a child's star. But the lines had variances at their ends, splitting into pitchfork-like branches, and crossed with bars or crescents. Geometric and symmetrical, each part seemed a bit more basic than most of the talismanic drawings Curtis had in his own books.

They weren't seals, nor was it some sort of pentagram, and the design didn't look much like it was inspired by Kabbalah, either.

I know I've seen something like this before.

This was the problem with having a triad instead of a coven. Curtis didn't want to admit it, but the reality was he had no idea what he was looking at and no idea how to break it.

"Not to mention how someone got a letter bomb into my house," he muttered.

"Pardon?"

Curtis jumped. Turning his head, he saw he wasn't the only person at one of the little study desks anymore. A young woman looked at him over her glasses, a small smile curling her lips. She had a disorganized tumble of black hair piled up on her head, held barely in check by two white chopsticks. The rest of her was the picture of tidy comfort. She wore a pale cream peasant blouse and a pair of black jeans. Her brown leather jacket was folded across the back of her chair, and a well-worn messenger bag was tucked beside the desk.

"Sorry," Curtis said. "Thinking out loud." He'd never encountered someone up here before.

"Ah." She turned back to her own work.

Blushing, Curtis tapped his finger on the desk and looked back at the stack of books.

"What the hell," he muttered, picking up the *Sternglantz Encyclopedia* at random. He skimmed through the pages, watching for the illustrations and trying to find something similar to his sketch of the Geas. By the end of the book, he'd seen nothing, though he definitely wanted to pick up a copy of the book for himself. Sternglantz knew her stuff. He put the encyclopedia to the left and looked at his sketch again.

Geometric lines. A couple of crescents. Crossed with bars, split into threes and fives... Simple, like something you could draw quickly, but deceptively so. The angles were pretty much perfect. It would take effort to create those symbols correctly, especially if you were carving them—

He remembered.

"Futhark."

He realized he'd spoken aloud again and glanced over at the young woman, but if he'd bothered her, she didn't react.

Futhark. Runes. The runic alphabet was made up of lines like these, except Futhark had no curves, only ninety- or forty-five-degree angles. Maybe this was some sort of bindrune? Curtis tried to remember. Runic magic hadn't come naturally to him. His elemental affinity was air, which left the more grounded earth magics a bit out of his reach. He'd learned pretty early on that he could affect the world around him with a spoken word much easier than he could craft a set of runes, so he'd tucked aside the topic for later study. Like so much else, it was still on his to-do list. Still…It was as good a place as any to start.

One trip to the linguistics stacks later, and he was in business. He sat down with a copy of *Germanic Languages of the Second to Eighth Centuries* and skimmed through the index. Sure enough, it had a piece on the Futhark alphabet. Curtis started reading.

❖

Much later, Curtis had followed the trail from one appendix to another until he'd reached a lengthy and patronizing tome on Galdrabók. Curtis had moved from continental Europe to Iceland now. On a page full of illustrations of various Icelandic symbols used in what the insufferable author referred to as "base pagan nonsense," he spotted something that was almost exactly what he had been searching for.

"Aha," he said, triumphant. But when he read the small text beside the symbol, he frowned. A symbol of guidance and protection? That didn't sound right.

"You found what you were looking for?"

Curtis looked at the young woman. She'd gathered her bag and put on her jacket, and was obviously getting ready to leave.

"I'm so sorry," Curtis said. "I don't mean to talk out loud. It's a bad habit. I hope I'm not driving you away."

She smiled. "It's been two hours since I got here. I'm hungry."

Curtis checked the clock on his phone. "Holy crap."

"You were in the zone," she said.

Curtis laughed. "Apparently." He pushed back from the desk and rose, stretching. The young woman glanced down at the open book.

"Is that Norse?"

"Yeah." Curtis was surprised. "Or Icelandic. It's called a *vegvísir*." He said the word carefully, making sure to hold tight to his magical gift. Being careful around words he didn't use on a daily basis was a reflex. The magic inside him wanted out, and sometimes it would take any available exit. Unsurprisingly, he felt it stir inside him when he spoke. He wondered what would happen if he were to cast the word. Not that now was the time.

"I don't know that one."

Curtis tapped the drawing on the page. "It's a kind of 'good travel' luck charm."

"Is it a good book?"

"No. The author is a complete dick. It's all 'backward pagan lifestyle' this and 'simplistic outlook on life' that."

"I'll keep that in mind." She had a nice smile. She slung her bag over her shoulder. "Is this something for Professor Mann's mythology and culture class? I don't remember seeing you."

"No," Curtis said. "But I have him for a poetry lecture on Fridays."

"Poetry," she said, making a face like she'd just sucked a lemon. "I prefer words that make sense."

"Professor Mann would say poetry makes the most sense," Curtis said. "The more words you use, the more untruths sneak in." He tried to make his voice rumble in the low growly way Professor Mann had of speaking, but he missed by miles.

She grinned. "Fair enough." She paused, as though she was about to say something else, and then her eyes shifted to something behind Curtis, and she tensed. Curtis turned. Three men stood at the end of the aisle, beside the long glass windows that divided the area between the bookshelves and where the carrels were organized in neat rows.

All three were handsome, tall, and muscular. They hadn't made a sound.

"Can I help you?" Curtis asked. He felt a vague unease. Two of the three men were wearing tank tops, and none of them had jackets. It was a little cool out for that, though he supposed they could be living on residence at the university and have used the tunnels. Still, they seemed a bit older than a typical student and—well, they were really hot.

Like, incubus demon hot.

When the men didn't respond, the woman beside him shifted her bag on her shoulder.

"Guys?" Curtis asked again. "Something you need?" Curtis wished he'd brought his glasses. Though it hadn't played to his strengths, he'd managed to enchant a pair of lenses. Looking at people while he wore them and concentrating would show him auras and let him know for sure if he was facing something more or less than human.

The man in the middle, a brunette with remarkable slate gray eyes, raised his eyebrows. "I got a message for you. Stop fucking around with stuff you don't understand."

Curtis frowned. "I beg your pardon?"

"Should I call security?" the young woman asked. Curtis glanced at her and saw she had her phone in hand. He bit his lip. The last thing he needed was to get a random student involved in something magical. He shook his head.

"Who..." Curtis's voice was a bit uneven. He cleared his throat. "Who sent the message?"

The gray-eyed man stepped forward. Curtis held his ground, but the man moved past him to the desk where the book lay open to the illustration of *vegvísir*. The gray-eyed man reached out a single finger and touched the picture.

There was a wisp of smoke, and the book began to smoulder.

Curtis stepped back, and the gray-eyed man, whose eyes were now the inky black of a demon, swung his hand at Curtis, a small arc of brimstone-scented flame flaring in the air after his fist.

Curtis ducked, raised his own hand, and said, *"Necto."*

The magic, teased for the last couple of hours by the words and symbols Curtis had been searching through, lashed out from his palm with an eager and gleeful rush. The air snapped with static, and the demon crashed back against the bookshelves, landing hard on the carpet as the binding tugged at him. Curtis wheeled to face the other two demons and saw the young woman beside him had pulled the chopsticks from her hair and held one in each hand out before her like weapons. The tips of the chopsticks were lit with a pale green light.

He glanced at her. She shrugged.

Huh. Okay.

The two remaining demons stepped forward.

"Back off, fugly," she said.

The two demons, their eyes telltale inky black now, stopped approaching.

"Sticks and stones, little wizard," the taller one said.

The young woman twitched one of her sticks. An entire shelf of linguistic arts journals tipped off the shelf above the two demons and crashed into them, the heavy books jarring their heads and knocking the taller one off balance. He had to grip the now-empty shelf to stay upright. He recovered, but a trickle of blood from a cut above his ear made a lie of his mocking smile.

"And words will never hurt you?" she said.

The two demons stood still, eyeing them, while the one Curtis had sent to the ground regained his footing. Curtis held out one hand, ready to level another spell at the three demons, but Gray Eyes rejoined the other two.

"Your book is burning," Gray Eyes said, with mocking sympathy. "Seems like that sort of thing is happening to you a lot."

The letter. The balefire. Curtis felt his temper rise. It was a rare thing. A temper didn't go well with magic, but Curtis couldn't quite help himself from giving in.

"Hiems osculum," he said. The blast of cold air that raced at the three demons was arctic. All three visibly recoiled despite their bravado, and Curtis gestured again. Sorcery sang through his blood and icy darts of wind gathered in the palm of his hand, visible trails of snowflakes drifting from his fingers to the floor. A low breeze filled the small corner of the library. Though the three tried to appear casual in their retreat, their movements were a bit too rushed. They passed by one of the narrow windows, and as they stepped into the shadow cast by the large trees in the quad outside, they vanished.

That could have explained their silent approach, Curtis realized. It would have been tricky, but they might have shadow-walked in. The library was a public place.

"Your book is still burning."

Curtis looked at the young woman for a moment and then took a step to his desk. Thankfully, books didn't burn particularly well, and nothing else was damaged. Curtis sent the frozen air in his palm at the book with a flick of his wrist and snuffed the flames out. Magic was dancing on his skin, and it took him a few breaths to calm it down and put it away.

Tempers and magic, he reminded himself. *Stay calm.*

"Couldn't have happened to a nicer author. At least the sprinklers didn't go off," Curtis said, turning again to look at the young woman. Her hair had fallen down past her shoulders, and she'd transferred both chopsticks to one hand. She looked a little shaken.

"Do demons attack you often?" she asked.

Curtis swallowed. "More often than I'd like."

She held out her free hand. "I'm Mackenzie."

"Curtis." They shook.

"So," Mackenzie said. "Icelandic runes, eh?"

Curtis nodded, looking at the mostly ruined book. "Yeah." He closed the cover and winced at the small spread of ashes that fell from the ruined pages. "At least I didn't check it out."

She waited while he gathered his things. He didn't know what to do with the ruined book, so he left it on the desk. He shrugged into his coat and picked up his messenger bag, slinging it over his shoulder. They stepped over the pile of journals, sharing a guilty glance.

"I really hate to leave a mess," Curtis said. "But…"

"Rather a mess than getting caught," she agreed.

They made it to the elevator without being seen. When the doors closed, Curtis exhaled.

"So," Mackenzie said. "You're cute. Not too tall. Quick with a spell, and fearless in the face of demons. I don't suppose you're single?"

Curtis couldn't help it. He laughed. "I'm gay."

Mackenzie nodded. "And my world returns to normal. You want to go get lunch and talk about Icelandic runes?" She started piling her hair back onto her head in a long twist and put the two chopsticks back into place.

"I'd love to. Nice wands, by the way."

Mackenzie smiled. "I bet you say that to all the girls."

"So, may I ask an awkward question?" Mackenzie said, taking a sip of a coffee that she had ordered with a litany of roughly eleven syllables. It smelled like caramel.

"Shoot," Curtis said. He'd ordered a green tea. He wrapped both hands around the paper cup, letting the warmth settle into his fingers. Water sorcery definitely left a chill.

"I've never met you before," Mackenzie said. "And I don't recall seeing you at a moot. Are you on your own?"

Curtis regarded her. There didn't seem to be any malice in her question, but he knew what she was really asking. She wanted to know if he was an Orphan, a wizard not born to one of the magical bloodlines. Orphans had a rough start. They didn't have anyone around them to explain what was happening, and the Families weren't particularly kind to them once they found them and brought them into the fold. They called it adoption, but in reality it was more like being hired help. There was a reason they called themselves "the Families." If you were an outsider in any way, at best you'd be tolerated. Assuming you were useful.

"I'm an Orphan," Curtis said. "In both senses of the word."

Mackenzie hesitated, and she looked pained. Curtis spared her the question.

"I didn't realize how seriously to take the threat from the Families," Curtis said. The wizards who'd first found Curtis after his magic had begun had told him he had a choice: ignore the magic, or join them and leave his family behind. He'd done neither, and his parents had had an "accident" shortly thereafter. When the wizards returned to offer the same deal, only this time threatening Curtis's life instead, he had refused, saying he'd rather never use the magic than go anywhere with people like them. But it had been easier said than done. The magic *wanted* to be used, and he hadn't known that at first. But he had known they'd been watching, waiting for him to slip up, and so he'd begun to learn everything he could. That had led to him discovering a different path to getting out from under the thumb of the wizard families, forming the bond he now shared with Luc and Anders.

Curtis tried not to think about his parents much. He knew he should blame the wizards for killing them, but he owned a share of the guilt himself. He hadn't realized just what the Families had intended, no, but if he had just been more careful…

He shook his head.

Mackenzie looked down at her drink. "I'm so sorry."

Curtis nodded. He didn't really know what else to say.

"Which family adopted you?" she asked.

Ah. Now this is awkward. "None of them," he said.

Mackenzie's eyes widened. "You're not still practicing as an Orphan?" It came out as a whisper, and she leaned forward. "Curtis, you can't. I saw what you did up there. You're not just a sorcerer, you can wield real magic. They'll kill you."

Curtis shook his head. "I'm not alone. I have a coven of my own. Sort of."

She frowned. "Sort of?"

"It's with a demon and a vampire." Curtis picked up his tea and took a swallow.

"Oh my God." Mackenzie stared. "You're *that* one."

He wasn't expecting a reaction like that. She barely seemed surprised. In fact, she seemed...interested? "Pardon?"

She smiled, though there wasn't a large amount of humor to it. "You've ruffled quite a few skirts."

"Among the coven heads?" Curtis laughed. "Rich old white men don't wear skirts."

"They're not all men," Mackenzie countered, with a little color in her cheeks.

Curtis raised a hand. "Fair enough. There was one woman there when I had to go meet them. She actually seemed pretty cool, for a coven head." Curtis had been "invited" to meet the coven heads twice. Once for them to test whether or not his triad should "count" as a coven, which they had to admit it did through their own laws, and once after an unfortunate incident where Curtis had conjured a thunderstorm in the middle of the day from an otherwise clear sky.

It had been self-defense, though convincing the coven heads of that had been a delicate discussion. The old men had seemed ready to throw him to the wolves. But the lone woman—Katrina, Curtis remembered one of the men had called her—hadn't been quite so bad. She'd also been about half the age of the other men—all of whom Curtis imagined were in their seventies or more.

Mackenzie looked down at her coffee again. "She's my mother."

Curtis flinched. He was glad he hadn't said anything too negative about her. "Like I said, she was pretty cool. She gave me the chance to speak up for myself."

Mackenzie smiled. "Good."

Curtis took another swallow, and then put his cup down. "So does that make you next in line?"

Mackenzie shook her head. "The position isn't inherited. It's…" She blew out a breath. "It's complicated."

"You grew up surrounded by magic, though," Curtis said, and a note of wistfulness he hadn't intended crept in despite his best effort to sound neutral.

She nodded. "Yeah."

"At least you knew what was happening," Curtis said. "I had to bumble around in the dark."

"You tossed that demon down hard. You throw a binding like a pro," Mackenzie said. "You use Latin?"

Curtis nodded. "Most of the time, but not always. I get more out of a spell if I use a different language. I'm studying languages, actually. They seem to come easy to me."

"It's an air thing," Mackenzie said. "Words, symbols…I'm guessing from the sorcery that air and water are your best elements?"

"Yeah. And you're more earth?"

She nodded. "Do you practice as a Wiccan or…?"

"Not really." Curtis smiled. He'd had no idea how much he'd wanted to talk about magic with someone else who knew it. "I do see magic as an elemental framework, and those kinds of traditions seem to work best for me. I'd say I borrow a whole lot from Wicca conceptually, but I've found some great pieces in other religions and spiritual frameworks, too."

She looked at him for a while, as if deciding something.

"You should come over some time. My family library has stuff this place obviously doesn't. I also host a craft night, if you'd enjoy something like that," she said. "I have a group of friends. We get together, work on stuff." She gestured to the chopsticks in her hair. "It's where I made these."

"I'm not very good at enchantment," Curtis said. "Though I did put a pretty good spell on a pair of glasses."

"You just might not be playing to your strengths. I'm brilliant with wood or stone, but my candle crafts are a mess." She smiled. "Air isn't an element that likes to be bound in place, but it loves symbols. You'd probably be great at talismans. And if water works well for you, too, then maybe some work with silver. Seriously, you should come."

Curtis felt a weight he hadn't really known he was carrying lifting from his shoulders. "I'd like that," he said.

Mackenzie nodded. "Good. Now, show me that picture again. Let's see if we can figure it out."

Curtis pulled out his sketch, and they got to work.

❖

"You're late," Anders said.

Curtis put his keys on the peg beside the door. "Nice to see you, too."

When Curtis turned, Anders wrapped his arms around him from behind and squeezed him in something a bit tighter than a hug. The demon also gave Curtis's ear a quick nibble.

"How was school?" Anders asked, his voice low and rumbling.

"Fine," Curtis said, trying not to be distracted by what Anders's stubble felt like on the back of his neck. "I skipped a class, but it was worth it."

"Skipped a class?" Anders squeezed a little and flicked Curtis's ear with his tongue again. "Naughty boy."

Curtis shivered. "I was researching the Geas. And I met someone who was a really big help."

Anders stepped back. "Who?"

Curtis turned and smiled at the dark look on Anders's face. "Mackenzie Windsor."

"Who is he?" Anders's dark look was turning into a scowl.

Curtis shook his head. "*She* is a wizard, like me. And she knows a crap-ton more about runes and bind runes than I do." He tried not to laugh at Anders's obvious relief that Mackenzie was a woman.

"You just bumped into her?" Anders crossed his arms. "Just like that?"

"Actually, no," Curtis said. "She was there when some demons popped in to pay me a visit."

Anders's scowl returned. "Did they hurt you?"

Curtis shook his head. "No. They delivered a threat. Or a warning. They basically admitted they were sent by whoever mailed us that letter bomb." Curtis rubbed his eyes. "Without, of course, telling me who sent us the letter bomb."

"What did they say?"

"To stop messing around with stuff I don't understand. Which is a giant list. Are we done with the interrogation now? I'd like to take off my shoes."

Anders blinked.

Curtis took a breath. "Crap. Sorry. I'm a bit tired and cranky. It's just—it means someone followed me. Someone is keeping tabs on me. On all of us, maybe."

"It's okay," Anders said.

"Let me boil the kettle, and then I'll try to go over everything with you. Did our houseguest wake up?" He went to the counter and picked up the kettle. He filled it up, put it back on the base, and flipped the switch.

"He was groggy for a bit," Anders said. "But not awake. I got him cleaned up, gave him some water, and shoved some soup down his throat."

Curtis leaned against the counter. "You gave him a sponge bath?" He couldn't quite picture Anders being so…considerate.

"Fuck no." Anders laughed. "We took a shower."

"You carried him into the shower?" Curtis felt his face heating up.

"He's pretty hot once you wash the grime off. Great ass. Nice dick."

"Fantastic," Curtis said. He didn't have the energy to be scandalized. Nor was he surprised. Of course Anders would have stripped their guest. The kettle started to whistle. He clicked it off. He filled a cup and popped in a tea bag, not wanting to bother with loose leaf. "I don't suppose the Geas washed off?"

Anders shook his head. "Water wouldn't touch it."

"Of course. Well," Curtis said, "I think I might have a shot at breaking it." He stirred some honey into the tea and waited while it brewed. "I'll wait until Luc is up."

"Sunset is in a couple of hours," Anders said.

Curtis yawned and rubbed his eyes. "I'm going to have this, then take a nap. This all-night, all-day crap is going to kill me." He laughed. "Assuming demons or letter bombs don't."

"No one is gonna kill you."

Curtis picked up the tea and took a sip. He closed his eyes. Sometimes he was pretty sure the most magic thing in the world was tea. He opened his eyes again.

"What's your job?" he asked.

Anders shook his head and walked away.

Curtis took another sip. He hadn't figured that would work, but it was worth a try. Still, he had time. And, if it came to it, magic. He'd find out.

But first he'd take a nap.

CHAPTER FOUR

L uc watched as Curtis flew back across the spare bedroom again and slammed hard into Anders, who'd braced to catch him. They both went down, the demon softening the blow and making sure Curtis didn't knock his head against anything like he had the first time. This was the third attempt, and Anders didn't looked pleased to be catching the wizard once again.

Luc helped them stand. *This isn't going well.*

"Okay," Curtis said, wincing as he stood back up. "That...that didn't work either. Plan C is officially off the list." Luc looked around and found Curtis's athame beside the bed. He picked the dagger up and handed it back to Curtis. The young man took it, still looking back at the prone man on the bed.

The lines drawn in blood on the man's chest were glowing with a dull light, pulses of darkish red that moved in a slow rhythm along the design. The bound man on the bed—who was now naked below the sheet, Luc noticed—was panting and turning his head as though pained. Curtis watched, standing a healthy distance back.

"You think?" Anders said.

Curtis waved a hand at him. "Be helpful or be quiet." He peered at the markings and the glow that moved around them. Luc watched Curtis work, finding the wizard's intensity very appealing. Luc could easily allow himself to forget how powerful Curtis might be, he seemed so very human most of the time.

"Oh, that's clever," Curtis said.

"What is?" Luc asked.

Curtis pointed, though he was careful to keep his finger from brushing the man's skin. "There are two layers of blood here. You can tell when it's powered up like this. There's the bind runes, a kind of a reversed *vegvísir* that leads him into himself, rather than to safety, but beneath that, some of these lines could be drawn to be a ward. Sort of a word within a word, like hiding 'tea' inside 'steam' and using a different color of ink for the three letters under a darker ink you use for the full five. Only with blood. And magic."

"Can you break it?"

"I think so," Curtis said, but he stepped back and lowered the blade. "But I'm going to get a second opinion first."

Luc raised an eyebrow.

"He made a friend today," Anders said.

Curtis nodded. "The daughter of one of the coven heads. She knows a heck of a lot more about the kind of runes being used here than I do. Every time I try, I can tell I'm hurting him. I need to get it right."

Luc looked back at the prone man. Sweat had spread across his forehead and chest, and he was panting as though he'd been running.

Or in pain.

Luc nodded. "Of course." The truth was, he'd rather Curtis had tried now and gotten it over with, but he knew better than to press him. Curtis wouldn't continue if it meant he might permanently harm their guest.

Anders sighed. "Does this mean I'm still the fucking nurse?"

"Please." Curtis rolled his eyes. "Like you're not perving out on him in the shower."

"Hey." Anders held up his hands. "He needed to be cleaned."

"Right," Curtis said. Then he yawned. "Okay, I know when I'm beat. I'll call Mackenzie in the morning." He looked back at the man on the bed. "Maybe nurse Anders can make sure he eats something?"

"Oh, fuck off."

Curtis grinned. "Good night." He started for the door, then paused. "Do you guys need anything before I go to bed?"

Luc shook his head. "No. I have business to attend to tonight."

Anders just grunted.

Curtis left.

"You wanna help me get him to the bathroom first? I'm sure he needs a dump."

Luc winced.

It should not have surprised Luc to find the home of Catharine Markham managed to be both beautiful and understated. It was one of the larger homes in Sandy Hill, closer to the Rideau River and the many embassies. It still retained its original character, which must have been both expensive and required a painstaking eye for detail. Luc guessed the home was from the nineteenth century, judging from its lines and the style of what looked like the original windows.

The fair-sized yard had been carefully groomed and included a water feature that seemed to circle the entirety of the property. The water trickled, running in an endless circle that Luc assumed was powered by something beneath the ground. Passing over the small bricked bridge that crossed it was a minor act of will.

Running water was rarely an impediment to a vampire with even a decade under his belt, but Luc still paused to admire the layout of the garden, the scent of the late-blooming autumn flowers, and the single stone birdbath that shone in the moonlight.

There was no doubt. The Lady Markham had class.

He approached the house, keenly aware that although the night seemed quiet and the streets bare, eyes were likely upon him. He lifted the knocker and rapped just minutes earlier than the time listed on the *billet-doux*.

❖

"I'm glad you could come."

Luc turned. Catharine was barely three steps behind him. He had not heard her arrive. Catharine, it seemed, had graces of her own.

"I thank you for your invitation, Lady Markham," Luc said, pulling out the small *billet-doux*. "What it lacked in detail it made up for in presentation."

"You are a welcome change." Catharine's smile seemed genuine.

"Am I?" Luc looked around the room. Like the entrance hall before it, the room was tasteful and understated, but its simplicity was elegant. The ceiling was Venetian plaster, and the wainscoting had obviously been carved by hand, not machine. The rich green of the walls was offset by the pale cream cushions on the dark leather chairs. The shuttered cylinder desk was either from the late eighteen hundreds or had been painstakingly recreated. Even the air itself seemed designed. A soft, earthy scent, perhaps patchouli, drifted through the room. Luc pulled air into his lungs and turned back to Catharine. "You have a beautiful home."

"Thank you," Catharine said. "And yes, you are. For one thing, you seem capable of speaking plainly."

"I am out of practice with vampire politics," Luc admitted.

"It is to your credit," Catharine said.

"And the other?" Luc asked.

"Pardon?"

"You said, 'for one thing.' That usually means there is another."

"Ah. Well." She smiled, this time revealing a hint of her fangs. "The other thing is less cordial. You, Luc, are a genuine threat to Renard."

It took an effort to keep his features plain. "He is very strong."

Catharine nodded. "He is that." She sat down on the love seat, moving one of the cushions and patting the space beside her. "Please, sit."

Luc joined her.

"What do you know of Renard?" she asked.

"Almost nothing. Thanks to your…introduction, I realized he was a wizard in life, but beyond that…" Luc shook his head. "Nothing."

Catharine didn't seem surprised. "I would say he prefers it that way, but that's not quite true. He lets enough of his nature be known to instill a healthy respect, by which I, of course, mean the vulgar man desires others fear him. But the details are always vague." She reached a perfectly manicured hand and touched Luc's knee. "You are the first vampire I've ever seen resist his will. And I have been in Ottawa since before Renard deposed the previous *Duc*."

"I see," Luc said.

"I don't think you do," Catharine said. At his slight frown, she patted his knee again. "I don't mean to insult, *chèr* Luc, just to inform." She paused. "When a wizard accepts the night and turns away from life, most of the magic they once wielded is lost. But for some, a little remains. Renard's gifts in life must have been considerable, because he retains more magical power than any other warlock I've encountered."

She leaned toward him. "He has access to minor sorceries, and his other elemental magics fuel graces rarely seen at all, let alone together in one man."

"Such as?" Luc asked. If Renard was going to consider Luc a threat, he wanted to know the man's capabilities.

"Understand, these are rumours," Catharine said. "But the sources are at least credible enough that I consider there to be more than a grain of truth."

Luc nodded.

"The flame you've seen—he can, in a limited fashion, call fire into being as well as perform other more intricate workings of fire spells."

Luc thought of the candle, not to mention the letter full of balefire.

"I've been told he's been seen to step into earth as though it were water," Catharine said.

"I've heard of that grace before," Luc said. "But I've never seen it."

"I have. Though I've not seen Renard do it." Catharine paused, and then met his gaze. "And he can mist."

Oh merde. Luc leaned back. "Are you sure?"

"No," she admitted. "But I consider the source to be somewhat reliable."

"Who is your source?" Luc asked.

Catharine smiled. "Membership in Renard's coterie is unusually short-term for one of our kind, especially for those who displease him. And at one point, it seems Renard replaced almost everyone. Certainly, anyone who knew him when he was alive."

"*Almost* everyone?"

"There is someone who was there at Renard's beginning. That was who told me of his graces."

"And Renard lets this person remain?" It didn't seem likely to Luc. If Renard was as careful about what others knew of him, why continue to let someone like that exist?

"She is no longer a part of his coterie. He cast her out, but unlike those who went before her, she remains." Catharine showed her fangs again. "I believe Renard considers her to be a cautionary tale for others."

"If he has all these graces…" Luc said, but then didn't know where to go with the thought. "Why are you telling me this?"

"Renard is a tyrant. He only honors tradition in the vaguest sense, and only as he is required." Catharine's voice rose just enough for Luc to realize she was holding anger in check. "You must understand. I have lost friends—friends I have treasured for decades and longer, all to Renard's sense of security. Those he deems a threat are soon gone, by accident to all appearances. He takes effort to leave no real traces, of course, as even a *Duc* must answer to those above him, but Renard is contemptuous of those of us with what he considers 'lesser' ability. I know some of the things he has done. He gloats to himself, and his thoughts—" She bit off her words, but Luc turned to her.

"You know his *thoughts*?" he asked. Luc was stunned. He'd heard of vampires who could read the minds of mortals, but of other vampires? That was a grace so rare he hadn't even believed it existed.

Catharine sat back and smoothed her long dress. "Sometimes. Rarely." She took a long, deep breath, something Luc knew full well as both affected and calming. It was a habit he had himself. "Often enough."

He couldn't help asking. "And mine?"

She shook her head. "No. Mortals are easy. Vampires, usually never. I believe it is because of his former life as a wizard that I sometimes hear what he thinks." She smiled. "I imagine he has no idea of that weakness. If he knew, I have no doubt I would vanish." She reached out and touched his leg again. "I play the coquette around him, as most do. I am a socialite and little else so far as our *Duc* is concerned. His thoughts of me—when he has thoughts of me at all—are the thoughts of a powerful man who sees a pretty woman and nothing else. And now you know something that could destroy me. Perhaps that is enough to earn your trust that I am not trying to lead you astray."

"For someone who can't read my mind, that was a very good guess."

Catharine shrugged. The gesture cracked her elegance, and Luc saw something in her amber eyes he had not expected from the calm, controlled woman.

Fear.

"I believe you are our first and, frankly, our only chance. If Renard comes after you, I would prefer that you be the victor."

"I have no designs on being a *Duc*."

"Luc," she said, squeezing his leg. "That does not matter. The *Duc* has designs on you."

Luc put his hand over hers. "I'm sorry if I seem suspicious."

Catharine shook her head. "It is not a surprise. You were alone for a long time, no? I can't imagine what that would be like. I've always had my coterie."

"Yes," Luc said. "I suppose mistrust is a habit."

"You need allies," Catharine said. "We all do."

Not friends, Luc noticed. *Allies*. Vampire politics. The *Duc* had decided he was a threat, or at least the triad he had with Curtis and Anders was a threat, which amounted to much the same thing. He'd figured that much from the way Renard had interacted with them at the *séance*, but Catharine's information confirmed his suspicions.

"Thank you," he said. "For the warning." *Not that I'm sure what to do with it.*

"You're welcome." She pulled her hand away and rose. "And speaking of welcomes, I know I have stolen the start of your night to meet me here. I have prepared a meal for us."

Luc raised a single eyebrow.

Catharine held out her hand, her smile playful. What was it she had said? For Renard, she played the coquette. It was a convincing act, if this was a rendition of it.

"Come," she said.

To not follow would be rude. Besides which, he was curious. Luc rose and took her arm.

Catharine led him down into the basement of her home, and Luc saw the careful period restoration that had occurred upstairs was not continued below ground. Here the home took on a more modern look, and Luc couldn't help but smile when he saw the large entertainment center against the far wall.

She saw him smiling. "I enjoy movies," she said.

Past this room was a hall behind a door, and once she closed it behind him, Luc could not hear even the ambient noises of the fine old house. His curiosity was piqued by the soundproofing, and it gave him a good idea of what might be ahead. At the end of the short hall, Catharine opened two opposing doors, and Luc regarded Catharine as the scents of sweat, fear, and anger drifted into the hallway. A delicate smile played at the corner of her lips.

"Guest's choice," she said.

Both rooms appeared to be two small saunas, finished in expensive slate and designed to work wet or dry, and each held a man bound to one of the four pillars that squared off the rooms. They weren't to his usual taste. Neither man looked remotely refined. They reminded him more of the sort Anders would enjoy. The one to the right wore a sleeveless gray shirt that revealed two full forearms of tattoos. He had a shaved head and a stocky build and was glaring openly at the two of them, more angry than afraid.

A fool, then.

The other wasn't as broad, but at least from his appearance and his scent, he had the sense to feel fear. His dark blond hair was buzzed short. His eyes widened when Luc looked in.

"Who are they?" Luc asked. He tried not to think of what Curtis would say about Catharine's generosity.

"Brutes," Catharine said, with a conviction that made him glance at her. She tapped her temple with one slender finger, and Luc understood. Catharine's grace gave her access to the thoughts of mortals. She could—and apparently did—judge their character. "I gave them both the opportunity to turn themselves in to mortal authority for what they have done to the women they have encountered." She paused and turned toward the man with the tattoos. He snarled into his gag. She looked back at Luc. "To their misfortune, they declined."

"Their misfortune, but not ours," Luc said.

Catharine's smile was no longer playful. This, he thought, was the woman behind her many smiles and gentle touches, a predator with a taste for brutes.

He felt a kind of admiration for her.

"I would like this one," Luc said, pointing to the smaller of the two men. Though she had offered him the first choice, Luc thought she would enjoy her time with the tattooed man more.

Her lips parted, and she revealed her fangs. "Take your fill. Justice's loss will be our gain." She went into the room with the tattooed man

and added, "The doors are sturdy and keep the sound from escaping."
She paused. "And my furnace is quite capable."

Then she closed the door.

Luc stepped into the room, and the bound man began to shake his
head wildly back and forth. Luc closed the door, took his jaw in one
hand, and held him steady until he opened his eyes and met Luc's gaze.

"Understand," Luc said. "You are done." The man's eyes widened,
and his whole body jerked with a sob that the gag barely contained.
"But I can make this end feel very pleasant for you." The man puffed
through his nose, his chest rising and falling rapidly in his fear. Luc
could hear the man's pulse, and he leaned in close, his lips an inch from
his ear. "It's up to you."

Luc let his glamour wash over his prey, a coolness that spread
across the man's skin and made him shiver. His panicked panting
slackened, and he sagged against the pillar. Luc turned the man's head
back toward him and pulled the gag from his mouth.

"I..." The man's confusion was palpable, his arousal fighting
with his sense of self-preservation. Luc extended his fangs and pressed
against the man. He slid his hand beneath the man's shirt and felt the
terrified heart hammering in his chest.

"Do you even regret what you did?" Luc asked, pulling the man
even tighter against him.

"Yes." His voice was raw with fear.

Luc took the man's shirt in both hands and pulled, tearing it down
the front, then pulling the ruins back over the man's shoulders and
down to his wrists. He stepped back, regarding the bound man, and
revealed his fangs.

"Oh, God," the man whimpered.

Luc decided the man was more to his taste than he had first thought.
Though he needed a shave, if he were dressed in better clothes and had
taken more care with his grooming... Well, it was too late for that.

"God, God." He was shaking his head back and forth.

Luc stepped up to him once again, and the man turned his head
away. Luc ran a hand across the man's exposed chest, his cool fingers
drinking in the warmth of the pounding heart, the racing blood. Fine
reddish hair covered some of the man's chest. Luc's glamour spread
from his fingers, and the man's back arched. He opened his eyes again

and looked at Luc. Though his eyes were wet with tears, desire was in his look.

"I don't want to die," he said.

Luc slowly traced down the man's chest, and then slid his fingers along the thin line of hairs that marked the man's stomach.

"You are going to die," Luc said. "I am going to end you."

The man shivered again, and Luc slid his hand farther, gripping him. Between the glamour and the fear, his prey was hard.

"I will make it feel good," Luc said again.

"Please…" the man said. It wasn't a plea for mercy.

Luc smiled, pulled the man's head back, and drank.

"This source of yours. The one who was with Renard at the beginning…"

"Lavoie," Catharine said. "I don't know her first name."

They were sitting on the elegant chairs again. Catharine's skin was flush with the heat and blood of her captive, and Luc knew he would look much the same. It had been a long time since he'd—how had Catharine put it?—*had his fill.* Since he had formed his bond with Curtis and Anders, he'd been free to partake every night and had been careful never to draw too much from one person.

This felt like luxury, and he had to admit to himself that he had enjoyed every moment. The man had begged, of course. They always did, even when they knew there was no hope. In the end, the man offered anything he thought might save his life, and Luc had taken every offering, each another course offered before the final, best, swallow.

Curtis can never know. The thought brought a new feeling to him, one he hadn't felt in a long time. Shame.

"Lavoie," Luc repeated, forcing himself back to the point. Now was not the time to revisit old moralities. "Is there a way I could speak with her myself?"

Catharine traced a finger along her bottom lip, though she had already cleaned off the last of the brutal man's blood. "I could tell you where she is. But whether or not she will speak to you? Well. That depends on how you feel about cats."

Luc blinked.

CHAPTER FIVE

A nders hated the cold. It wasn't winter yet—he fucking *despised* winter, but the way the Ottawa weather plunged in fall was almost as bad. He shoved his hands into his jacket and looked up at the sky. The clouds were rolling fast, and there might be rain later, but right now the sun was breaking through in places.

That was all he needed.

The large maple that grew in the backyard of Curtis's house cast a solid shadow, even now that the leaves were spilling onto the ground in messy yellow piles. When the sun broke free of the clouds, a shadow appeared beneath the tree, and Anders stepped inside.

The complete silence of shadow-walking had terrified Anders when he'd first fallen into a shadow. After weeks of the shadows seeming to whisper and call to him, he'd expected more of the almost-language, not the startling sensory deprivation. An inky endless midnight lacking stars spread all around him. He could see nothing at all, even though he knew the shadowed version of the maple was still right beside him. He brought flame behind his eyes, and his vision sharpened. In the past, the hellfire had colored the shadow world a dull bluish-purple, but ever since forming his bond with Curtis and Luc, Anders saw things differently. A pale yellow-white shine surrounded the objects within his line of sight. Just one more difference he couldn't explain and didn't really care to.

He turned to face the Glebe, leaned, and began to move.

Despite what they called it, demons didn't walk through the shadowed version of the world so much as *flow* through it. In the pitch darkness, an oily cold seemed to brush along his skin, and the black world shifted around him. The complete lack of color left signs useless, and even landmarks were often hard to discern, especially as Anders leaned more and picked up speed. It was easy to get lost, though the various eddies of shadows pulled and tugged at him hard enough that he knew he'd never be trapped here. Now and then, he saw a bluish purple flash streaking by in another direction. Some other demon shadow-walking. Every time, he tensed. He did not want to face an enemy surrounded by silence and an almost absolute darkness.

The other demons, however, moved on, slipping past him in a blink. Most gave him a wide berth. He supposed he looked strange to them, golden white instead of hellfire blue. He wondered if anyone knew it was him at all, or if they were just avoiding him because they didn't know what he was.

Either way, it made him smile.

Moments later, he was pretty sure he was where he wanted to be. The layout of buildings seemed right, and he saw the large park divided by Bank Street that he liked to use as a return point. He waited beside another tree—only natural shadows cast by natural things were gateways—and when it pulled on him, he let himself be carried through.

"Fuck." The light of day made him blink, and he closed his eyes and pulled on a pair of sunglasses. His eyes always took a while to recover from a shadow-walk. He opened them slowly, adjusting, and looked around. He was in the right place.

He heard a growl. Anders turned, ready to defend himself, and saw a young woman holding the leash of a large yellow lab.

"Sorry," she said, giving the leash a short tug. "He's usually friendly."

"It's fine," Anders said, holding out one hand.

The dog stepped back.

"Zaphod, what's wrong with you?" the woman asked.

Anders pushed a little of his allure to the surface of his skin, heat seeping from his pores and chasing away the last of the cool, still silence of the shadow walk.

The dog began to wag its tail and moved forward to lick his hand.

"That's more like it," the young woman said. "Sorry about that."

That's right, Anders thought. *I'm the boss.* He rubbed the dog's head. It looked at him with adoring eyes.

He never got tired of that.

"It's fine," Anders said again. He waited for the young woman to walk away—she nearly had to pull the large dog, who kept looking back at Anders and whining. He turned to go and felt a strange coolness brush the back of his neck. He glanced back at the tree just in time to see a pair of eyes lit the dark blue-purple of hellfire watching him from the shadow underneath the tree. They closed and vanished.

Anders froze.

It took a lot of effort to pierce the shadows to look out at the real world without returning from the shadows yourself. It also took strength, and power, and practice. Anders hadn't met many demons who could do it. *Fuck, I can't even do it.* Anders scowled. Curtis was right. *Someone's keeping tabs on us.*

And they're strong.

❖

The small foursquare house looked like many of the others on the street, a perfect example of the overpriced gentrified neighborhood. Not a single lawn had weeds, and even the leaves seemed to have fallen in an orderly manner. Multiple homes had paper bags of garden waste lined at the curb, like soldiers awaiting deployment.

Anders rolled his eyes and knocked on the front door.

The man who answered was tall, blond, and broad-shouldered. The long-sleeved shirt he wore was tight on his frame. He oozed a kind of confident masculinity and an unflappable calm.

Until he saw Anders. "What do *you* want?" he said, a line appearing between his eyebrows.

"Hi, David. I'm great. You?" Anders peered past him. "Can I come in?"

"No."

Anders smiled. He'd known David wouldn't invite him in. Residency was a powerful barrier, and not one David would casually part with. "Fair enough. Take a walk with me."

David scowled. "I can't."

"You can't?" Anders didn't buy it for a second.

"It's Ethan. He's..." David shook his head. "Never mind. Just a second." He turned his head. "I'll be back in a few minutes," he called. No one replied, but David didn't wait. He tugged a jacket off a row of hooks beside the door, and stepped outside.

David strode right past Anders and started down the sidewalk. Anders caught up. "David," he said.

"What do you want?" David repeated. He stared straight ahead and didn't slow.

"Someone took a shot at me."

David laughed. "Well, it wasn't me."

"I know it wasn't you. For fuck's sake, slow down."

David stopped walking and glared at him. "What kind of gun?"

Anders shook his head. "Wasn't a gun. It was a letter. It blew up in my hands, tried to eat me. Balefire, Curtis said."

David frowned. "Magic?"

Now I have your attention, Anders thought. "Yeah. Big magic, and it was delivered to our house. It got through the front door." He frowned. "Well, into the mailbox, anyway."

David crossed his arms. "So why are you telling me? I doubt you want to file a police report."

"No." Anders counted to ten and tried to find some of that "patience" shit Curtis was always going on about. David was definitely in a foul mood.

He tried again.

"Look, I just wondered. You seen anything like that before?" Anders watched him carefully. David was a rare thing: an incubus without a pack who was tolerated. He'd come into his demon heritage much later than most and had already been a cop by then. Having a demon on the police force—even a lone demon who'd normally get torn apart for preferring men—was useful, and he was pretty much at the beck and call of the Families. He was a mole, and Anders knew full well he had connections with the various nonhumans that moved through the city. Especially ones who didn't want to be seen by those more powerful.

David was shaking his head. "No. Getting an attack like that past a residency…That's a pretty big deal."

Anders sighed. "Tell me about it. Curtis was pissed." Anders took a breath. "Someone also sent three demons to shake him up. At his school. That's not the first time someone sent demons after him."

David shook his head. "No demons would strike at a wizard without the okay from one of the Families. Then again, he's an orphan, right?"

"No. We're…" Anders shrugged. He wasn't sure what the fuck his group was, but Curtis had definitely shown the other covens that their group counted. The wizards had had no choice in the matter.

"Maybe he needs to take a hint?" David said.

"What hint?" Anders said. "They burned one of his books and made a crack about the letter bomb. As far as hints go, that's pretty fucking weak."

David raised his hands. "I don't know. Obviously someone's pissed off at you guys. I'm just saying the demons and the Families might not get along, but they don't take potshots at each other without some sort of order from one side or the other. Malcolm Stirling doesn't take kindly to demons going rogue."

David said Stirling's name with a level of disgust that made Anders raise his eyebrow.

"Believe me," David said, not answering the unspoken question. "If demons took a shot at you three, Stirling either knew about it or is going to blow his stack when he finds out. No one wants that kind of trouble. You said they'd attacked him before. Who was behind it last time?"

Anders exhaled. "One of the Families, we think. Maybe even Stirling himself. Before they believed Curtis that we were a coven. But after that, Curtis made it pretty fucking clear that we were a coven and they needed to stay away from us. Since then, we've been staying out of their way, too, and there's been nothing for almost a year."

They reached the end of the street.

"Until now," David said. He stopped walking.

"Until now," Anders agreed. "I know you hear things, and I know you can find things out. I just want to know if you hear something that might have to do with us. You see a lot working clean-up," Anders said.

David's scowl made it clear what he thought about his "obligations." Despite everything, Anders was pretty sure David still just wanted to be a good cop. It didn't matter he had to feed on souls, or that he could conjure hellfire, or even that he didn't have a soul of his own. Somehow, some part of the human that David had been was still there. Anders wasn't sure if he pitied him for it or not, but it sure made him useful.

"Oh, and if anyone reports a missing guy, Native, tall, nice ass—it's okay. He's recouping with us."

"I'll keep an eye out for anyone matching that description," David said. He sighed. "I need to talk to you about Ethan." The change in subject made Anders blink. Ethan was another incubus, younger than either of them and brand new to his heritage. He'd only started changing last winter, and Anders had connected him with David, hoping that he could help Ethan survive. They were both packless, owing to their preference for men, but while David's occultation meant he had a use, Ethan would be considered disposable.

So he'd convinced him to hide with David.

"Yeah?"

"He took a beating. A bad one."

Anders scowled. "Where was he? What was he doing? That kid has to learn to stay out of the way."

"He knows. We both know. But he has to draw soul." David ran a hand through his hair. "He's getting by. But things are really tense out there right now. The packs are really riled up, and he's pretty much just blood in the water."

"The demons are riled up?" Anders frowned. "Why?"

David shrugged. "Hell if I know. Tempers are running high. I've had more clean-up this month than I've had in the last six." He paused. "You know, if Stirling isn't the one messing with you—and, if I'm going to be honest, as much as I hate that fuck I don't think he is, since you're still standing here—then someone else is really screwing the status quo."

Anders heard the frustration in David's voice. He swore.

"Yeah," David said. "And if Stirling doesn't find out what's going on soon, he's going to crack down on everyone. You know he can't look weak."

"Fantastic," Anders said. "I don't suppose he needs to know about the letter bomb if he had nothing to do with it, then. Though that probably makes it harder for you to find out if he did."

"You never bring me good news," David said.

"It's a gift."

David looked at him. "Are you sure you don't want to join us?

Three of us would make a pack. And we'd be no threat. 'Cause what you've got with the bloodsucker and the wizard? That's a threat, Anders." He rubbed his chin. "And threats don't last in this city."

Anders thought about it. Not being a threat? That sounded pretty fucking fine to him. But... *My fire isn't blue anymore,* he wanted to say. *No brimstone. I have no fucking idea what that means, but I like it.*

"I know," he said instead. "But no. We're good."

David shook his head. "Your funeral." He turned to go.

"Hey," Anders said.

David paused, his back to him. "What?"

"What about demons who can watch from the shadows?"

David turned and stared at him. Any incubus worth shit was a master of hiding what they were thinking or feeling, but Anders caught the surprise and the fear in David's eyes. It was there and gone again in a second, but Anders had seen it.

"What?" David asked, his voice betraying none of what Anders was sure he'd just seen.

"On my way here," Anders said. "I caught someone watching me."

"From shadow."

Anders nodded.

"You are in some serious shit." David stuffed his hands into the pockets of his jacket. "I know maybe five demons who can do that. You gotta be old, Anders. And you gotta have a lot of soul to pull that off. What the hell have you three done?"

"Nothing," Anders said, and the frustration made him raise his voice. "We've been trying to stay the fuck out of the way. But obviously, that's not good enough." He sighed. "Which five demons?"

David shook his head. "Not on your life. Or *mine.* But they're all in some pretty large packs, so they can draw on the group if they need to. So far as I know, they don't puppet for the Families, though." He frowned. "You sure the letter is related to the spying?"

Anders sighed. "We're not sure of anything."

David's voice softened for the first time since he'd opened his front door. "You want my advice? Get out. Whatever you get from those two, it ain't worth it. Me and Ethan, we could be a pack with you at the next full moon." He snapped his fingers. "And it's over."

"You sound pretty sure of that," Anders said. Something wasn't right here. David was offering something that would solve the problem, sure, but David barely tolerated him on the best of days. And Ethan couldn't stand Anders, even if he had saved the little shit from being wiped out.

David stiffened. "Whatever. Offer's on the table."

"Yeah," Anders said. "I noticed. Twice." He took a step toward David and met his gaze. David looked away.

"Something you're not telling me?" Anders asked. "'Cause we all know you don't like me much, and Ethan fucking hates me even though I saved him from a world of hurt when he was changing."

"You ruined Ethan's first love. The only guy who'd ever treated him nice, and you set it up so he'd catch Ethan with someone else in an alley," David said. "What, he's supposed to thank you?"

"You and I both know he would have killed his boyfriend if he'd tried to stay with him. He wouldn't have been able to resist drawing on him. Not when he was changing."

"And instead of explaining that to him, you set him up to fail," David said.

Anders rolled his eyes. "You ever try 'explaining' anything to a nineteen-year-old who just found out he's a demon? I didn't have the time. Curtis knew Ethan, and I didn't want to explain to Curtis how that other kid he knew at school sucked his boyfriend dry because I didn't stop him."

"You're such a hero. Did you tell Curtis you broke them up?" David asked.

Anders shrugged. "He knows they broke up."

"Because of you."

Anders nodded. "Yeah. Because of me."

"Well, aren't you just a saint these days?"

David turned to go again. Anders reached for his shoulder, but David shook it off. "Let me look into the letter," he said, his voice once again gruff and angry. "But don't expect much."

"This demon watching me," Anders said. "He watching you, too?"

"Ethan said he saw some eyes in the shadow before he got jumped." David walked away.

Anders let him go, more confused than before he'd arrived.

Someone's riding David to get me to leave Curtis and Luc, he realized. And then it hit him. *They don't give a shit about me. It's Curtis or Luc they want out of the picture.* He wasn't sure if he was insulted or not. Still, if he went with Ethan and David, like David said, the next full moon, they could form a pack and the triad would be undone, and Anders wouldn't be a threat to whoever the hell it was that was riding their ass.

Luc and Curtis, though, would be completely on their own.

Anders started walking, fists buried deep in the pockets of his jacket. He stared at the ground ahead of him, a thick knot of uncertainty twisting in his stomach. It wasn't the danger that made him nervous. It was knowing he had a way out if he wanted one.

CHAPTER SIX

Curtis parked his car on Acacia, checked the address on his phone one more time, and then got out and started walking back up the avenue. He hadn't often come near Rockcliffe Park, and he was mildly amused at the lack of sidewalks. Apparently, the richer elite of the city didn't deign to walk very often.

Or maybe they just didn't want visitors.

Curtis was pretty sure he knew which house it was. Even when he'd driven past, he'd felt *something* brush against him. A coven head from one of the Families would take warding seriously. Sure enough, when he got to the large Tudor revival house at the corner, he could feel a pressure in the air before he even made it to the front gate. Looking up at the imposing structure from the front gate, he had to force himself to maintain his gaze. It was a beautiful home, with herringbone brickwork on the ground floor and beams above, but it took effort to fight the desire to look away.

That's some serious magic, Curtis thought. *I have so much to learn.* He wasn't sure he could manage a ward as strong as the one he was feeling. By the time he made it to the front door, he was leaning forward like he was walking headlong into a strong wind. His own magic was twisting around under his skin. The pressure of the ward made him feel claustrophobic and exposed. His magic wanted out.

Breathe. He closed his eyes, took a few cleansing breaths, and forced himself to relax. He opened his eyes again.

He rang the doorbell.

Mackenzie answered the door, her tangles of hair once again held up by the two chopsticks but without the glasses she'd been wearing in the library.

"You're early," she said. She didn't sound upset, though. She sounded delighted.

"It's a bad habit." Curtis smiled. "But I barely made it up the front path. Quite the wards."

"Oh, right," Mackenzie said. "Curtis, I would like to extend you an invitation to visit our home today, so long as you are willing to act as a guest and bring only trust and compassion through our door."

Curtis blinked. "Uh, sure. I mean...I do?" The pressure of the ward remained.

Mackenzie grinned. "You pretty much have to say it all back."

"Oh," Curtis said. "Okay. I, uh, accept your invitation to visit your home today, and I'll act like a good guest and bring trust and..." He shook his head, not remembering.

"Compassion."

"Compassion. Through your door." The wards faded around him, and he gasped. "That's incredible."

"It's a temporary visa." Mackenzie stepped aside, and Curtis entered her home. The entrance hall was understated. Clean and painted a pale yellow, a single bench lined the long wall, which looked like a refurbished pew from a church. Small glass hanging vases were placed along the wall, each sporting a fresh-cut day lily.

Curtis was starting to feel like he should have put on something other than his Hello Kitty Stormtrooper T-shirt with the rainbow Death Star.

"Can I take your coat?" Mackenzie asked.

"Sure, thanks." Curtis shrugged out of his jacket and handed it to her, blushing. If she noticed the shirt, she didn't say anything. She pulled a hanger from the closet and had it put away in a moment. Next time, he was definitely going to wear something with a collar.

His skin was still humming a little. Curtis shook his head. "I've never felt a ward like that. I can flicker mine up and down, but yours has a built in dimmer switch."

Mackenzie laughed. "Yeah, with teeth. If you try to do anything violent, the wards will smack you down." His awe must have shown on his face, because she added, "It wasn't me. It was my great-grandfather. This place is a chantry."

"Oh," Curtis said. Finally, something that didn't make him feel ignorant. A chantry was a home that had been built by a wizard, and built to last. It could only be owned by a magical bloodline, so it was passed along through generations of those who had the gift. Each time the home was inherited, the power of residency only grew stronger. The magic, it was said, sang louder with each generation, hence the borrowed term "chantry." It was one of the things he was struggling with in his own house. His parents hadn't owned it long, and they had not been magic. It made warding the place harder, since it had officially only been his residence since they had died.

"Come on through," Mackenzie said while Curtis pulled off his shoes. She led him through the high ceilinged hallway and they reached a small parlor through a glass-paneled door. There were four other people all around their age in the room, and Curtis felt all of their eyes turn to him as they entered.

"Guys, this is Curtis." Mackenzie gestured to him. "That's Rebekah," Mackenzie said, pointing to a tall black woman who smiled at him in a way that made him wonder if his fly was open.

"Hi," Curtis said.

"Hi," she replied. He couldn't decide if she'd mocked his tone.

"That's Dale and his girlfriend, Tracey," Mackenzie said, continuing despite the chilly vibe filling the room. Dale put his arm around Tracey as though he wanted to drive home the point that they were together. They didn't seem like a likely couple. Dale was tall and broad and had a bland, forgettable face. He wasn't ugly, but he wasn't handsome. Tracey, on the other hand, was beautiful. Everything about her seemed "just-so," from the carefully toned highlights in her hair to the perfect manicure done in a pale rose varnish.

The two nodded at Curtis. Dale didn't hide a small scowl, and though Tracey's smile was sweet enough, it didn't reach her eyes.

"And that's Matthew," Mackenzie said, indicating a slender young man who was shrugging into his hoodie.

Matthew finished tugging his hoodie on and pulled back the hood. "I'm the last and least," he said. He was cute in a lean and clean-cut way.

"Hardly," Mackenzie said.

To Curtis's surprise, Matthew held out one of his hands and offered it for a shake.

"It's nice to meet you," Curtis said and meant it. Other than Mackenzie, Matthew was the only person here giving off a remotely welcoming feeling. They shook. After, the four gathered up their coats and bags. Curtis couldn't help but notice the sounds of glass and metal clinking, and there was an awkward moment when everyone was ready to go, and Curtis felt more and more like he'd done something wrong.

"I'm sorry to have interrupted you all," he said.

Mackenzie shook her head. "We were done anyway. It's craft night."

"Kenzie," Rebekah said, with a weight of warning in her tone.

"Guys, Curtis is cool." Mackenzie crossed her arms. "He's the one that made the coven with the vampire and the demon. He's not gonna snitch on us."

Matthew whistled. Curtis looked at him with alarm, but the young man was smiling. "Props," he said. Curtis felt himself blushing.

"It was nice to meet you," Tracey said. Even her voice was elegant.

The four took that as a cue and left the room. Mackenzie walked them to the door, leaving Curtis to stand where he was, feeling all the more an outsider. *They grew up with magic*, he thought. *I'm definitely on a lower playing field.*

"I'm sorry about that," Mackenzie said, coming back through.

Curtis shrugged. "It's fine. Besides, they seemed nice."

Mackenzie laughed. "You're a terrible liar."

He blushed. "Well, Matthew seemed nice."

Mackenzie nodded. "He's, like, the only nice Stirling. I think he got the whole family allotment."

"Stirling. As in Malcolm Stirling?" Malcolm Stirling was the head of the largest coven in the city. He looked like a high-powered CEO on the downward side of sixty and was, Curtis knew, the man most responsible for pretty much everything magical that happened in Ottawa.

Especially to Orphans. Curtis tensed. If Matthew reported him back to Malcolm Stirling, nothing good could come of it.

Mackenzie nodded. "Right. I forgot you've met him." The mischievous smile that lit up her whole face made Curtis relax a bit. "Matthew calls his great granddad the Iceman."

"Because of his charming personality?" Curtis said.

Mackenzie tapped her nose.

They stood quietly for a moment.

"Listen," Mackenzie said. "I'm really sorry about them. They're nervous about anything making it back to our folks or the coven heads, anyway. Strictly speaking, us gathering and playing around with magic isn't technically against the rules, but we're not from the same covens, so it's...unusual."

"And we all know how the coven heads feel about unusual," Curtis said.

Mackenzie nodded. "Yeah. Rebekah and Dale get really worried about something getting back to their parents."

"I can't say I blame them," Curtis said. "Anders says the Families are like the mafia."

Mackenzie's eyebrows rose. "That's...Wow. Is it awful that I don't think that's a terrible comparison?" She shook her head. "Don't answer that. Anders is, uh, the vampire?"

"He's my demon," Curtis said, then cringed at the way it sounded. "A demon. The demon. In my group. Coven. Triad." He took a deep breath. He was sure he was blushing.

Mackenzie had the grace not to tease him. He decided she was his new favorite person. Then he wondered if that was a good idea, but before he could wallow too much in paranoia, he decided to blaze ahead.

"So, I didn't manage to crack the Geas."

"Really?" She sounded almost offended. "I'm sure we figured it out. What do you think we missed?"

"We didn't. Or, you didn't. I did." Curtis pulled out the new sketches he'd done of the blood binding and put them on the table. He pointed to the one on the left. "This is what we thought we were dealing with—which, by the way, is still true. But if you look at the other drawing, I used two colors, to show how—"

"Oh, that's legit smart," Mackenzie said, looking at the second sketch. "Hiding something inside the binding by building the binding on top of it with some of the same runic lines?" She frowned at it for a while. "So, the top layer is the Geas holding the person trapped inside themselves, and this bottom layer is sort of a ward, isn't it?"

Curtis breathed out. "I think so. But it's got that same outside-in problem as the Geas. It aims back inside, back into the man caught in the Geas."

"So when you push, it punishes him."

"Exactly."

"I can't imagine how long it must have taken to come up with a bind rune based on the same framework of the Geas like this. This is... This is pretty epic finesse." Mackenzie leaned back and crossed her arms. "It's also really cruel. Curtis, who did this?"

Curtis hesitated. He liked Mackenzie. He really did. But he'd been known to misjudge people before, and he wasn't eager to let the Families into his life a second time. Still, he didn't have a lot of other options for this kind of problem. Mackenzie had been learning about magic for most of her life. She had a giant head start on him, and he had a man in his basement who couldn't survive forever on what Anders could make him eat and drink.

He took a deep breath. "I know I don't know you well enough to ask you not to share this, so if it's okay, I'm going to leave names out of it."

She frowned, and he held up his hand.

"But. I can tell you this: it was a warlock."

Mackenzie's eyes widened. She looked back at the sketches, clearly shaken. "Wizards who become vampires usually lose most of their magic."

"Usually isn't always," Curtis said. He realized he sounded defeated when Mackenzie looked back up at him and smiled. If she'd been thrown a few seconds before, she seemed to have recovered quickly. Once again, he felt relief at having met her.

"We'll crack it. But we're going to need some tools."

"I'm not very good with tools. Even my athame and I barely get along."

"That's an air thing." Mackenzie laughed. "But I was thinking more along the lines of Dr Pepper and cheezies."

Curtis smiled.

❖

Hours later, at the front door of the Windsor chantry, Curtis thanked her again.

"Enough," Mackenzie said. "You did just as much of the work as I did. I hope it helps."

"It has to," Curtis said. He rubbed his eyes. It was long into the night, and he'd been burning the candle at both ends lately.

"Go home," Mackenzie said. "Get some sleep. Don't try to crack it until the morning."

"I'm stronger when Luc is up," Curtis said, and then he winced. That wasn't the sort of thing he should admit to someone connected with the Families. It was official. He liked Mackenzie too much.

"Luc is the vampire," she said.

Curtis nodded. "Yep."

"Not *your* vampire? Just *the* vampire." She smiled to show she was teasing. She had left the room at one point to take out her contacts, and she was wearing her glasses again. She looked as tired as he felt.

"They're both mine," Curtis said. His face heated up. "It's... complicated."

"Uh-huh. Which means they're both hot?" She asked.

"Oh my God, you have *no idea*," Curtis said, and they both laughed.

"Good luck," she said. "And keep in touch?"

"I will." He nodded. "Thank you. I mean it. I couldn't have done it without you."

She waved a hand. "You would have gotten there eventually. You're a talented flick, Curtis."

"Flick?"

Mackenzie flourished her fingers, and a pale green light surrounded her fingertips. She flicked her wrist, and it vanished.

"Ah," Curtis said. "Flick. Gotcha. Thanks again for my continuing education. You have a good night."

"You, too," she said. Then she added, "Oh, and sorry about this part, but I have to say it. Your invitation to my home has expired."

"Wha—?" Curtis began, but then the push of the chantry's wards were pressing into his chest again. He took a step back, leaning into the press of it. "Seriously. Best wards ever."

"Good night, Curtis," she said.

"Good night."

Curtis turned and walked down the path back to the gate, the ward pushing him all the way, lightening only in increments until he closed the gate behind him. He walked back to his car, looking up at the beautiful houses that lined Acacia.

"A chantry," he said, impressed. It must be wonderful to have that level of security. A house with a residency so strong, it was built to be magic from the foundation up...

Wait.

"From the ground up," Curtis said. He grinned. He aimed his keychain at the car and beeped open the doors. Despite how late it was, he decided he had a stop to make before he went home.

❖

It took him a while to find a gas station—did the rich not need gas?—but it had maps, which was a start. He climbed back into the driver's seat, looking at his bag on the passenger seat. He'd tucked the maps inside, but now he felt the urge to spread them open and get started. Now wasn't the time, of course, but the more he thought about this, the more it made sense.

"They're gone," Curtis said. The two words seemed loud in the car, but this time, he felt no crushing guilt, no overwhelming pain, and no shame. His parents were dead. The house he'd lived in for the last few years was just that: a house. It hadn't even been their house that long. It wasn't a home, not really.

And it sure wasn't a chantry.

"Talk to the guys," Curtis said. Luc, especially. If anyone knew the value of a long-term plan, it was Luc. Curtis knew damned well no one could get a magical letter bomb into Mackenzie's house—not with those wards—and if things were going to continue to be dangerous, why should he settle for anything less?

So, maybe they needed to start over.

Curtis hit the power button and did a shoulder check while his hybrid sang out the little tune that let him know it had started.

Something moved.

He froze, twisting farther around, but he didn't see anything. He bit his lip, slowly gripping the wheel. The car pinged—he hadn't put on his seat belt.

It could have been a cat. Or just someone walking down the sidewalk.

He looked up and down the street, leaning forward in his seat. Nothing.

He pulled on his seat belt, still looking around.

Nothing.

He tapped his finger on the top of the steering wheel. Reaching into his jacket, he pulled out the pair of glasses he'd enchanted. He slid them on and took another look. He'd get a headache if he wore them too long, but he didn't see anything other than humans.

In fact, he didn't see anyone.

At least, not anymore.

Curtis exhaled and pulled off the glasses. He put the car in gear and started for home. Pulling out onto the street, he took another long look around him but didn't see anything or anyone.

"Paranoid," he said. But he couldn't shake the feeling like someone had been there. Someone who was now gone. And the problem was, the only "someones" he knew who could do that sort of thing were vampires and demons; vampires because they were fast, and demons because they could step in and out of natural shadows. The trees were big enough here, and the moon was up. At least he had the roads almost to himself at this time of night.

He'd gotten onto Colonel By and had finally relaxed when he heard a ping and the "check engine" message appeared on the dashboard screen.

"Of course," Curtis muttered. That was all he needed. The car felt okay, but you never knew what—

A series of pings and bells startled him, and he looked down to see the dashboard screen lighting up in various shades of orange and red. Tire pressure. Oil warning. Fuel low, which was impossible, since he'd just gotten gas. Temperature light. Air bag failure.

What the hell?

Something was burning.

"Crap," Curtis said. He looked up quickly to see if any other cars were coming up behind him, but the road was empty. He aimed for the shoulder and hit the brakes.

The car barely slowed. The brakes felt like slush.

He jerked the wheel back to the road before he hit the grass median. Wisps of smoke were coming from the vents, and he saw blacker smoke from under the hood.

Curtis stabbed the power button. Nothing. He yanked on the lever to put the car into electric mode. The lever wouldn't budge. The engine began to whine. Thicker smoke started to pour in through the dashboard vent. Gritting his teeth, he tried the hand brake. It wouldn't budge.

Curtis pulled on the wheel. He needed to stop the damn car, and at that point, he didn't care if he all but wrecked it, so long as he could get out. He braced himself, aimed for the grass median, and tried to bump his tires into the concrete curb to kill some of his speed.

He coughed. The smoke was foul and getting worse.

This is how they died. The thought came unbidden and was very much unwelcome. His parents. Their car had struck a lamp post and burst into flame.

The wheel lurched in his hand. It was like the car had a mind of its own and was avoiding his attempts to slow it down. Fighting him.

Trying to kill him.

"Tardus ad statur," Curtis said, letting the magic ride his fear. The wheel stopped fighting him, and he slammed his foot hard on the brake. It had even less effect than before.

Crap. He needed to slow the bloody car down. He balled the magic in his chest and then imagined it bursting out in front of the car. *"Ventorum."* Outside the car, a sudden wind whipped at the hood, and though it blew the smoke right up the windshield, the car shuddered in the face of the strong gale, slowing some. He heard a guttural woof, and open flames appeared on the dashboard vents.

Curtis looked. The car was still moving, but he'd managed to knock the speed back. Good enough. He reached for his seat belt, coughing in the thick black smoke that was now pouring into the car.

The seat belt wouldn't come loose.

Curtis covered his mouth with his sleeve, trying to get a half-decent breath, and then bellowed, *"Procella venti!"*

The magic rose to his skin and sparked there, sorcerous energy crackling with static across every surface before erupting out from him in all directions. The windshield, driver's side window, and rear window shattered out onto the street. Clear air blew into the car, and Curtis sucked in a lungful.

Curtis grabbed his bag with one hand, still trying to fight the car to the side of the road. The wind he'd conjured battered at the hood, and the plumes of black smoke were growing thicker. The smell of burning plastic was heavy in the car, even with the wind blowing through the broken windows.

"Aperta," Curtis said, letting the word take as much of his magic as it wanted. It was an inelegant casting, but he didn't care. The magic hammered at the clasp, and the seat belt snapped open. He threw himself at the driver's side door. It resisted at first, but the second time he shoved, it gave way, and he was out of the car.

He managed a quick sorcery that thickened the air around him like a cushion, and then he hit the ground, left leg first and going down hard.

For a few seconds, the world was filled with pain and motion. He rolled and rolled, asphalt tearing at his cheek and hands. His left leg burned from the impact. Curtis grunted, holding himself in a tight ball.

As soon as he could tell which way was up, he crawled from the middle of the road to the far side. Still no traffic, thankfully. A loud crash made him jump and he turned to look. His car had crossed the median and hit the railing bordering the bike path along the canal. It was finally at a stop. There was still no one around. Curtis fought off a hysterical giggle. It was a good thing Ottawa wasn't exactly a party town, or he might have hit someone with his car.

Just as he pulled himself onto the sidewalk, flames filled the inside of the car with a loud whoosh. He rolled onto his side and then managed to sit cross-legged. He watched the flames lick the inside of his car for a few seconds.

His skin raw and fingers shaking, Curtis reached for his phone and hoped it had survived his flying roll.

❖

Luc opened the door and stepped into the small hospital room. The relief on Curtis's face was obvious, as was the annoyance of the large blond man, pen and notebook in hand, who was talking to him.

"Are you all right?" Luc asked.

"Bumps, bruises, and road rash," Curtis said. "Luc, have you met David Rimmer?"

Luc regarded the man again. *Ah.* So this was the detective the Families kept handy to deal with anything inconvenient. He was certainly handsome, though as an incubus, that was hardly a surprise. "I think we may have met in passing once," Luc said and offered his hand.

David shook, squeezing a little tighter than he needed to. If Luc remembered correctly, David and Anders had some sort of history.

Apparently, it wasn't friendly, which was neither surprising nor immediately important.

"What happened?"

Curtis puffed out a breath. "As far as I can tell, someone whammied my car. It locked up tight, started smoking, burst into flame, and tried to stop me from getting out."

Luc reached out and touched Curtis's cheek. It was raw and red.

"I had to roll out while it was still moving," Curtis said.

"First the letter and now this," David said.

"Also demon attack. It's been a pretty crappy week," Curtis said. "I thought I saw someone when I was at the gas station, but…" He shrugged. "I couldn't make anything out, and I thought I was being paranoid. Ha."

"I'll check to see if the gas station has cameras, just in case."

"Do you have any idea who might have done this?" Luc asked David.

David shook his head.

"Oh please," Curtis snapped. "This is exactly how my parents died."

"The Families have already told me they had nothing to do with this," David said.

"Oh, well then," Curtis said. "If they say they didn't do it."

Luc put his hand on Curtis's shoulder. "If not the Families?"

David tapped the pen on his pad. "If not the Families, then you've still got vampires, demons, weres—"

"Except the letter bomb and the car were both some serious fire magic," Curtis said. "It's not like the Families allow that level of magic without their say-so…" He stopped, trailing off. He glanced at Luc, and Luc felt his worry through their bond.

They knew someone with fire magic who wasn't a member of the Families.

"What?" David said.

Curtis let out a puff of breath. "I was just thinking that no matter how bad you think it might get, there's always room for worse."

David didn't reply, though he narrowed his eyes.

"What will happen with the car?" Luc asked.

David waved a hand. "It'll be dealt with as quietly as possible, then buried. Something plausible but unlikely, I'm guessing."

"Super. Does anyone give me a new car?" Curtis said. "Or do I just put down 'magic' on the insurance forms and hope for the best?"

"I'll find out," David said, and he offered up a small smile. "Hey, if they really don't want you thinking it was them, I'm willing to bet the Families will work out something to your advantage."

Curtis snorted.

"I'm serious," David said. "If this wasn't a sanctioned attack, the Families will be pissed. The last thing Malcolm Stirling wants is for people to think they can smack folk around without Family approval. If you're willing to help them make it look like it didn't happen, they'll meet you more than halfway."

"I don't think they like me that much," Curtis said. "But I'm willing if they are, and if it gets me a new car on their dime? All the better. As long as it's another hybrid."

"I'll let them know." David closed his little notepad and rose. "And I'll keep you in the loop." He pulled his jacket from the back of the chair.

"While we have you," Luc said, "anything on the letter?"

David shrugged into his jacket. "What Anders told me was right. It's called balefire, and it would take a lot of skill to wrap it up tight in an envelope like that. There would have to be a separate enchantment to destroy the evidence—balefire doesn't burn paper—but that would be easy to pull off. Even a sorcerer could do that, with enough effort." He paused. "There aren't that many people in the city with the magical know-how to make balefire happen, though, and none I know of outside of the Families. And before you get pissed, I spoke to my contact with the Families and, again, they had nothing to do with it."

"So they say," Curtis said.

"So they say," David said, zipping up his jacket. "Look, I've been doing this a long time. If I'm honest with you, then yes. The Families could have done both. The car thing is absolutely their style, like you said."

Luc frowned. "But you don't think they did it."

David shook his head. "No. Because you're alive. The Families wouldn't screw up twice." He left, closing the door behind him.

"If that was supposed to make me feel better," Curtis said, "it needed way more puppies. Or something from the chocolate family."

Luc smiled. He put his hand back on Curtis's shoulder. "Are you okay?"

"Yes. I mean *no*. I'm sore, and I'm pissed off, but I'm okay." Curtis shifted on the bed. "I'd like to work some healing magic, frankly. Though I'm not knocking the painkillers they gave me. I want to go home."

Luc heard the tremor in his voice. "Okay," he said. "I'll go find out who I need to talk to to make that happen."

"Thanks," Curtis said. "Hey, where's Anders?"

"He stayed with our guest."

"Ah," Curtis said. "Probably had to give him another shower. I guess I won't be trying to break a Geas tonight after all."

"Probably not," Luc agreed. "There's always tomorrow evening."

"True," Curtis said, and then spread his arms wide. "Can't wait to see what blows up in my face next."

Luc didn't reply. It certainly did seem like whoever was trying to break them was aiming for Curtis first.

CHAPTER SEVEN

Sparks crackled on the end of the athame, but Curtis didn't seem at all bothered by their sting. The string of Latin he spoke was too quick for Luc to catch, and it seemed to have other words mixed in as well, from at least one other language.

Magic, as always, was fascinating to watch.

Their unconscious guest shivered on the bed but this time wasn't thrashing around in obvious pain. As Curtis traced patterns in the air above the man's chest with the crackling and snapping knife, the pattern of dried blood began to change. It wasn't pulsing as it had, and it almost looked wet.

It was. Luc took in a lungful of air and could smell the blood.

Finally.

Luc looked up at Anders, who stood behind Curtis, ready to catch him if the Geas fought back as it had before, and smiled. Anders relaxed a notch.

Curtis drew the blade down toward the man's skin, until the tip touched the edge of the Geas. Curtis spoke again, his voice hard and demanding, and the blood began to flow up the edge of the blade.

The Geas was coming undone. Pooling back into liquid and drawn up onto the athame. When the blade was full of blood and the man's smooth chest was clear of even a single drop, Curtis reversed the blade, aiming the point up at the ceiling. He pulled a small glass bottle from his pocket and uncapped the cork with his mouth. Taking the cork and the bottle in his free hand, he looked up at the blade.

"*Utrem.*" At the word, the blood leapt from the blade and poured itself into the bottle. Curtis smiled, lowered his athame, and then stoppered the small glass vessel.

On the bed, Renard's once bound "treat" inhaled deeply and began to snore.

"You're welcome," Curtis said. He pressed hard on the cork and stepped away from the bed. "I think we can wake him up now." Curtis closed his eyes for a moment. He looked pale, the red scrapes across his cheek standing out in stark contrast.

"The Geas is undone?" Luc asked.

"Both halves. The trap and the binding. Score one for team us."

"You look exhausted."

"I am," Curtis said. "I need to sleep." He put his athame back in the velvet-lined box and closed the lid. "But first I need to go cleanse my athame. I don't want any trace of that crap on her."

"Her?" Anders said. "Big pointy knife and you call it 'her'?"

Curtis shrugged. "I'm not big on obvious metaphor. If it helps, I think of my wand as a 'he.'"

"Do you name them?" Anders asked. "Like 'Stabby' and 'Pointy' or something?"

"They're tools of arcane power," Curtis said. "Not stuffed animals."

"I name my toys," Anders said. "There's 'Mr. Fisty' and 'Mouthful' and—"

"Gentlemen," Luc interrupted, pointing at the bed.

Their guest was waking up.

❖

The man's eyes fluttered. He put his hand to his bare chest and then he reached for his neck. He found only the smooth skin that remained after Luc's tongue had worked its healing.

The man opened his eyes. First he saw Curtis sitting by the window. Curtis offered him a wan smile. Then their guest turned his head and saw Anders and Luc. He froze.

"Now, what are we to do with you?" Luc asked.

The man lowered his hand slowly. "You're a vampire," he said. He frowned, like he was struggling to think clearly. "I was taken by vampires, but I don't remember you."

Luc waited.

"I was surrounded, and then…" He shivered, looking around. Curtis had said the Geas would have dulled his mental awareness, and it appeared to be true. "I can't remember." He took a deep breath. "Where am I?"

"Ottawa. My house," Curtis said. "You're safe. I'm Curtis. This is Anders, and that's Luc."

"What are you going to do to me?" His voice was bitter but held more than a measure of strength. He was in no position to make demands, yet he was trying to take control of the conversation. He was not easily broken, Luc realized. He granted him some grudging admiration.

"We're not going to hurt you. Oh, and I wouldn't—" Curtis raised his hand.

But the warning was too late. The man had obviously tried to call on his abilities. He yelped and clenched his teeth, his hands balled into fists.

"Sorry," Curtis said.

"Curtis freed you," Luc said. "But he also warded this chamber against powers not his own. We don't know you any more than you know us. It seemed wisest."

"You have a pet mage, too?" His tone was one of disgust.

Curtis bristled. "I'm no pet." Anders smirked. Luc shook his head at them, then turned back to their guest.

"It's more complicated than that," he said.

The man regarded him. Cleaned and awake, it was easier to see his heritage. He definitely had Native ancestry, though it was diluted. Métis, Luc thought, remembering the man's tattoo, the blue flag with the white infinity symbol, from years far less pleasant.

"You're going to feed on me, then?"

"No," Luc said.

"How about we skip the guessing game?" His voice was strong. Anger had crept in now, and with it, courage. Luc admired his comportment again. "How long have I even been here?"

"Three days. And frankly, I don't know what to do with you," Luc admitted. "I'm afraid we won you as a prize." The man looked horrified. Luc held up his hand. "I assure you, I need no…pets." When that made him scowl, Luc went on. "I know you're gifted. Curtis's warding wouldn't have worked had you not tried to call power. You're a wizard?"

The man shook his head, tight-lipped.

"You can sense spirits, then? And call them?" Luc said. Renard had said this man's type were *trouble* to the vampires. It would only make sense.

"Yes," he said. He almost spat the word.

"You've nearly died before, then?" Luc pressed.

The man hesitated. "At birth." He frowned. "Wait. My cousin. She was with me."

Luc shook his head. "We've only seen you."

The man's voice was raw. "I think he took my cousin. The vampire who had me," he said. "She was eighteen. Here for university. I came down to speak to her music class. I play the fiddle..." He shook his head. "I need to know if she's okay. I need to call my uncle, my aunt...It's possible she got away okay..." He shook his head, eyes wet. "Probably not."

"What happened?" Curtis said. His voice broke on the question. "Why did they come after you?"

"We didn't attack, if that's what you're asking." The man laughed, but there was no humor to it. "I don't even live here. Chantale, she... Like I said, she's here for school. She knew not to do anything to attract attention from *your sort*." The words were less spoken than they were growled.

"She's like you?" Luc was surprised.

"When she was fourteen, she tried to kill herself."

Luc nodded.

"As for why the vampires attacked us? We feel spirits. We can see them, call them. All spirits are visible to us. That's enough reason."

Curtis shook his head. "I don't understand."

"Those with his gift," Luc said, "can see the movement of spirits or souls. When a vampire wakes at sunset, or sleeps at sunrise, someone like..." he waited, looking at their guest.

"Eli," the man said, after a short pause.

"Eli," Luc repeated. "Someone like Eli can sense it."

Anders clarified. "They sniff out vampires."

"If we're close enough," Eli said. "Vampires are dead. Their spirits don't stick around during the day."

"Oh," Curtis said. He looked surprised. "I've never read about this before."

"What a shock," Eli said.

Curtis frowned. "What's that supposed to mean?"

"You're a rich white boy reading books by other rich white guys who wrote history they wanted remembered," Eli said. "When was the last time you gave a shit about someone you didn't know who didn't look like you?"

"About three nights ago when I stopped a vampire from draining you dry, and then, what, five minutes ago when I freed you from a Geas," Curtis snapped.

"Was that before or after you chained up my gifts?"

The two glared at each other.

"I like this guy," Anders said.

"Of course you do. He's half-naked and has a pulse," Curtis said.

Luc stepped forward. "Enough." Eli looked at him, and Luc finally saw some of the fear behind the bravado. "Is there someone you can call?"

Eli started to shake his head. "I don't know. If she didn't get away…" He swallowed. "She lived alone, and the scholarship she was on meant she didn't have to work this semester…" He shifted in the bed, muscles working across his chest and arms, but he was shaking and grunted. "I can try…I can try her cell and her apartment. I need to know." He paused, steeling himself. "I need to know either way."

"Here," Luc said, drawing a phone from his pocket. "It's pay-as-you-go. I had it loaded in hopes you would recover."

They watched in silence as Eli dialed and waited for a response. No one answered. Eli tried a second number. Luc caught the recording of a young woman's voice requesting a message. Luc could see Eli's fears grow. Then Eli tried a different number. Again, there was no answer, though this time a man's voice suggested they'd get back to him. The uncle, Luc assumed. On the fourth call, finally, Eli got a person. Luc listened, and Eli's quick glance at the vampire let Luc know Eli was well aware he could hear every word.

"Mom?" As much as Luc thought the man was trying to avoid it, Eli's voice cracked on the word.

"Eli!" On the other end of the line, the woman's voice was a mix of laughter and a sob. "Oh, thank God. Eli..." Her voice grew quieter. "It's Eli. He's okay. It's Eli."

"Mom," Eli repeated. "Mom, is...I tried Uncle Pierre's number, but no one—"

"Where are you?" she interrupted. "We'll come get you as soon as we can."

"Mom." The word was a demand.

There was a long silence. Luc could just barely hear Eli's mother breathing on the other end of the phone.

"Your aunt and uncle are here with us. Chantale, she..." She choked on a word, then cleared her throat. "There was an accident, the police say. A hit-and-run. But no one could tell us where you were, and we knew you were supposed to be with her. I kept calling, but the police gave me the runaround. Your brothers drove down to get Chantale's..." Words failed her then. She started to cry. "They brought her back here. We called her back, to ask her if she knew where you were, but she didn't. Your brothers went back to Ottawa, and they tried to find you."

"I'm okay," Eli said. He closed his eyes. "I'm with some people in Ottawa. They took care of me while I was out of it. Are Tristan and Nic still here?"

"No. We're at the cabin," his mother said. "They had a run-in with some demons."

"Are they okay?" Eli's voice rose.

"Nicolas is okay. Bruises, mostly, and...and some burns. Tristan will be okay. He just needs some rest. He has a broken arm and wrist. I can leave Nicolas with him, and I'll drive down to come get you."

Eli looked at Luc again. "Mom, I don't want you on your own. I can come to you. I'm a bit messed up myself, but I'm okay."

"Messed up?" Her voice rose. "What do you mean? Eli? What happened? Chantale's spirit said vampires attacked her." Luc heard the woman take a steadying breath. "She was only eighteen."

"I'm okay. I'm weak, and I feel pretty awful. Bloodsuckers did something magic to me."

"It's called a Geas," Curtis said quietly.

Eli frowned at him and held up his free hand. "Mom, it doesn't matter. I'll call, okay? Don't come here. I'll come to you. You guys just stay safe, okay? I'll keep in touch, every night, every morning. I just need to get back on my feet, and I won't let this shithole city hit my ass on the way out. I promise."

"Don't swear. What aren't you telling me?" Her voice had an angry edge to it now. "Don't you do something stupid, Eli."

"I need to go now. I love you. I'm safe." He tipped up the phone and thumbed it off, holding it in his hand for a few seconds before putting it down on the bedsheets beside him.

It started to vibrate a moment later.

"I'm guessing that's your mom," Curtis said.

Eli nodded. "Yep."

"You don't want to get it?" Curtis said.

Eli shook his head. "She'll keep trying to get me to go home."

The phone continued to buzz. "And you don't want to go home?" Curtis said.

Eli took a breath. "Not yet. I want those bloodsuckers punished first." He shifted his gaze to Luc. "No offense to your friends."

"None taken," Luc said. "And believe me, Renard and his compatriots are not my friends."

"Renard," Eli said. It sounded like a vow.

The phone stopped buzzing.

Eli tried to sit up straighter, but his arms buckled, and he slid back down again. "Damn it," he muttered.

"You've basically been asleep for three days," Curtis said. "At least. I don't know how long Renard had you out before we got you. You're going to need to eat and drink something. And take it slow."

He didn't look happy about it, but Eli nodded. He looked at Curtis. "Would you...Can you take off whatever it is you did? I can't defend myself if I can't even call on a spirit, and I can get better faster with their help. There are curing spirits I can call."

Curtis looked at the other two. Anders shrugged, but Luc nodded. Curtis reached behind the headboard of the bed and pulled out a piece of paper. The markings on the paper were intricate and done in confident slashes of black ink. He tore the paper in half. There was a single blue spark.

Eli leaned back in the bed, closing his eyes. "Thank you." The relief in his voice was obvious.

The phone began to buzz again.

"She's persistent," Luc said.

Eli didn't open his eyes, but he smiled. "It's a family thing."

❖

"Question."

Luc had been waiting for Curtis to ask. "Okay."

"Why did you ask him about nearly dying?"

"The gifts he has only come to those who've been close to death themselves," Luc said.

Curtis raised his eyebrows. "Oh. So…it's not inherited, like magic?"

"Your magic wasn't inherited," Luc said.

Curtis nodded. "True. But most of it is."

"It's some mix of the two, I think," Luc said, admitting that he wasn't sure. "But every spirit-speaker I've ever heard of has been one who has nearly died. They've all also had some ancestry, but…" He shrugged. "I don't know if it's the same elsewhere. I've only lived in Canada."

"Huh," Curtis said. Luc could tell he was storing the information away for future reference.

"Regardless, we've got a house guest for a while longer," Luc said.

They were in the living room. Curtis was sitting on the floor, carefully cleaning his athame. Anders sprawled on the other couch.

"He's going to need a couple of days to recover," Curtis said. "What did his mother say?"

Luc shrugged. "She was concerned about him. Also, his cousin was killed. It sounded like Renard's people surprised them."

"Oh God. They murdered her? I don't understand," Curtis said, and Luc could feel the echo of anger along their odd bond. He glanced at Anders and saw the demon was also looking at Curtis with concern.

"So he could have Eli at the *séance*," Luc said. "It was a way for him to show off, I think. A way to show everyone what he can have and what he can deny them in one stroke."

"People die so he can show off?" Curtis scowled. "I think Eli has the right idea. Renard needs to be punished. With a vengeance."

"Lapin," Luc said.

"I know," Curtis said, raising a hand. "I know."

"The last thing we need is Renard coming after us," Luc said.

"You forget the magic letter bomb?" Anders snorted. "You don't count that or setting demons on Curtis as coming after us? Or blowing up his car?"

"We don't know that's Renard," Luc said, and then he frowned. "And Eli's mother said demons attacked his brothers when they came to look for him."

"The last time demons attacked us, it was the coven heads," Curtis said, though grudgingly. "And that balefire letter would have taken some genuinely badass fire magic to craft." He leaned back, stretching his arms over his head. "Renard used to be a wizard, and he still has magic. Do we think he has enough magic to craft that letter bomb?"

"Fuck if I know," Anders said. "Magic's your job. But how's this: If the letter bomb didn't come from Renard, that means multiple people are pissed off at us at the same time. Those demons told you to back off, Curtis, and what's watching us is definitely demonic. So we've got a vampire problem—Renard; a wizard problem—the letter; and a demon problem—our stalker. You know what's better than three problems?"

"Puppies?" Curtis offered.

"One problem," Luc said. Anders nodded.

"Right," Anders said, and it was a measure of his mood, Luc thought, that the demon had agreed with him. "One problem is better than three. The bloodsuckers are too afraid to do anything about Renard because they're not strong enough, and then we come along. Suddenly demons and exploding mail? I don't think it's a coincidence."

"Technically, the letter came first. Why invite us to a meeting but blow us up before we come?"

"Plausible deniability?" Anders shrugged.

"So what do we do?" Curtis asked. "I can't finish my degree if demons keep attacking me in the library. And why would the demons do what Renard wants, anyway? I thought demons and vampires didn't get along."

"We don't," Luc said, and Anders smirked. "But it could be as simple as intimidation. As you said, Renard retains magical abilities. Wizards can force demons to do as they want, yes?"

Curtis exhaled. "Only if they really think it through. It's like playing with fire." He paused, and then groaned as what he'd just said sank in. "Though, come to think of it, binding a demon to a contract is pretty much just a different kind of Geas."

"See?" Anders said. "Renard."

"So what do we do?" Curtis repeated his question.

Luc leaned back in his chair. "For now? We learn. Catharine was kind enough to give me the name of someone who has known Renard a long time. Perhaps this person can tell us how to avoid his attention."

"Right," Anders said. "Because we've got a great track record of flying under the fucking radar."

Curtis groaned and put his head in his hands.

"Anders," Luc said.

"What?" the demon scowled. "Let's be honest. When Curtis bound us together, he didn't know we were going to light up like fucking fireworks. We're powerful, guys, and there's nothing we can do about that. It's going to piss people off. It pissed off the covens, and now it's pissing off the vampires. Unless you want to break our little threesome up, there ain't no way we're going to avoid this shit."

"Gee, Coach, thanks. Now I'm totally ready to play my best." Curtis's voice was thick with sarcasm.

"Curtis, babe, you *are* the best," Anders said.

Curtis looked up, surprised.

"He's right," Luc said.

"Vampire just said I'm right. Someone note the time and date," Anders said, but Luc ignored him.

"He's insufferable, but he's right," Luc repeated. "I'd hoped we could sidestep vampire politics, but I was naive. When you saved Eli, we declared ourselves a threat to Renard's rule. A vampire *Duc* is not going to sit idly by while there is a threat. He will try to make us misstep. We cannot attack him."

Anders shook his head and opened his mouth. Luc raised one hand.

"We cannot attack him, as then he could put us down without reprisal. But we need to learn everything we can about him and how he's got the demons under sway, if indeed that's what he's done. We need to protect ourselves and act carefully and calmly." He stared at Anders, who raised his eyebrows.

"What? I'm all about calm and careful."

Curtis laughed. Anders glared at him, and Curtis laughed even louder. The more Anders scowled, the louder Curtis laughed, until Anders crossed his arms and Curtis toppled onto his side, holding his stomach. Luc watched, amused. It took Curtis a few moments to recover.

"Man, I needed that," Curtis said, wiping at his eyes.

"Asshole," Anders muttered.

"Sorry," Curtis said, but a little half-laugh came out with it.

"So we're agreed?" Luc said.

Curtis nodded. "Watch, listen, learn. Oh, and get a new car."

"You can borrow the Mercedes if you need to," Luc said.

"Thanks." Curtis smiled. "So. Researching Renard, eh? How do we go about doing that? Is there a vampire's who's who book or something? A convenient website? Vampires dot com?"

"Not likely," Anders said, still grumbling.

"No, but I have a lead. And though I'll meet with the Lady Markham's contact alone, that's the last thing any of us do alone," Luc said. "Catharine made it clear she wouldn't appreciate more than one visitor. But after this, we need to stick together." He rose. "And on that note, I need to feed." He looked at Anders and tried not to let his distaste affect his voice as he added, "We should go out together, Anders."

Anders grinned. "A double date? I thought you'd never ask. I'll drive. Though, remember the last time we tried to pick up together? It all went to shit."

"Hey," Curtis said. "I'm sitting right here. I can hear you."

"Exactly," Anders said, smiling at him. "We picked you up, took you home, and you tricked us with a binding." He leaned back in his chair. "It was not our proudest moment. And worse than that? We had to share."

Curtis rolled his eyes.

"What?" Anders said. "I don't do sharing."

❖

The pub was deplorably common. Wood paneling, neon beer signs, a jukebox filled with what only the most base of listeners could refer to as "music," and over it all a thin layer of grime that Luc could sense more than see. Luc worked hard not to let his distaste show and instead focused on the clientele.

It didn't help.

None of these people seemed to have any sense of the sartorial, Luc thought. While he understood himself the allure of the occasional lapse of style for comfort, the jeans-and-a-hoodie look was for home, not the public. The same for jeans-and-a-hockey-jersey. And jeans-and-a-sweatshirt.

Frankly, he was fairly certain he was the only person in the pub who wasn't wearing jeans, with the exception of the bartender, who was—unfortunately—wearing leather pants.

Luc tipped the glass of red wine against his lips, allowing only the briefest taste to sneak through. The bouquet was terrible. He swore he could scent petroleum in this "vintage," and the flavor had all the subtlety of a rutting incubus.

Speaking of which, where had Anders gone now?

Luc spotted the demon at the far side of the room, playing pool with one of the younger men in the pub. The man had a short beard and tattoos that began at his wrists and vanished into the sleeves of his T-shirt. As the young man leaned across the table to make a shot, Anders pressed close to him and "helped" the young man's aim. He also muttered something, and the young man blushed before taking the shot.

He missed.

"He's here quite a bit, though he doesn't go home with the same guy twice, as far as I can tell."

Luc had detected the approach of the man, of course, but pretended to notice him now. He turned and was pleasantly surprised to see the man was wearing a pair of blue suit pants and a white collared shirt. Off the rack, of course, but for this pub, that was still light-years ahead of the others.

"I'm sorry?" Luc said, smiling.

"The pool player," the man said with a knowing smile. "The whole room watches him whenever he comes here."

"Oh," Luc said, realizing what the man was implying. "Oh, no. I promise you. He's not to my taste." *I only sleep with him once a month or so, but it's more of a contractual obligation.* "Please, join me."

The man's eyebrows rose. "Thanks," he said. Luc studied him as he joined him at the small table. The man didn't suit the rest of the pub, and it wasn't just his suit. He was clean-shaven, and his russet-colored hair had seen a barber with at least middling skill. He might not be strictly handsome—he suffered the affliction of freckles like so many redheads did—but in this pub, he stood out. More, his drink, which he set on the table, had come in a glass, not a bottle.

Luc took in some air and caught the scent of rum and the sickly sweet syrup of some sort of cola.

"I'm Luc," Luc said, offering a hand to the man.

He took it. "Corey." Corey had a decent handshake. "I haven't seen you here before."

Luc nodded. "I'm here with a...friend."

"Oh," Corey said, leaning back a bit. "I'm sorry."

"No." Luc smiled and let his glamour bridge the gap between them like a cool wind across flushed skin. "My friend is the one playing pool you were talking about earlier. We are very much just friends."

"Oh man." Corey blushed. "I basically just called your friend a slut, didn't I?"

Luc leaned toward him. "We've known each other a long time. It's a fairly accurate assessment."

Corey took a sip of his drink, hiding an awkward smile. "Well, I'm glad he brought you." His blush deepened. Luc always found men who blushed to be so very appealing. And on the fair-skinned, it was all the more apparent. The heat of the blood moving beneath the skin was tantalizing.

"I'd thought I was perhaps in for a disappointing evening," Luc said. "At first."

Corey swallowed. "You've changed your mind?"

"No," Luc said. He let the silence go on just long enough to capture Corey's gaze with his own. Luc's glamour stroked the man again, a coolness that did anything but chill them both. "You did."

"Ah," Corey said. The skin beneath his freckles warmed even more.

Luc picked up his wineglass and tipped the foul red against his lips again. He glanced briefly across the bar. Anders had his arm over the shoulders of the scruffy young fellow he'd been playing pool with, and the two were moving farther back into the bar, no doubt to find a darker corner. Luc spotted a dartboard.

Luc turned to Corey. "Do you play darts?"

"I've never tried." His self-deprecation was charming. "I'm not sure you should trust me around sharp pointy things."

Luc smiled. "You can trust me with them."

❖

Trouncing Corey at darts hadn't dulled either of their moods, and Luc found himself genuinely warming to the young man. When Corey asked, hesitantly and with more of his guileless authenticity, if Luc might want to "walk together," Luc agreed. He hadn't needed to give the man much of a nudge with his glamour beyond their initial contact, just enough to bolster Corey's courage to make the first move.

"I'll just go find my friend and say good night," Luc said.

"I'll get our coats?" Corey offered, and Luc gave him his ticket.

He found Anders in a darker corner of the bar, with one hand down the back of the pants of the scruffy inked trash he'd been playing pool with earlier. The bearded man was moaning into Anders's neck while Anders moved his hands in a way that left little to the imagination as to what was happening.

Anders met his gaze over his plaything's shoulder. Even in the dim corner, Luc could see Anders's eyes had blackened. He was drawing on some of the young man's soul even here. Luc supposed he should just be glad it was only Anders's fingers inside the younger man, and they both weren't naked and fucking against the wall.

"I'm heading home," Luc said, ignoring the way Anders's movements picked up speed, and the moans increased in volume. "I'm going to walk. You'll drive back?"

Anders smiled. "I think we're probably ready to head home soon ourselves, aren't we, little Otter boy?"

"Yes, sir." The man's voice was muffled against Anders's neck. Anders winked at Luc, and Luc left them to their public groping.

He rejoined Corey at the front of the pub and took his coat. They stepped out into the chilly autumn air, and Luc smiled at him.

"It's cold. Are you sure you wouldn't rather take a cab?"

"I don't mind," Corey said, putting his hands deeper into his pockets. He had a longer coat, and though it had a nodding similarity to a duster, it didn't look particularly warm. He had looped a green scarf around his neck, however.

"I live off Riverside," Luc clarified, and Corey nodded again.

"I like a walk," he said.

They started walking. "I never asked," Corey said. "What do you do?"

Luc smiled. "I was trained in woodworking," he said. "But that was a long time ago. Mostly I deal with antiques now."

"Oh." Corey was obviously genuinely interested. "I co-manage a small gallery. Paintings, mostly, though some sculpture."

Luc looked at him. "If you don't mind me saying, you seem far more cultured than the rest of the clientele at that pub." That was an understatement.

"Well, maybe." Corey looked down at his feet for a few steps. "I'm not always…uh…comfortable at some of the other bars."

Luc slowed to a stop, and Corey followed suit, looking up at him shyly. Luc glanced around. Once he was sure they were alone, he stepped up close to Corey and nudged him back until he was pressed against the brick wall of a closed restaurant. He lowered his lips to kiss Corey, and the man responded—hesitant at first, but soon deepening the kiss. Luc loosed more of his glamour, and as the coolness spread from his lips, Corey gave him a small murmur in return, pressing more firmly against him. Corey's hardness was obvious against Luc's thigh. He broke off the kiss, and Corey blinked at him a few times.

"Are you comfortable now?" Luc teased.

"Uh, yeah," Corey managed. "I'm…" He frowned suddenly. "Ow!"

Luc caught the scent of something burning before he felt it, and he moved back from Corey just as smoke began to rise from the redhead's coat. His own jacket was also smouldering.

Luc drew his speed to the surface, the world slowing around him as his body sped up. He tore his coat off, flinging it away before he leapt at Corey. Already, small licks of flame lapped along the long jacket's edges like candles stirred by a gentle breeze. He gripped the front of the jacket and pulled it open with both hands, tearing it with his unnatural strength and drawing on the blood that fueled his graces.

Corey cried out. Luc loosened the draw on his graces. The world was picking up speed, and the coat hadn't come completely free yet. He forced Corey to turn and tore at the flaming jacket, pulling it hard to get the young man's arms free at last and tossing it aside just as it burst wholly into flame.

"Holy shit, holy shit..." Corey pushed back away from him, though his back was to the wall, and he was struggling to keep his feet. "Ahh," he hissed. Luc could see scorch marks on the man's shirt and on his pants across his thighs where the coat had burned him.

"We need to get out of here," Luc said.

"What the hell?" Corey stared at him, eyes wide. "You just set me on fire!"

Merde. This wouldn't do. Luc took a step toward Corey, and Corey slid farther away, finally tripping over his own feet and half falling against the wall. He slid down and landed hard on his ass. He was pale with fear and wide-eyed, angry red marks on the back of his trembling hands.

"Don't hurt me!" he said. "Please!"

Luc met his gaze. "It wasn't me," he said, and he let the full force of his glamour wash over the prone young man. They didn't have time for this. They were out on the open streets of the city next to two burning coats on the sidewalk. Not to mention Corey's cries.

"Forget about the coats." Luc pressed his glamour harder. "We have better things to think about."

Corey blinked, and his breathing slowed from the fevered rush of fear. He opened his mouth slightly, and his whole body shivered.

"Come here," Luc said, holding out one hand.

Corey took it and let Luc pull him to his feet. He continued with the momentum and pressed against Luc, once again hard and willing.

"We need to cross over a few streets," Luc said, smiling down at him. "I'll call a cab."

"Okay," Corey said. His voice was full of need. "I..." He frowned a little, and again Luc allowed his glamour to wash over the young man. The frown smoothed, and the redhead smiled up at him again. "I like you," Corey said.

"I like you, too." Luc led the young man away from where their coats burned on the sidewalk. He fished his phone out of his pocket and dialed Anders first, to warn him off from the coat check at the pub. Hunger coiled deep inside him. He would have to be careful with Corey when he got him home. He'd fed a lot of blood into his speed and strength and glamour, and he needed to recover some strength.

Anders answered his phone, and Luc forced himself to ignore the pangs. He warned the demon, who swore colorfully about how much he liked his leather jacket. Luc hung up and called a cab.

"My hands hurt," Corey said. His voice was a bit foggy and lost. Luc's glamour was by far his strongest grace, and it had always served him well. Luc wrapped his free arm around the younger man and pulled him in close, enjoying the warmth and the scent of him.

"I'll make you feel better soon," Luc promised, but he couldn't help but remember the feel of the coats as they'd ignited around them. If he'd been a little slower or hadn't noticed the scent for a few seconds more…

Once again, fire was the danger.

Hunger clenched inside him, unexpected and sharp. He tightened his hold on Corey and hoped the cab would come soon.

❖

They moved through the door together, Luc steering Corey through the hall and into the kitchen, then the sharp turn to the stairs. Corey gave him a shy look as they started down the stairs, and Luc paused with him long enough to lean down and share a short, light, kiss.

"Hiding me in the basement?" Corey said. His voice had returned to normal, the glamour having effectively washed away his fear and the memories of the sudden fire.

"Keeping you to myself," Luc said, and Corey ducked his head, a flush spreading under his freckled skin. Luc's jaw ached with the pressure of holding his fangs in check. He guided Corey down the stairs, and they were inside his basement bedroom in a few hurried moments more.

"I don't normally…" Corey said, his voice trailing off when he met Luc's gaze. The young man swallowed.

Luc stepped forward and slid his hands under the suit jacket Corey wore, pushing it over his shoulders. Corey let the jacket slide down his arms and fall onto the floor. Luc traced his hands up across Corey's shoulders, then cradled Corey's neck, leaning in again for a kiss. The young man wrapped his arms around Luc's neck, pulling him into the kiss with an eagerness that wasn't all to do with the glamour's power. He then mimicked Luc's movements, pulling the jacket off the taller man's body and throwing it over the back of his desk chair. Luc turned back to Corey, and with a small smile playing on the corner of his lips, began to work the small white buttons of Corey's shirt.

The man was trembling now, and a shiver ran through Corey's entire body when Luc pulled the unbuttoned shirt free from his trousers. Luc's smile grew, and he pressed against Corey, kissing his throat while he slid his fingers beneath the opened shirt and drew it off him.

Below Luc's lips, Corey's heartbeat felt like a painful pleasure. He wanted to feed right there and then, to open his mouth and sink his fangs into the young man and swallow greedy mouthfuls of blood. But with a great effort, he pulled back and let Corey try to work at the buttons of Luc's shirt.

He leaned back, letting the young man undress him. Corey's body was trim and his skin pale, dusted with freckles across his shoulders. He was pleasantly built, well groomed, and—if the trembling in his fingers was any clue—not greatly experienced. Luc found all those things very appealing.

When his own shirt had fallen to the floor, Luc pressed their bodies together again. Nervous or not, Corey was hard now, and when Luc teased his fingertips across the small of Corey's back, dipping them below the waist of his pants and inside the elastic of the young man's underwear, Corey responded the same.

Luc licked and kissed the side of Corey's throat, finding where the blood flowed hardest, and just barely nipped at his skin. It was driving him crazy; the hunger and desire were mixing into a single need. He'd already been hungry before this evening had begun, and now he was ravenous.

"Oh," Corey whimpered, when Luc's teeth grazed his neck a second time. Luc knew he didn't have much temperance left. He reached down between the two of them and tugged at Corey's belt. Corey returned the gesture, but together they were fumbling a bit, so Luc stepped back and started to work on his own trousers.

Corey did the same, and they were soon naked before each other.

Corey stared at him with no slight surprise. Luc knew Corey was still dazzled by the glamour, but he also knew his body was sculpted and strong. Corey swallowed again, looking down at Luc's obvious arousal, and bit his lip.

"You're really hot," Corey said. "I think maybe I won the prize here." His voice was the slightest bit uneven, and Luc was charmed all over again by this sweet red-haired man.

"What would you like?" Luc asked. He had to work to hide his fangs now; they were extending despite himself. He was fighting the urge to push Corey backward onto the bed and bite down hard into his lean thighs. The man had very little body hair, whether from grooming or genetics, and Luc could imagine all too easily the veins that ran through the man's thighs near his hard, upright cock.

"Uh," Corey said. He laughed, though he was still hard. "Can I maybe suck you?" His face was blazing red by the time he'd asked the question.

"I would like that," Luc said. "And I would like to fuck you, Corey, if you would like that, too. I would like to lie you down on my bed, roll you onto your lovely smooth stomach, and fuck you." He paused while Corey swallowed again. Corey's dick had visibly reacted to the words, raising higher up toward Corey's stomach. "And then I'll roll you back over again, and suck you till you come. Would you like that?"

Corey managed to nod, mute.

Luc smiled and Corey slid down to his knees. He was not an inexpert cocksucker, Luc realized, pleasantly surprised that his shyness wasn't born of inexperience. Once he'd adjusted to Luc's cock, Corey was soon swallowing him as deeply as he could, using one hand to stroke Luc's length in opposition to his mouth. Corey's tongue was talented, too, teasing Luc's cockhead with some skill. Luc closed his eyes and let a hand rest on Corey's hair, bucking only slightly into the young man's mouth, but he knew he would not be able to stand waiting for long. The aching need was only growing the more he felt the heat of the man's mouth working his cock.

Luc murmured in appreciation. He opened his eyes and looked down, and found Corey doing his best to look up at Luc while he worked.

Enough, Luc thought.

Luc reached down, pulled Corey up from under his shoulders, and kissed the young man when they were standing. He moved him back onto the bed and knocked him gently on his back when they bumped the edge of the deep red blanket. Corey looked up at him, breathing heavily, biting his bottom lip again, and it was all Luc could do not to leap at the young man's throat.

He went to the antique bedside table and tugged open a drawer. Condom and lube in hand, he slid onto the bed on his knees, and Corey moved up on his elbows just long enough to accept one more kiss, harder and deeper than the others, and then the young man obediently rolled onto his stomach.

Luc settled between the young man's lean legs and worked the lube into him with a single finger, rubbing gently, opening him as slowly as he could force himself to go. A second finger joined the first, and soon Corey was pressing back against him, taking long, even breaths while he shifted almost languidly on the blankets.

He opened the condom and sheathed himself, and then he pressed the full length of his body against Corey's back. He kissed between the man's shoulder blades, then the side of his neck. The pulse there was fast and so very tempting. Luc shivered above him.

"You're cold," Corey said, a breathy exclamation.

"Let's warm up, then," Luc said. Reaching down to guide himself, he pushed slowly into Corey, who exhaled hard as Luc pressed. Corey shifted under him once, then twice, but didn't resist as Luc buried his length into him. When they were together, Luc's stomach against the small of Corey's back, Luc slid one arm up tight around Corey's chest and squeezed.

Corey moaned.

"Yes?" Luc asked.

"Yes," Corey said.

He began to fuck the young man in earnest, slowly at first, but they soon found a rhythm that worked for both of them. Luc squeezed tight with every rocking thrust, and Corey braced his elbows against the pillows, arching his back and gasping out little noises of pleasure. Luc kissed the young man behind his ear, then licked his way down the side of his neck. Corey turned his head, willingly twisting to give Luc easier access.

They moved faster now, Corey's cries growing louder and deeper as Luc's thrusts grew harder. And when Corey shifted just enough beneath him that Luc felt the pulse beneath his lips, he thrust deep into the young man, who cried out in pleasure just as Luc opened his mouth and sank his teeth into the soft flesh of his neck.

CHAPTER EIGHT

L uc's coat blew up?" Curtis frowned.

Anders shrugged. "It caught on fire. He picked up this prissy ginger trick, and when they got too close to each other, their coats caught on fire. He didn't give me the full rundown, just told me not to put my coat on when I got it back from the coat check. He said I should give it to you. I stole the other guy's coat, too, just in case."

"The other guy…The guy Luc brought home?"

"No, the one I fucked in the bathroom. Luc's guy went home already."

Curtis glanced at the hallway. "You had sex in the bathroom?"

"No, not here. At the pub." Anders spoke slowly, like he was explaining something to a particularly slow child.

Curtis rubbed his temples. He was still wearing boxers and yesterday's Totoro T-shirt, and he'd barely been awake ten minutes. "I haven't even had a cup of tea yet." He glanced over at the kitchen table, where Anders's well-worn leather jacket was draped over the back of a chair. The light windbreaker of the lucky fellow who'd enjoyed an evening with Anders in some random toilet stall was folded up on the kitchen counter.

And they say romance is dead.

"Sorry." Anders pressed up against him and wrapped him into a strong hug. "Did you sleep okay?"

Curtis smiled. "I did. I was pretty wiped. I didn't even hear you guys get home." It was comfortable in Anders's arms, just like it was to be held by Luc. Some days, that bothered him. He wasn't sure what the hell the three of them were outside of their mystical bond, but he knew "friends" didn't cover it. But right now, in the cool autumn morning, he didn't care. He leaned back against Anders. Anders had one of his seemingly endless supply of sleeveless black shirts on, and his thickly muscled arms felt amazing. The demon always ran hot.

But that reminded Curtis of the coats, and the car, and the letter bomb.

Moment ruined, he thought. Curtis sighed and pulled free from the hug. "Okay. So, more fire."

Anders nodded.

Curtis shook out his hands and took a deep breath. Some instinct had come with his magic, a gift of words and language that he could feel rising to the surface. He'd slept well and felt refreshed even if he was a little groggy and hadn't had a cup of tea yet.

The magic wanted out, and was felt good to feel it stirring beneath his skin, rising up his spine.

"Revelare."

He looked at the coats, holding his hand palm out, an inch or two away from the leather jacket. He moved it slowly as he repeated the words to hold the magic in place, keeping the reins taut. Twists of deep amber and orange began to shift across the surface of the black jacket, knots and ropes of magic bound into the leather. It wasn't subtle, and it wasn't anywhere near as intricate as the Geas had been.

Curtis turned his hand over. *"Retexere."* He slowly closed his fingers, and the twists of magic were pulled out of the jacket and drawn into his open palm. He squeezed his hand shut, the bound magic swirling in his open palm a moment before bursting. A rush of heat and wisps of smoke drifted from his closed fist.

Then nothing.

Curtis nodded, then turned to look at Anders.

Anders leered at him. "God, that is so fucking hot," he said.

Curtis blushed. "Thanks."

"I'm serious. You should get naked."

"Uh, good morning."

They both turned. Eli, looking wan and leaning against the opening to the hallway, gave them an apologetic smile. He wore one of Anders's sleeveless shirts and a pair of Luc's cotton pyjama bottoms, both of which weren't quite the right fit on him, but still better than anything

Curtis could have offered. Curtis couldn't help but notice Anders wasn't the only man in the room with impressive arms. Eli was fit.

"Morning," Curtis said, stepping toward him. "How are you feeling?"

"I still feel like crap," Eli said. "But I was hoping there'd be coffee?"

"Ha!" Anders said. "A coffee man. Finally. I'll make it. You are shit at coffee," he said to Curtis.

Curtis exhaled. *So much for being fucking hot.* He turned to Eli. "Have a seat." He moved Anders's jacket and then carefully picked up the windbreaker and put it on the kitchen table.

Then he finally filled the kettle, putting it on the oven to boil.

"What was that you were doing?" Eli asked, nodding to the jacket.

"Someone put an immolation spell on it," Curtis said.

"Which is sort of stupid, since I'm pretty much fireproof," Anders said. He was grinding some beans. The smell of the ground coffee was pleasant, Curtis thought, even if he'd never liked the taste of coffee itself.

"It would have still been inconvenient to your date," Curtis said. "Y'know, if you'd taken him home, rather than…" He waved a hand.

Anders shrugged. He filled the coffeepot with water. "Didn't feel like being patient. Sometimes you just wanna fuck 'em against the nearest wall."

Eli's eyes were wide. Curtis wasn't sure whether or not he should apologize to him. "Did you want some breakfast?" he asked instead. "Are you hungry?"

Eli blinked, looking at him. "Um, yeah. Okay."

"Eggs? I was going to make myself an omelette."

Eli nodded. "That'd be great. Thanks." The thank-you felt a little forced and tacked on, but Curtis decided to let it go. Eli wasn't going to be Curtis's best friend any time soon, whether or not he'd freed the man from the Geas.

The kettle started to whistle. Curtis moved it to the trivet and threw a couple of tea bags into a teapot. He turned off the oven-ring and then frowned.

"I get trying to burn Luc," Curtis said. "But you're right. Trying to hurt you—or your date—with fire, it's pretty weak."

"Don't ask me, I'm not the warlock with the hate-on," Anders said. He was leaning against the counter now while the coffee brewed.

Curtis tapped his finger on the teapot, and then he turned to look at the windbreaker. He called the magic again, feeling it coil happily in the palm of his hand. Repeating the words that had come to him earlier, he moved his palm out over the jacket that had belonged to Anders's "friend" and waited.

Nothing. There was no magic on the windbreaker.

"You said that Luc's jacket burst into flame when he was kissing the guy he picked up?"

"Yeah," Anders said, watching him.

"It's missing half," Eli said.

They both turned to look at him. Eli was looking at the two coats, lips twisted in distaste.

"You can tell that?" Curtis asked.

"The fire was made to wait for another of its kind," Eli said. His eyes were a little out of focus. Curtis realized he was looking at something in the air between them. Something Curtis himself couldn't see. "It was forced into the leather to wait." He tipped his head. "You can go now."

Curtis waited for something to happen, but nothing seemed to.

"What did you do?" he asked.

Eli exhaled. "The spirit of the flame was still nearby. Your magic"—his words were thick with disapproval—"leaves them disrupted and confused for a time."

Curtis blinked. "I can't see or feel anything."

Eli's smile wasn't warm. "I know."

"Now you know how I feel," Anders said.

Curtis touched the leather jacket. "So, the idea was for your coat to end up near Luc's, in case the guy Luc was with didn't go home with him, or whatever. I think maybe you were a backup to trigger Luc's immolation."

"You sure about that?" Anders asked.

Curtis shook his head. "I'm just guessing, really. But there's nothing on this coat, and you're right—fire against a demon is sort of pointless. But it's very effective against a vampire. Or me. Or my house…" He took a deep breath. "Because if the coats had just ended up beside each other in the hall closet before they'd gone off..." He let the rest go unsaid.

"Someone really wants you three dead," Eli said.

"No," Curtis said. "Someone just wants any one of us dead. They only need to take one of us down to make the rest of us not a threat." He turned back to the teapot and poured himself a cup.

"What are you going to do?" Eli said.

Curtis looked long and hard at the leather jacket.

"Breakfast," he said. "Breakfast, and then recon."

❖

"So, I don't mean to be rude, but...What are you guys?" Eli asked, after they'd finished eating.

Anders grinned and leaned back in his chair, obviously willing to let Curtis field the question.

"I'm a wizard," Curtis said. "He's a demon. And Luc's a vampire."

Eli nodded. "I know that, but they've both got part of your spirit."

Curtis blinked. "What?"

"Your spirit. It's spread out between the three of you."

"They have part of my soul?" Curtis's voice rose. He cleared his throat.

"You didn't know?" Anders said.

Curtis gaped at him.

"I've never seen it before," Eli said. "That's why I thought maybe you were the vampire's pets."

It was Anders's turn to frown. Curtis was staring. He realized his mouth was open, and he shut it.

"Um," he said. "We're more like a coven. Or coterie, or a pack, I guess. Something like that. I call it a triad, but it's really just a bond, like a regular group. Only instead of us all being wizards or vampires or demons, we're..." He shook his head. "Can we go back to the part where they have my soul?"

"Spirit," Eli said.

"Soul, spirit. Whatever," Curtis said. "Is it dangerous?"

"Dude, I'm not gonna get it dirty," Anders said.

"Says the man having sex in public bathrooms."

"Oh, like you've never—"

"I've never," Curtis said.

Anders leaned back. "Really? It was like a rite of passage in the seventies."

"I wasn't alive in the seventies." Curtis gritted his teeth. He looked back at Eli. "Is it dangerous?"

Eli stared at the two of them, and Curtis figured he was deciding whether or not he should just make a run for it, weakened or not. "I don't think so," Eli said. "You can't harm a spirit, not really. They can change, and they move on, but sharing a spirit isn't unheard of. I've seen it done for deep curings and in some special ceremonies. It's just usually not done with…" His voice drifted off. "Uh, people who don't have spirits."

"I swear I was only trying to make us count as a coven," Curtis said.

"Why?" Eli asked. His voice, already deep and rough, was low with disbelief.

Curtis took a moment to gather his thoughts. "If you're magic—all the way magic, not just a sorcerer, say—the Families only let you use the magic if you're in a coven. But they control the covens, so really, they control the magic—so they control you. They're not good people."

Eli snorted, so Curtis assumed he didn't need the rundown on the various infamous qualities of the Families.

"Anyway, I didn't want to sign up. I found Luc and Anders during a full moon. See, the covens and packs and coteries have to get together on full moons—"

"I know."

Curtis bit off his words. "Right. Okay. Well, they were alone, and all the research I'd been doing came back to three. Three wizards, three vampires, three demons. And it occurred to me that nothing in the tradition said it had to be a matched set. Or at least, nothing prohibiting it. So…" He shrugged. "Here we are."

"You bound yourself with a demon and a vampire," Eli said.

Curtis nodded. "Yeah."

Eli looked at him for a few seconds.

"Anyway," Curtis said. "That's what we are."

Eli exhaled. "I guess that explains your spirit, then." He rubbed his eyes, and Curtis saw the deep shadows underneath them.

"You should probably get some rest."

"Who knew being asleep for three days would be so exhausting?" Eli said. He didn't sound pleased. "I just want..." He yawned. "You're right." He rose, and Curtis could see the effort it took.

"If you want, I could work a healing spell, maybe?" Curtis said.

"I'm calling on curing spirits," Eli said. It wasn't a completely curt dismissal, but it was a good imitation of one.

"You need help getting back to bed?" Anders asked.

Eli frowned at him.

"Just ignore him," Curtis said. "We're going to be heading out. Did you need anything?"

"I wish I had my fiddle," Eli said. "But no, I'm okay. I'm just going to go lie down again." He left, and Curtis heard him climbing the stairs to the second floor.

"Oh, you're welcome," Curtis said. "It was just an omelette. Don't worry about it."

"What?" Anders asked.

Curtis sighed. "Nothing."

"I like him," Anders said.

"I'm not surprised. He's rude and dismissive and handsome. Come on, help me clear the table. Then we're heading out." Curtis started picking up the plates.

"Is it okay if I bring your soul with us?"

"I will hurt you."

❖

"You're sure we're okay leaving Eli by himself?" Curtis asked.

"He'll be fine. You've warded the house." Anders wrapped one arm around Curtis's neck and gave him a squeeze and a quick tickle. They'd parked his SUV near the park where Anders had seen the demon peering at him from out of the shadows. Curtis had wanted to give the spot a magical once-over, which Anders figured couldn't hurt.

"Right," Curtis said. He ducked out from under Anders's arm. "Because that worked so well with the letter bomb."

"He's not going to collect any mail," Anders said. "The guy barely managed walking to the kitchen this morning." He smiled. "I wonder if he'll still need help with a shower later?"

Curtis rolled his eyes. "You give and you give."

"It's my nature," Anders said. "Okay, here's where I stepped out."

"That tree?" Curtis asked.

Anders nodded. He watched Curtis look around, but it was another cool day, and the park was empty except for the two of them. Curtis reached out his hand and started to mutter under his breath in what Anders assumed was Latin. He turned in a slow circle, still muttering, and walked around the tree trunk.

As far as Anders could tell, nothing happened, but magic was sometimes like that. He'd seen Curtis pull black clouds and a torrential downpour out of a sunny sky, but he'd also seen him slam someone to the ground with a word and a gesture. When a demon used their powers, anyone paying attention would know something was up. For one, the demon's eyes turned an inky black, swallowing up even the whites if the demon pulled out the really big guns. For another, claws and hellfire weren't subtle. Demonic power wasn't easy to hide.

Magic, on the other hand, wasn't always obvious.

He shoved his hands in his pockets and waited.

A minute or so later, Anders felt a pulse of something from Curtis. Satisfaction? It ran like a shiver up his spine. He'd never get used to the way he could sometimes catch a piece of what was going on in the wizard's head.

"Gotcha," Curtis said.

Anders grinned. "What'd you find?"

"Demon," Curtis said. "You were right. Someone pumped so much demonic power in this area, I'm still getting a little trace of it. Given how much time has passed, that says a lot. I don't feel any trace of you." Curtis rolled his shoulders. "And you're powerful, too."

"I can't do that 'watch from the shadows' trick."

"Not yet, you can't," Curtis said, still peering at something Anders didn't see. "Give it time. We're all getting stronger." He crossed his arms. "It's worn."

"What?" Anders said. He moved beside Curtis, but still saw nothing. *Fucking magic.*

"I think…" Curtis reached out a hand, but shook his head and drew it back. "It's hard to explain, but I think this isn't the first time the shadow under this tree got used as a spy-hole. It's not like scrying, where you bring a vision of a place to you. That doesn't really leave a trace. But this..." He bit his lip. "This spot has been used a lot. It's left a mark, like a weak spot between the world and the shadowy place you go where things have been rubbed a bit thinner."

Anders grunted. "Makes sense."

Curtis looked at him. "It does?"

"Sure. This park is a great spot to end up, and it's easy to know where you're at when you're on the shadow side. I bet a lot of demons use this place." He knew the park was popular. Shadow-walking needed natural shadows. You couldn't pop in and out of a shadow cast by a house. A tree, a mountain, something that had time untouched by people—that's what it took. Anders looked around. He'd chosen Central Park as the easiest spot closest to David's house. But Central Park and both halves of Patterson Park were pretty central in the Glebe, crossing Bank and O'Connor, and offering a lot of trees and even some cliff sides. The three parks had no shortage of natural shadow. No doubt they saw a lot of demon traffic.

"I can't really tell anything else," Curtis said. That sense of satisfaction was gone now. "Sorry. I was kind of hoping I'd be able to feel something about who was doing it. 'Demon' isn't really specific, is it?"

Anders shrugged. "Worth a try."

"Wait," Curtis said. "How often do you come here?"

Anders frowned. "Not often." He knew of much easier places to track down a willing piece of ass than the Glebe. As far as Anders was concerned, the Glebe was a bad mix of pretentious hipsters trying to find meaning in the bottom of overpriced lattes and organic fusion restaurants and had nothing better to do than drive expensive cars and mortgage their old homes to renovate the character out of them.

"But before the other day? How often?" Curtis asked.

Anders shrugged. "A year maybe? Nine months ago, I guess. I don't know." He did know. It had been when he was trying to find Ethan somewhere to be safe, when the kid had started to come into his demon heritage. He'd come to talk to David about it, last winter.

"Okay," Curtis said. "Okay. Well, this spy-hole has been in use way more often than that, especially over the last few weeks, I'd say."

What had David said? *Blood in the water.* Something was up with the packs. Anders frowned. "So it's not just me that's being spied on."

Curtis nodded.

"David said there's been a lot of shit going down lately with the demons," Anders said.

"Huh," Curtis said. "I guess he'd know. He's sort of the cop in the pocket of the Families, right?"

"Right."

"Okay," Curtis said. He shook his head. "Wait, though. Why would a demon spy on other demons?"

"Fuck if I know. But it can't be good," Anders said. But then he frowned. "Unless it's David."

"Doing the spying?" Curtis said. "I thought you said he wasn't in a pack. Would he be strong enough to pull off that trick?"

"No," Anders said. "No, I mean what if it's someone watching David?" He turned his head. "He lives a little bit over there. This must be one of his most-used ways in and out." *Ethan, too*, he thought darkly. Ethan, who'd had the shit kicked out of him even though he'd been trying to stay out of harm's way.

"I'm confused," Curtis said. "I thought David was pretty much in line. He doesn't have a pack, but he's got a deal. Everyone uses him to help keep things on the down low if there's magic or demons or whatever. And he gets left alone."

"Except someone took a swing at Ethan," Anders said.

"Stop." Curtis held up his hand. "You said Ethan was safe. I haven't seen him in months, and his ex-boyfriend is still a mess over what you did to them. And what the hell does Ethan have to do with David, anyway?"

Anders exhaled. "Look, it's complicated."

"Simplify it." Curtis was pissed. Anders didn't need their bond to know that.

"Ethan started to change," Anders said.

"Yeah, I remember. You spotted him, helped him—and by 'help,' I mean you broke him and his boyfriend up with a public display of indecency."

"Had to be done." Anders shrugged. "Anyway, Ethan needed somewhere to lie low. He didn't have a pack. He was going to finish changing pretty soon, and then it'd be open season on the twink demon, and I knew you'd be pissed if he ended up dead, so…"

"So…?" Curtis said.

"I sent him to stay with David."

Curtis stared at him. "You sent Ethan to David. Ethan who is in danger. You sent him to David, the cop who is under the thumb of the Families, the vampires, *and* the demons."

"When you say it like that, it sounds dumb."

"Anders."

"He's learning the ropes," Anders said. "Besides, David is the last place the Families or other demons would look for trouble. And if they can find another demon with no taste for pussy, then they can make a pack. David gets out from under that thumb, and he owes me a solid."

Curtis opened his mouth. He made a little choking noise, then closed his mouth again.

"See? Genius." Anders crossed his arms.

"Anders, that's…that's not a plan. That's a series of actions designed to break rules and spit in the faces of the people in charge."

Anders grinned. "I know. Perfect, right?"

❖

"They won't let you in."

Curtis just shook his head and didn't slow down.

Anders swore, then caught up. "Look, David's taking care of him."

"You said he got beaten up." Curtis's voice was carefully even. *Uh-oh.* He was pissed.

"That's what David said," Anders said.

"And you just left him there, beaten up." There was a complete lack of inflection in any of the words. Anders tried not to flinch, then got annoyed at himself. He'd done the right thing, for fuck's sake. Why was Curtis pissed at him? He'd saved Ethan, who'd been completely ungrateful and a total snot about it. Curtis should be singing his praises.

"I left him with David. David wasn't about to let me in," Anders said. "I'm sure David's got it under control. But if you want to check in with him this much, then we will."

"Good." It sounded anything but.

They paced each other for a while.

"It's the next one on the left," Anders said.

Curtis's expression was grim. "Nice house."

"Yeah," Anders said.

Curtis took a deep breath and went to the door. He knocked and waited.

"He might be at work," Anders said.

"He works nights," Curtis said. "You told me that already."

Anders grunted. Damn wizards and their damn memories. "Then he's probably asleep."

"Maybe," Curtis said, and he knocked again.

Anders shoved his hands into his pockets. He was about to say something else when the door opened.

"Yes?" A decidedly sleepy-looking David loomed in the doorway. His hair was ruffled, and he was wearing a pair of jogging pants and a white undershirt. He smiled at Curtis. The entire package looked more or less like the cover of a fitness magazine promising a great workout, tips for a new and improved sex life, and a tell-all about what it was like to have a far-greater-than-average penis length.

Curtis made a noise somewhere in his throat that Anders usually liked to hear, but he was used to being the source of it. He bristled.

"Hi, Dave," Anders said.

David looked past Curtis, and his smile vanished. "What do you want?" he asked.

"Curtis wanted to check in on Ethan," Anders said. "I told him you wouldn't let him in, but—"

David took a single step back. "I wouldn't mind."

"What the fuck?" Anders growled.

Curtis turned and glared at him. "Anders."

"He doesn't go in without me." Anders crossed his arms.

David took a moment to think about it. Then he nodded. "Okay. But you stay out of sight, Anders. Ethan can't stand you."

"Not uncommon," Curtis said.

Anders rolled his eyes. "Fine."

David took a deep breath. "You two can come in for the next hour. Not a second longer."

Anders felt a ripple of power against his skin. Residency was a powerful thing. Even letting someone in with a caveat was dangerous.

"Thank you," Curtis said.

They went inside.

Anders had never been in David's house, but nothing was all that surprising. The furniture was straightforward and basic. David had probably bought it all in flat packs and assembled it himself, Anders figured. The entrance opened into a living/dining room, through to a kitchen, and had stairs leading up to a second level. It was a small and simple house.

"You have a lovely home," Curtis said, and Anders barely stopped himself from smirking.

"Thanks," David said. "Ethan is upstairs. Come on up."

They followed him up the narrow stairway. David hesitated at a closed door in the upstairs hall and nodded sharply to Anders. Anders scowled but stepped out of the line of sight. He could see into the master bedroom from there. It was just as plain and boring as the rest of the "lovely" house, Anders thought, then he caught sight of a framed picture on the bedside table. It was David, smiling and laughing, with his arms around a man who was smiling up at him with a look of adoration and pride. It was a black-and-white photograph, but Anders knew the man's short hair had been a deep red and his eyes a dark brown.

Chad. After all this time, David still kept a picture of him? Anders sighed and looked back out the hall just in time to see David and Curtis step into the spare bedroom. He waited. He could hear David's low voice, and then Curtis's, but the answer that came to them was pale and weak. Ethan was obviously not in good shape.

Minutes passed.

Anders itched to go look through the door. He even took a step toward it, but then David was backing out of the room, Curtis in tow.

David closed the door quietly.

Curtis's expression told Anders all he needed to know. "That bad?" he asked, doing his best to keep his voice down.

Curtis nodded. "I thought demons healed fast?"

David exhaled. "We do. If we've drawn enough soul."

"And he hasn't," Curtis said.

"He gets what he can on the full moons," David said. "And we try to make sure he's okay the rest of the time, but..." His voice trailed off. They all knew the reality. Without a pack, Ethan was scraping by. David had a measure of freedom owing to the way he was of use to the movers and shakers of the supernatural world, but even he could only help Ethan so much.

"What about, uh…bringing him someone home?" Curtis suggested. He blushed to the tips of his ears. Anders chuckled.

David nodded. "He's got apps on his phone. We make sure I'm around, and we don't do it often."

"Well, then…" Curtis shook his head, obviously confused.

"Looking like that?" David raised his eyebrows.

"Oh," Curtis said. Then, a second later. "*Oh*…He can't change how he looks?"

"Too weak still."

Curtis bit his lip. "But he can't get strong without…" He blushed again. "You know."

David nodded. Anders knew him well enough to know he was fighting a small smile.

"There's gotta be someone who's into bruises," Anders suggested.

"Ew," Curtis said.

David took a breath. "I'm sure there is. But that's not really the kind of visitor I'd like in my home."

"All he needs is enough to allure himself into looking better. Then he can top up on whoever he wants," Anders said.

"Looking better," Curtis said.

David and Anders both looked at him. Curtis was smiling.

"I don't suppose you've got a calligraphy pen?"

David frowned. "No."

"How about a marker? Preferably a red one."

"I think so," David said, but he didn't move.

"What do you want a marker for?" Anders asked.

"Because I don't use blood to draw something magic on somebody's skin," Curtis said. "Ethan can't change how he looks, but I'm pretty sure I can. Kind of."

"Kind of?" David crossed his arms.

"Trust me," Curtis said. "When I'm done, you can fire up his app and get him a date."

"If he's really bad, you might want to line up two or three," Anders said.

Curtis's ears went pink.

❖

When they came back out of the room, David was scowling.

"I need you to go look at him," Curtis said.

"I thought he didn't want to see me," Anders said, keeping his voice low.

"He doesn't. And the spell didn't work—" David muttered.

"It worked," Curtis said. "It's just—"

"He looks the same. You said—"

"No, it's because we saw him before. If someone who doesn't know—"

Anders held up his hand. "Stop."

They fell silent.

Anders nodded at Curtis.

"I'm not great at illusions, so this is more like a misdirection. There's a suggestion on his skin to not notice the bruises."

"But it didn't work," David said.

Curtis exhaled. "It did. But you can't not notice something you've already seen." Curtis shrugged. "We can test it by letting someone who hasn't seen Ethan all banged up see Ethan now."

"Ah," Anders said. "Is he awake?"

Curtis nodded. "I needed to explain what I was doing."

Anders rubbed his chin. "Okay," he said, and he *changed*. He let his allure reach out to David, and the heat washed over his skin in a wave. His view shifted, and he fought off a wave of vertigo as he grew shorter. An ache burned through his arms and chest, spreading lower and across his stomach and then down his legs, and he grunted.

"Whoa," Curtis said.

Anders took a second to recover, then looked at David. "Good enough?"

David stared at him for a heartbeat, then nodded. "Just don't talk." His voice was gravel.

Curtis led the way.

The bedroom was as spare and plain as the rest of the house, but Anders saw traces of the young man lying in the bed. A laptop on the small desk covered in stickers. Pop cans. Clothing tossed across the floor.

Anders looked at Ethan and saw nothing wrong. He was lying down on his bed, blanket and sheet pulled up to his waist, head propped up with a few pillows. A tablet lay beside him, though the screen was dark. He turned his head, and although his skin seemed smooth and unblemished to Anders, Ethan winced.

"Sorry," Curtis said. "Last time we bug you, I promise. I just want to take another look at what I did. Make sure it set."

Ethan looked at Anders, but there was no sense of recognition in his soft blue eyes. His dark hair was a bit longer than the last time Anders had seen him, and he'd continued to fill out. His shoulders were wider, his chin stronger. The demon was emerging. Incubi were all handsome and masculine. Though Ethan would likely always have a quality of youthful good looks to him and would probably keep those baby blues, he was definitely losing his baby face.

Ethan nodded. "Fine." He sounded angry. He drew out his left arm from below the sheet, and Anders could see the red lines Curtis had obviously drawn on the young demon's forearm. It might have just been a red marker, but it was beautifully done. There were three words, though Anders didn't have a clue what they said. Ethan's arm, like the rest of him, appeared fine. Tan. Healthy. No bruises.

Anders looked at David and nodded.

David tilted his head to the door.

Anders took the hint. On the way out, he caught a reflection of himself in a mirror beside the door. He was shorter, which he'd already known, but his skin was also much fairer. He was slimmer, nowhere near as bulky as his natural state. And apparently, even though his first boyfriend was now long dead, David still had a thing for redheads.

"Thank you," David said at the front door.

"You're welcome." Curtis shrugged. "I'm happy to help. Ethan and I used to know each other. Before…" Curtis seemed to struggle for a word, then shrugged again. "Before." He bit his lip. "Listen, the demon watching from the shadows. Can I ask you something?"

Anders wasn't sure if David was going to answer or just close the door, but after a few seconds, he sighed. "Ask."

"How long ago?" Curtis asked. "The first time you noticed someone watching you, I mean. Because I looked at the spot under that tree in the park, and it's been used as a peephole *a lot*. And I think for quite a while."

David thought about it. "Maybe six months ago. For sure, anyway. Before that, I had a feeling sometimes like I was being watched, but the first time I saw the eyes, it was definitely spring."

"And Ethan?"

"About the same, I think. I can ask him once he's better."

Curtis smiled. "Thanks."

David held out his hand. Anders blinked, surprised. Curtis shook it.

When they let go, David said, "He didn't mean half the stuff he said to you. He's just angry."

Curtis smiled. "I know. Aren't we all?"

"Lately? Seems like it," David said. He stepped back into the house and closed the door.

Anders led the way, Curtis beside him. He looked out onto the street out of habit, but nothing seemed amiss. A couple of guys were walking some bikes along the sidewalk toward them, but that was it. He wondered how David could stand living in such a pretty, *boring* place.

"What did he say to you?" Anders asked.

"Huh?" Curtis was obviously deep in thought.

"David said Ethan didn't mean what he said to you. What'd he say?"

"Oh, he was mad I never told him I was a wizard. Back in university when we kinda-sorta knew each other at the LGBT Center." Curtis laughed. "Because it's a great icebreaker. 'Hi, I'm Curtis. If I'm not careful, when I swear things explode.'"

Anders raised his eyebrows. "Really?"

"Really," Curtis said. "Wizards and tempers don't mix."

"Huh," Anders said, then he paused. The two young men on bicycles were close now, and a slow smile spread across his face.

"What?" Curtis asked. He looked at Anders, then looked ahead.

"Give me a second," Anders said. He left Curtis behind and walked up to the two young men. They wore identical white dress shirts and neatly pressed black pants. Little black name tags were clipped to their shirt pockets.

"Excuse me," Anders said, and he let his allure briefly wash over him—a quick pulse of heat that was more of a tap than a touch. "I was wondering if you two had time to check in on a friend of mine?"

Both of the young men openly gaped at him. One licked his lips. Anders barely stopped himself from laughing out loud.

❖

"David? Two inbound for Ethan. Repressed Mormons. You're welcome." Anders didn't even give David time to reply before he ended the call and put his phone back in his pocket. He turned to Curtis, who was still shaking his head.

"That'll help Ethan out," Anders said. "Get him back on his feet." *Because if it all goes to shit, I want him strong.*

"How common is it?"

"Mormons secretly wanting blow jobs? It's like coffee shops. One on every corner."

"No! You, and Ethan, and David." Curtis blushed again. It was adorable. Every time Curtis blushed, Anders wanted to see how much more uncomfortable he could make the young man. Not that now was the time.

"Not very."

"So then it might be a while before Ethan and David find a third," Curtis said.

"Yeah," Anders said. Then he remembered David's offer to join them. *Or not long at all.*

"Do you ever get…" Curtis started, then stopped. "Never mind."

"Do I ever get what?" Anders asked. He grinned. "Mormon ass? Blow jobs? Boy, I swim in blow jobs."

"That doesn't sound as appealing as you think it does," Curtis said. "No, not blow jobs. I was going to ask if you ever get tired of it?"

"Tired of blow jobs?" Anders frowned.

"No!" Curtis said, annoyed. Anders laughed, and Curtis shoved him.

"It's how my clan feed," Anders said. "Lust, sex, hedonism…It's all good. And it feels fucking fantastic."

"So that's a no?" Curtis said.

"No. I don't get tired of fucking and sucking and making cute things such as yourself squirm and beg and…"

"Okay, okay!" Curtis held up his hands.

"It's better than the other options," Anders said.

"Sorry?"

"Lust. Best way to feed."

"But there are other ways?" Curtis looked surprised. "What other ways are there? You can draw on souls without sex?"

"No, I need lust," Anders shook his head. "I'm an incubus. Sex and pleasure. But there are other clans of demons."

Curtis leaned back. "You're kidding. Seriously? What other kinds of demons?" He was grinning now. Anders almost laughed. Trust Curtis to be excited that more demons were out there than what he already knew about.

"Pick a deadly sin," Anders said.

"What?"

"Pick a deadly sin."

"Okay," Curtis said. "Sloth."

Anders leaned away from him. "Seriously, all those good choices, and you go for sloth?"

"Since joining with you and Luc, I have become a big fan of the nap."

"Okay, well, some demons can feed on your soul through your dreams or even your daydreams. Your inspiration. They mostly stick to the hot places, where it's easier to find people willing to pause and rest. Like a siesta or whatever. And they love artists and creative types. In fact, they've been called muses."

"A *soul-sucking* muse," Curtis said. "Which sounds less appealing than the traditional muse."

"Some of the best artists had demons. Actors, musicians..." Anders shrugged. "But you don't want to hear about that."

"Yes I do."

"Maybe I'd feel like telling you more after a blow job."

"You? The worst. Completely the worst."

"Nah, I'm the best," Anders said. "Anyway, all that to say different demons can get at your soul any number of ways—all your baser instincts. The seven deadly sins are oversimplifying things, but it's a pretty good list. Envy. Wrath. Gluttony. You get the idea."

"I guess it shouldn't surprise me that lust is the most common."

"You calling me common?" Anders said.

"You are a unique and special snowflake."

Anders snorted.

They walked in silence for a bit. Anders could tell Curtis was thinking about everything he'd said. Digesting the new information. He could feel the young man's intense concentration through their bond as he placed this new knowledge in some sort of organized fashion in his bright, sharp mind.

Then Curtis chuckled.

"What?" Anders asked.

"You said hedonism. That's four syllables." Curtis smiled. "Good for you."

"You can be a snobby little thing, you know."

"But I give good head," Curtis said.

"Prove it."

"Maybe when we get home. If you keep using words with four syllables." Curtis let out a breath and stretched. He winced.

"You okay?" Anders asked.

"My neck's still a bit sore from jumping out of the car." He stopped walking. "Wow."

Anders paused beside him. "What's wrong?"

"I jumped out of a car," Curtis said. "If you'd have asked me a few years ago to list the ways I could hurt my neck, 'jumping out of a car' wouldn't have been on it."

Anders nodded. "You're an action hero."

Curtis laughed. "Right." He started walking again. "Let's get some tea and head back to the park. I want to take another look at that peephole."

"Tea is worse than moose piss."

"Coffee, then. This is the Glebe. We'll find an overpriced café."

It didn't take them long. Curtis got himself a green tea while Anders held his nose. The demon ordered himself a dark roast and explained to the barista that he didn't want any no-fat dairy anything in it, no fucking agave-nectar or stevia leaf or even goddamn sugar. Just coffee. She looked shell-shocked by the time she handed him the cup, but she stopped suggesting ways to "improve" his drink.

The park was the same as when they'd left it; no one had arrived in the middle of a chilly workday to spend time outside.

Curtis went back over to the tree and circled it another time, muttering to himself. Then he came back to Anders and sat down on the wooden bench, staring at it while he drank his tea.

Anders joined him on the bench. "I should have told you about Ethan."

Curtis swallowed some tea. "I guess I just didn't know how bad it could be for a demon on their own. The Families are bad enough—scratch that, they're freaking awful—but they don't beat the crap out of you just because they can."

"It's hard," Anders said. "But he's tough. He'll make it."

"Assuming they find a third."

Anders didn't know what to say to that. It wasn't like he could tell Curtis that he'd been thinking of Ethan and David as plan B. He took a swig of his coffee. It was already cooling off, so he aimed some heat from his palm into the cup. He looked over at the tree again.

Something was looking back. A pair of eyes, darker than the shadows of the tree, almost too black to notice. No hint of the face, just the eyes, rimmed with blue hellfire. It wasn't enough to recognize, and Anders had no idea how long they'd been scrutinized.

Anders raised his cup in front of his lips again and said, "We're being watched. The tree." He took another swallow of the coffee.

Curtis pretended to rub some grit from his eye and managed to look across the park without being obvious. He smiled at Anders and pushed some unruly hair off the demon's forehead.

"I can't see anything," he said. Then he spoke a few words in another language and gave the tree a second, briefer glance.

Anders heard him suck in a breath. He leaned back on the bench and put his arm behind Curtis, then leaned in and gave him a peck on the cheek. "What do you see?"

"A demon," Curtis said, bringing his tea up to cover his mouth and pretending to sip. "But like one made out of blue fire."

That made sense. It was how demons appeared when they shadow-walked. Except for Anders, who'd been glowing gold-white ever since he'd bonded with Curtis and, according to Eli, had managed to score a bit of permanent soul.

"So now what?" Anders said. "Can you figure out who it is?"

"No," Curtis said. "But..." He put his cup between his knees and seemed to stretch for a second, raising his hands above his head like his neck was stiff. Then, he turned to the tree, reached out both hands, and said, *"Apricum."*

The flash of light that burst just in front of the tree made Anders's eyes water. He swore, turning his head, and blinked as white afterimages glared against his eyelids. "What the fuck was that?" Anders asked.

"That was satisfying," Curtis said.

Anders blinked a few more times. "What did you do?" He looked at the tree, but the eyes were gone. No surprise.

"It was just light," Curtis said. "But it probably hurt." He sounded smug.

"Didn't Luc say we weren't supposed to attack?"

"I didn't attack." Curtis shrugged. "I annoyed."

"Right."

"I won't tell if you don't."

Anders leaned over again, and spoke into Curtis's ear. "What's my silence worth to you?"

"Seriously? I finally score a shot at a bad guy, and you're negotiating for blow jobs?"

"Just a blow job?" Anders leaned away, then laughed at Curtis's mock scowl. "Fine. Though I was hoping for something a little kinkier."

"What? With Mr. Fisty?"

"Aw, you remembered his name."

"Let's go home, you blackmailing bastard," Curtis said, though he couldn't quite fight off a smile.

"I love it when you call me names."

Chapter Nine

L uc recalled when the first bridge had been constructed near here. They'd called it Union Bridge, and it had been a wooden arch. It had been lovely. Had he ever crossed it?

He looked down at the Ottawa River that ran below and doubted it. It was a wide river; it could run quite fast. This was no garden feature. A natural river, and a strong one, would have been difficult for him in the eighteen hundreds.

Gatineau was on the other side of the river, but it was the island between the two he wanted.

He approached the Portage Bridge and looked to the green space on Victoria Island. He couldn't recall if buildings had been on the small island back when the Union Bridge had stood just upriver, but now a few had been devoted to hydropower and a small First Nations center. It was long past midnight. All would be closed.

He couldn't see any point delaying. Also, he had to admit he was curious. The triad had given him so many pleasant surprises, and he wondered if he was about to enjoy another. He hadn't quite been sure enough of himself to drive—and also couldn't recall if you could get a car down onto the island from the bridge—so he'd parked his Mercedes on the Ottawa side.

Luc stepped onto the bridge and began walking. He knew the moment he was over running water because a paralysis threatened up and down his limbs. He gathered his will, and the impulse parted around him. He barely felt any resistance at all.

Luc smiled in the dark and walked the rest of the way without stopping.

Coming down off the bridge, Luc sought the area Catharine had described, ducking away from where the buildings and lights shone. Sharpening his predator vision, he looked at the old mill.

It had been classified as a heritage building, a term that always made Luc think of darker times and a scoffing French voice.

"What does Upper Canada know of heritage? You have no history. There is nothing here older than me."

Shaking off the voice and the memories, Luc went to the mill. The windows had been bricked up, the walls were solid limestone, if he was correct, and for all that it looked like a piece of history from over a century ago, Luc knew it served a darker purpose now.

As a jail.

Luc found the stones Catharine had told him to look for and caught the first hint of the damp smell she'd described. He tried to look above the pile of apparently random stones to the wall where they had seemingly fallen, and couldn't do it. He felt his gaze slide left, then right, or down at the rocks again.

Catharine was right. Magic was shrouding the way. Curtis had once said illusion was a fire magic. Renard's "diminished skills" again.

Luc closed his eyes, forced air into his lungs, and reached forward. By touch, he found what he needed, an opening in the lower part of the limestone, with even some of the steel framework revealed, if he believed his hands. Ducking through was a bit of an effort. He was too tall for this opening, really, but he managed.

Inside, the smell was no better, and no light came through from outside. Luc moved as quietly as his graces would allow, feeling his way down a slope that was steep and slick, and tried not to displace any of the detritus that had built up along the uneven floor. It was a wretched place. It wasn't lost on him the only reason the poor soul had to exist here was Renard.

All this, just to send a message.

Luc heard something move, and he came to a stop, waiting. Down here, his predator sight was fully engaged, but even then he almost missed the small, guarded movement of the cat as it slunk around the bend. It stopped, sat, and regarded him.

It was incongruous to the place—a sleek-looking thing, lithe and graceful. If the near lack of scent he was getting from the cat was any indication, it was also both clean and healthy. Even in the near-perfect dark it was meeting his gaze, a soft redness behind its eyes.

He would get no closer undetected, he realized.

"Lavoie?" he called out. "I would speak with you." His voice echoed up and down the rough-hewn stone. The sound told Luc there were multiple branches in the tunnels carved inside the island.

The cat didn't move, but a second joined it. Then a third. By the time the fifth had appeared, and Luc could hear the padding of even more soft feet from all around him, he realized Catharine's odd warning was dead on.

He was glad cats didn't bother him.

They gathered past counting, and sat, unblinking, a series of softly reflecting eyes aimed at him from all directions. What little light there might be was aimed back at him in tiny red pairs. Ledges he hadn't noticed, nooks and corners lost to the darker shadows, were all filled with the creatures.

He remained still and waited.

"The *Duc* has forbidden me from being harmed."

The voice was a woman's, and yet it was off—choked or blurred by something. He could not see her, and from this place in the carved out tunnel, the voice seemed to come from many directions at once. He concentrated, allowing his hearing to take on a measure of his vampire graces. Thankfully, he'd fed well these last few evenings.

"My understanding is the *Duc* is the reason you are forced to remain here."

"Who are you?" The words were sharper this time, less blurred. Angrier, too.

"My name is Luc," he said. "I am a friend of Catharine."

The long silence was broken only by the soft steps of a few more arriving cats.

"Catharine…is kind," the voice said. Luc turned his head. Every word Lavoie spoke made it a little easier to figure out from which direction her voice came.

"She is," Luc agreed, though he thought of the "brutes" she had so cheerfully dispatched. "May we talk?"

The silence stretched on long enough that Luc wondered if he had blundered somehow and scared Lavoie off. Finally, though, her voice echoed again.

"What do you want to talk about?" She sounded almost childlike. Or broken.

Luc hesitated, but he had no choice. "The *Duc*."

Some of the cats began to growl, a low, rumbling sort of noise that threatened pain.

"The *Duc* has forbidden me from being harmed," Lavoie repeated. Luc was fairly sure he knew which branch of the cave she was hiding in now. He didn't turn his head to face her, though. He didn't want her to bolt.

"I know," Luc said. "I give you my word I will not harm you."

He waited for her. The cats slowly quieted, though from the way their ears had pulled back, their attention was even more sharply focused on him. Their backlit eyes were all around him.

"Can you call animals?"

The childlike note was back in her ruined voice, and Luc blinked at the sudden shift in her tone and the topic both. But he answered honestly. "No. I don't have that grace."

"Oh." She sounded disappointed. "One of Catharine's coterie can call the vermin. Rats. Mice. My cats feast. Catharine is very kind. When my cats feast, I can feed a little. I can't get past the water."

Luc frowned into the darkness. He'd found himself occasionally forced to take the blood of an animal or two to make it through to the next full moon, when he was somewhat safe to come out and be among humans. It was a desperate thing, though, and didn't slake the thirst the way human blood did.

Nor did it help the mind.

He wondered how long Lavoie had been reduced to surviving on the blood of cats. Had people ever gone missing here on Victoria Island, or had Renard forbidden her even that?

"I will ask her if she would send that person here soon," Luc offered, though he wasn't sure he wanted to owe Catharine any more than he already did.

"He burned me."

The three words were full of such misery that even Luc's unmoving heart pained him. Fire. Again.

"I'm sorry," Luc said. And to his surprise, he meant it.

"What do you want to know?" The ruined voice was angry once more, hardened by a conviction that Luc understood. This was someone who had been pushed to the edge of destruction and, through will alone, did not allow it. Renard kept her alive as a warning to others.

Which, Luc thought, *may well be Renard's first true mistake in all this.*

"How did you meet him?"

A few of the cats moved. Luc tensed, but they moved down the branch of the cave where he was sure Lavoie herself was hiding. To comfort her, perhaps. He wasn't sure.

Her voice, when she spoke next, was much quieter. "We were in the same coven."

Lavoie was a wizard? And perhaps now a warlock, then? "The same coven," he repeated, not sure what else to say.

"He was old then, and growing sick. It was a bad winter, very cold, and the war...We were a small coven and many of us childless. It made him angry that our coven would be the last of our lineages. The Families—oh, he hated the Families. The *Anglais*."

"You weren't part of the Families, then?"

As ruined as her voice was, it didn't prepare him for her laughter. It was like a drowned gurgle. Luc flinched.

"No," she said. "Renard was proud of his heritage. Of all our heritages."

That word again.

She let out another hideous gurgle of laughter. "Really, I was barely French. Just my father. But it was enough for Renard. By then, the Families were making it harder for the magical bloodlines to hold true to any but their orders. Orphans were adopted or destroyed. Many returned to Quebec, to New Brunswick, even to France."

"So he became vampire?" Luc shook his head. It was a desperate move. Renard only had a small chance of keeping his magic if he turned vampire, and even then the power he'd known would be lessened considerably. He had to have known that.

"He knew of a way. A magical way. He was so strong then." She gurgled. "He's strong now, too. So strong." Her gurgles descended into choked sobs. "He let me burn. He burned us all."

Luc took a step toward the opening where he was certain Lavoie was hiding.

"No," she said, recovering. "Please. No."

He stopped. "I won't hurt you," Luc said. "Renard has decided I'm a threat."

Lavoie moaned. "He'll burn you, too."

"Help me. Tell me what happened. Anything you can. I intend…" Luc drew air into his lungs. Beyond the slight scent of cat, the heavy thickness of rot and dampness was strong enough to taste. "I intend to withstand him."

"He knew ways to bind power," Lavoie said. "Runes. Old runes twisted with blood and ink. He told us that we could still be powerful when we turned, and we believed him. The vampire he brought to us, she was alone. He offered to have her join us when we turned, if she turned us, but he told the rest of us he wanted her destroyed as soon as she made him like her. She was so desperate to have a coterie. She agreed. He worked his runes and she turned him and we destroyed her."

The regret in Lavoie's voice was painful. Luc understood. A vampire's sire held sway over their progeny. If they hadn't destroyed Renard's sire, they might have been able to control him. He knew what was coming next, even before Lavoie said it.

"He turned us all, one a night. The bindings worked, but not the way he told us they would. Oh, we had our magic still. He was right, he knew how to make sure we kept it. It was less, but it was there. But he bound our magic to him, too. He'd turned us, so we couldn't even fight back. Ink and blood under our skin, under my skin. To hold our magic, he said, but he was lying. That wasn't all it was."

Geas, Luc thought. *He used a Geas on every single one of them.*

Lavoie's broken voice grew softer. "I was one of the last. I tried to warn the other two, but I couldn't even speak against him. My magic— most of it was gone—but what I had left, Renard told me I could only work magic when he wanted me to. It was like being blind. And deaf. And burned…"

Luc closed his eyes. Freshly made, a vampire could barely think a thought if the sire didn't allow it. He could only imagine Renard's level of domination, backed with the same kind of magic that had left Eli nearly comatose. A vampire under the sway of her sire *and* a Geas? It was so far beyond overkill.

"I'm so sorry," Luc said. Then he frowned. "Wait. Renard turned your coven. You were his coterie."

"Yes." The word was leaden.

"But he turned on you. If he'd destroyed you, he wouldn't have had a coterie of his own. He needed three, or he could have been easily destroyed, even as a warlock."

"We thought we were safe," Lavoie said. "But he used us, even then. We were there, in the library. The Families came. I don't know how they knew he was going to be there. He said there was a book he needed, a book that could end the Families. Something about the Accords. He wanted it. But they were there."

"The library?" Luc wasn't sure what Lavoie was talking about. The Accords had happened centuries ago, when the wizards and vampires had finally stopped warring—territories, coteries, covens—it had all been laid out in those meetings. What book could possibly matter enough to Renard? Ending the Families? What could that even mean?

"He tried to get to the library. The Families stopped us. He was furious. He burned everything. Everyone. The whole building, almost. The bell rang before it fell, and I barely crawled out. I was on fire. He could have helped me, but he didn't. He let it all burn. Let us all burn. He burned so much." She sobbed again, her wet gurgles echoing around him.

The bell rang before it fell.

1916.

Luc grew very still. "Lavoie, do you mean Parliament?"

"Yes," she said.

Luc was stunned. He'd been in Ottawa then, and like so many, he'd stood in the ice and snow on a frigid February night and watched the buildings burn. For a few days, they'd heard rumors the fire hadn't been an accident, that it had perhaps even been caused by spies. But eventually, the culprit had turned out to be a cigar, if he remembered correctly. A cigar, freshly polished wood, and ill luck. He'd believed it. But of course, that was just the sort of talent the Families had always had: making you believe nothing was amiss.

Warlocks fighting the Families in the middle of Parliament on an icy February night. He'd had no idea.

"The Families had books there. In the library, because of the war. To keep them safe. Renard wanted one. He said it could undo everything. But then he set everything on fire—he could pull the fire out of nothing, so much fire, so fast…" Her voice dipped into a wretched series of gurgles, and Luc realized she was weeping. "He just left us there to burn. All of us. He turned into mist and he just left us to die."

He can mist.

Luc shook his head. What book could be worth all that death or the risk? Renard left himself without a coterie, though obviously he'd replaced those members who'd died in the Parliament fire. And the library had been saved. Great iron doors had been built onto the library, and someone had managed to close them before the fire spread, though now he wondered if there'd been some magic involved as well.

"The book," Luc began. If Renard wanted something, it could be a bargaining chip, but Lavoie cut him off.

"He didn't find it. The Families moved it. When he found out I was still alive, he came back for me, but I was burned, so as soon as he made others he tossed me aside."

"I'm sorry," Luc said. Fire was anathema to a vampire. Healing a burn took more blood than any other wound. Still, it was not impossible. Had Renard actually cared for Lavoie in the slightest…

"He doesn't know everything," Lavoie said.

Luc paused. Her ruined voice strengthened for the first time since Luc had arrived. Around him, the cats had stopped moving. Not a single one so much as swished a tail.

"What do you mean?" Luc asked.

"I have to obey him," she said. She was whispering now, and the gurgle in her ruined voice was less apparent. "But it gets easier to resist. When I'm stronger, as I get older." She paused. "He doesn't come here very often, just enough to tell me I'm not allowed to leave. But I can get a little farther than I used to. Catharine told me why. I'm getting older. He demands I tell him who visits me, and I tell him no one visits me." She giggled, a horrible, wet sound. "Visits are face-to-face, you see. What we're doing is talking, not visiting. And I tell him my only friends are cats, and he thinks that's the same as me saying nobody helps me, nobody feeds me. He doesn't know about Catharine. Or the rats her friend brings me. And he won't know about you."

"I thank you for that," Luc said. He understood. A sire's control over his progeny begins as an absolute, but it wanes. The stronger the progeny, the faster the control slips. But Lavoie was not strong. He was honestly surprised she'd managed even these small rebellions.

"He doesn't know his ink burned away." This was said the quietest of all, and Luc blinked.

"Your Geas is broken?" he said.

"Fire," Lavoie said. Her voice shook again, and she grew louder with every word. "It burned me. Burned my skin. Burned his ink and blood. He doesn't own me, but he still has me. I can't stop him. My magic is almost nothing now, and I can barely use it at all without blood. And there's so much fire. So much burning. You can't stop him. He'll burn you. He'll burn everything."

Her sobs echoed through the woman's dank prison.

"He always burns everything."

CHAPTER TEN

"You're still up," Luc said. The sun had just dipped below the horizon, and he'd been surprised to find Eli standing in the kitchen, a cup of coffee in one hand. It looked like Anders had let him borrow some more clothes, though the jeans were a bit loose on him, and the sleeveless shirt didn't suit the man at all.

"Barely," Eli said. He still sounded tired and had shadows under his eyes.

"You should skip the coffee," Luc said, moving past Eli. "Something healthier would be better. Something with iron." He noticed Eli tensed as he drew close, and he couldn't help but feel a small measure of pride. Even as the one who saved him, Luc obviously felt like a threat to Eli. Curtis would no doubt tell Luc he shouldn't enjoy being perceived that way, but Curtis hadn't lived powerless.

"You're safe here," Luc said, not ungently.

Eli scratched the back of his neck. "Sorry. It's…" He let out a breath. "Well. Sorry."

Luc gestured to the kitchen table as he sat down. Eli pulled out a chair and joined him.

"It's understandable," Luc said. "Vampires have not been kind to you."

Eli chuckled. "Well, yeah. But it's not just that. You bloodsuck… Uh, vampires just feel *wrong* to us. Well, most of them. You're a little different."

"Different?" That was news to him. He'd met few with Eli's gift over the years, but none had ever had anything other than antipathy for his entire kind. Luc had certainly been no exception.

"You and the demon both," Eli said. "You have spirit."

"At night," Luc said, tilting his head.

"No, that's just it. You have some all the time." Eli took a long draw from the coffee. "At first I thought it was just because I was so worn out, that I was feeling things wrong. Curtis said there was a lot of magic in that thing your buddy did. I figured it was still messing with me."

"Geas. And Renard is not my 'buddy.' "

Eli smiled, and the rare show of humor made him quite attractive. Luc surprised himself by smiling back. He made an effort to ensure he didn't let his fangs show, which had extended just a little when Eli had smiled. Eli's skin had a burnished warmth that made Luc think of the man's blood, which had tasted so very sweet.

"Right," Eli said. "Well, I'm getting better. There was some leftover crap from that Geas but I've cleansed it. The only spirits I'm working with right now are ones to cure me faster, to get my strength back after being knocked out for so long. There's nothing else interfering with what I can feel, though Curtis's wards make me feel like I'm trapped in an iron box. I can't feel anything outside."

"And nothing outside can feel *you* inside," Luc said. "Which is the point."

Eli nodded. "I get it. I do. It's just not what I'm used to. But neither are you guys."

Luc leaned forward. Once again, he saw Eli tense, and once again, he felt a flush of arousal. There really was nothing quite like someone who was a little afraid of you.

"Our spirit?"

Eli nodded. "Most of yours flees with the sun, like all...vampires. But not all of it. And with the demon..." Eli paused. "It's hard to explain. I can always tell a vampire. Even at night, there's a 'temporary' feel to their spirit. Also, the way other things react to a vampire—animals, wood, streams—I can feel them all, their wariness and confusion. You're a part of the world, but you're not quite natural." He gave a little shrug of apology.

"So I'm told," Luc said dryly.

"With demons, it's less obvious, but it's more like I can tell the spirit they've got isn't right for them. It takes time, and it's not something you notice right away. And the spirit fades."

"They draw on soul to survive," Luc said. "Or spirit, as you'd say. And feed on it over time."

Eli nodded. "Right."

"And you can sense that."

"Yeah. Like I said, it's not obvious, but given time, I can spot a demon."

"I can see why our ancestors didn't get along," Luc said.

"Didn't get along." Eli's voice was cold.

"Perhaps that was an understatement," Luc allowed. The sound of a key in the door interrupted them, and Luc looked up to see Curtis and Anders step inside.

Eli grunted, and what little humor he'd shown was gone. "Didn't get along," he repeated.

"Who didn't?" Curtis asked, tugging off his coat. He went into the hall to put it away. Anders went to the coffeepot and poured himself a cup.

"Our kin of old," Luc said.

"Oh," Curtis said, coming back into the room. "Right."

Eli finished his coffee. Anders reversed a chair and sat beside him. He leaned over and nudged Eli's shoulder.

"Looking good."

"Thanks for the clothes," Eli said. He looked uncomfortable.

"Are you hungry?" Curtis asked. "I'm not a great cook, but even I can't ruin a stir fry."

"Thanks." Eli exhaled. "I hate being a burden. I'll be back up on my feet tomorrow, I'm sure."

"No worries," Anders said. "On your back is good, too."

"Way to master the single entendre," Curtis muttered. He pulled out a wok, put it on the stove, and then went to the fridge.

Eli twitched under Anders's gaze.

"Eli was telling me that our spirits are different than typical demons' and vampires'," Luc said. He tried to catch Anders's attention so he could aim a meaningful look at him, but the demon was still staring at Eli.

"Yeah," Anders said. "He told us. Apparently we're borrowing Curtis's soul."

"It's more like he's letting his spirit overflow into both of you."

Eli nodded at Curtis, who stopped, a package of chicken breasts in one hand.

"Still creepy," Curtis said. "Because it's *my* soul."

"Your spirit," Eli said. He looked even more uncomfortable now that all three of them were paying attention to him. "And you're not missing any—you're sharing the extra with them. It sort of bleeds from you into them, and they're keeping it. Even in the day, I can feel it in him." He looked at Luc and nodded at Anders. "And there's some inside him that doesn't get used up."

"Our triad," Luc said.

"Wait, I have *extra* soul?" Curtis raised an eyebrow. "Like...soul plus ten percent?"

"Spirit," Eli said. "And we all have more spirit than we need. It enters the world around us, joining the natural flow. But yours goes to them. It's a part of how you're all tied together. I've never seen anything like it before."

Curtis put the chicken on the counter. "I'm giving my soul to a vampire and a demon. But hey, it's okay, it's just the extra."

"You're making too much of it." Eli shook his head. He sounded annoyed now. "And it's *spirit*, not soul. Soul is something religions use to keep you coughing up the cash and feeling superior to other people."

"Sing it," Anders said.

"Spirit is like a font," Eli said. "You have enough to share. You're sharing it with them. It's not something I've ever seen done this way. We usually share spirit with those we love."

"Oh, he loves me," Anders said. "In many different and interesting ways."

"Anders," Luc warned. Curtis just rolled his eyes.

Eli went on as though he hadn't been interrupted. "But with you three, it wouldn't work that way. Or it *shouldn't*. A vampire's spirit leaves with the sun, and even when it's present, it's not permanent. A demon has no spirit of its own, and draws spirit from others to burn through. But now they both have a bit of your spirit, and it's staying during the day, and it's not being burned up, and it's sort of becoming theirs as much as it's yours—and you're all three sharing it."

"I...That's..." Curtis said. "I don't have the slightest idea if that's a good thing or a bad thing."

"Hey," Anders said.

"No offense, big guy," Curtis said. "Just don't know how I feel about trusting you with some of my soul." He saw Eli's look and raised his hands. "Sorry. Spirit. Whatever."

"I would say it explains some of our unexpected growth," Luc said. His ability to rise before sundown, for one. And also the way they could feel snatches of emotion from each other.

They sat in silence for a while.

"So," Anders said. "Dinner?"

"Right," Curtis said. He still sounded dazed. "And over dinner we can fill you in on what we found out, and hear how it went for you last night with Catharine's friend," he said, looking at Luc. "And maybe after that we can figure out how to get you back to your family?" Curtis smiled at Eli.

Eli frowned. "I'm not leaving."

"Pardon?" Curtis said.

"Renard killed Chantale." Eli looked at the three men around him. "I told you, I'm not going until he pays for what he did. I want him dead."

❖

Luc toyed with a glass of wine while the others had dinner. Anders ate with his usual gusto, and Curtis stared at his plate. Eli ate slowly, obviously tired, but the look of determination never left his face.

Finally, they had to broach the subject at hand. They had all finished, and Curtis cleared the plates with nervous energy.

"How did you imagine to accomplish killing Renard?" Luc asked.

The silence that greeted his question spoke volumes.

"My understanding of your kind is that your abilities are…" Luc hesitated for words that wouldn't seem overtly insulting. "Fairly passive in nature."

Eli frowned but didn't disagree. "That son of a bitch killed my cousin and nearly killed me. For no reason."

Curtis exhaled. "We're not arguing that. And I don't think we disagree. I'd like to see Renard punished, too. How do you recommend we do it?"

Eli scowled at him, and Curtis shrugged.

"Cut off his head? Stake him? Drag him into the sunlight?" Eli said.

"Sure," Anders said. "You sniff him out, and we'll do that."

"Anders," Luc said.

"What?" Anders said. "I'm with him. Let's off the bastard. We know he wants us dead. Didn't your lady friend tell you as much?"

"I can't," Eli said.

They all looked at him.

"I have to be near. To sense a vampire's spirit." He sighed. "If it's dawn or sunset…" He leaned back from the table. "Look, I know it wouldn't be easy."

"It wouldn't be possible," Luc said. "Renard is stronger than us. Yes," Luc raised his hand, forestalling Eli's arguments. "We're powerful. What we have is different. But we've already faced him once, and the best we managed was a standstill. And that was in a civil match with onlookers. Renard has abilities we haven't even seen."

Eli shook his head. "So he gets to kill her. And maybe you guys. And what? You just take it?"

"He has a point," Anders said.

"No," Curtis said. "We don't just take it. We're going to figure out a way."

"A way," Eli said, smirking. "To what? Avoid him?"

"Something like that." Curtis said. "We just want to be left alone."

Luc had to admit, it sounded hollow.

The doorbell was a welcome break from the deadlock with their guest.

"Expecting anyone?" Luc asked the other two. They shook their heads. When no one made any signs of moving, Luc rose. He shared a brief glance of warning with Anders and went to the front door himself.

The young man who had taken their coats at the *séance* regarded Luc with a frightened expression when he answered the door.

"Yes?" Luc asked. He had no idea why the young man would be there.

"I'm sorry to intrude," the young man said. His voice wavered. He seemed uncertain, and almost afraid. Luc frowned. This couldn't be good. "But I hoped I might speak with Mr. Baird."

Luc raised an eyebrow. "Curtis."

The young man nodded.

"Curtis, there is someone at the door for you," Luc said, raising his voice. He didn't move. The young man looked away from his gaze.

"Who is it?" Curtis asked, arriving behind him. Luc stepped to the side, and Curtis stopped.

"You were at the *séance*," Curtis said. "It was Tyson, right?"

The young man nodded again.

"How can I help you?" Curtis asked. His voice was clipped. He sounded angry. Luc was surprised, and he laid a hand on the wizard's shoulder. Curtis looked up at Luc, his expression cold, and then regarded their young visitor again.

"I can't answer that," Tyson said, his voice strained.

Curtis blinked. "Pardon?"

Tyson looked like he wanted to say more, but his face reddened. Finally, he sighed. "It was a mistake to come," he said. He turned to leave.

"Wait," Luc said. Tyson stopped, his gaze aimed at his feet. "Why are you here?"

Luc looked at Curtis, who was frowning now.

"I…" Tyson seemed to struggle with his words, then shook his head.

"Did Renard send you?" Luc asked. Something wasn't right here, and it wasn't just a case of hesitation. Tyson seemed genuinely unable to reply.

Tyson looked at Luc for just a second. The misery on his face was painful, like he wanted to speak, but couldn't. The realization struck Luc then, and he remembered Lavoie's words. *I tried to warn the other two, but I couldn't even speak against him.*

"He can't answer," Luc said. "Curtis, check his chest."

Tyson looked at Luc, eyes widening. He crossed his arms over his chest and took a half-step away. Luc called on his vampire graces. The night blurred as he moved behind the young man and pulled Tyson's arms away with ease. He was stronger than Luc thought he would be, but in moments he had pinned his arms behind his back. Tyson struggled when Curtis reached forward to undo the buttons of his shirt but ultimately fell limp in Luc's arms. Curtis pulled the cloth open.

Luc couldn't see what Curtis saw, but he saw the surprise and anger that crossed the wizard's face.

"He has you in a Geas," Curtis said, disgust in his voice. "Why would he...?" He locked eyes with Luc. "You said he did this to his old coven." He turned back to Tyson. "Are you a wizard?"

The young man slumped in Luc's arms. "No. I...I...can't..."

"Let him go," Curtis said.

Tyson nearly fell away from him when Luc let go. The young man refastened his shirt with trembling fingers, but not before Luc saw the dark red spiderweb of lines and runic symbols that crisscrossed his lean chest. This was not just blood smeared on the skin. The Geas was tattooed on Tyson with black and red lines. Curtis had struggled with the Geas on Eli, and that had been far less permanent layers of blood. When Tyson was done, he looked up at Curtis, and Luc saw Tyson was on the edge of tears. He had closed his eyes.

"Renard doesn't know you're here, does he?" Curtis said.

Tyson took a deep breath, eyes still closed. "He told me at the party...He...asked me to make sure you saw me." He swallowed, struggling for each word as though it pained him. For all Luc knew, because of the Geas, it did. "But he didn't say *when*. Or how long. He said I should 'allow you to see me.' He wants me to make you angry."

"Success," Curtis snapped. "Why haven't the covens rescued you?" His voice was shaking. "Are you an Orphan?"

Inwardly, Luc cringed, hoping it wasn't the case. Curtis's own history as an Orphan would color his already livid response. They needed cool heads for dealing with whatever this was, and Curtis was nowhere close right now.

"I can't do real magic..." Tyson said. "He uses me for fire."

"You're a sorcerer." Curtis looked at Luc. "I think I get it. Renard bound him to gain access to his natural ability with fire sorcery. It would explain the balefire and how Renard's pyromancies are still so strong even though he's a vampire. Tyson doesn't have enough ability to really qualify as a wizard." He took a breath. "And if he's not powerful enough to be a fully fledged wizard, even if they did know, I don't know that they'd care." Curtis was angrier than Luc had ever seen. The scent of ozone was building around them, and the air crackled with static. "Go on back," he said to Tyson. "I don't want Renard to know you were here, if you can help it." His voice softened. "Don't give him any reasons to hurt you, okay?"

Tyson turned, his face aimed down at the ground again.

"Tyson? Wait. Listen to me."

Tyson looked up. The misery in his eyes made even Luc feel pity. If it was possible, he looked even younger than before.

Curtis touched the young man's shoulder. "I'll break the Geas. I promise."

Tyson breathed out, his eyelids fluttered down, and a single tear escaped. He turned and left without a word.

They watched him go. Luc could feel the pulse of anger radiating from Curtis. This, more than anything else, had piqued the wizard's ire. The way the Families treated those they considered "lesser" had been most of the reason Curtis had bound them in their triad. Luc struggled to think of something he could say that would ease the young man's temper but found nothing.

Curtis had every right to be this angry.

"How do we find out where Renard sleeps during the day?" Curtis asked. The air crackled with static electricity. Luc had never seen Curtis like this.

"I have no idea," Luc said. "*Lapin*, please. You need to calm down." He reached for Curtis's shoulder, only to be shaken off.

"Eli's right, Luc. Renard killed Eli's cousin. She was eighteen years old and had done *nothing* to him. He has Tyson—who's what, nineteen?—enslaved in a Geas because he's got a gift with fire that Renard wants. You said that woman you spoke to was trapped in a wet cave below a bridge to serve as a warning. The rest of the vampires are too weak and too scared of him. This has to stop."

"Renard wants you angry for precisely this reason," Luc said. "Tyson said so. If we attack Renard, he could put us down and not a feather would ruffle in the rest of Ottawa. It would be within his rights as *Duc*."

"And if *we* put *him* down?" Curtis asked, crossing his arms.

Luc stared. "Think of what you're saying. There are traditions, yes, but—"

"I know what I'm saying, Luc. My parents were killed, remember? Eli's cousin. You and Anders were in hiding for God knows how long. Ethan gets beaten almost to death, David is danced around like a puppet on a string...All of that is tradition, too, right?" He frowned when Luc nodded carefully, conceding the points. "Well, just because something's always been done a certain way doesn't make it right. In fact, most of the biggest wrongs are all about *tradition.*" He nearly spat the word.

Luc tried to make him understand. "If we break with tradition..."

Curtis shook his head. "We're not going to. He draws power from that link he's got to Tyson. Renard has all the finesse—the magical ability—but if I break that Geas, he's going to find himself much less powerful all across the board, but especially with fire magics. We had him at a standstill before. But if I free Tyson, I think you could take him."

"If I dominate him, I would take his position. That doesn't remove him as a threat, it just makes him angry I took his place, and he'd likely be more determined than ever to get it back." Luc shook his head. He wanted to avoid vampire politics, not engage in them. Curtis couldn't know, but Luc had to make him understand.

"But it puts you in charge, right?" Curtis held up his hands, frustrated.

"Of Ottawa, yes, but—"

"Good enough. Become the leader, banish Renard."

"Lapin," Luc started again.

"Don't give me that bunny crap, Luc!" He pushed at Luc, and sparks of static flashed in the air all around them. Luc took his wrists, and though Curtis struggled against him, the vampire gathered him in his arms and held him while he tried to shove free. Curtis fought only a short time, then pressed against Luc's chest, breathing heavily and shaking. Luc stroked his back. The anger finally bled away. The pain beneath it was harder for Luc to sense, but he knew it was there, whether their bond would show it to him or not.

"I'm sorry," Curtis said. "That kid has a gift, but instead of being invited to a coven, he ends up chained to a vampire. All because the Families are so tied up in their own elitist crap and only use sorcerers as hired thugs, if they bother to think of them at all. My magic is stronger because of you and Anders. My fire magic used to be pretty terrible. It was my worst element. Now, especially if Anders is around, I can draw on his fire if I need to. But it's sharing, not stealing. What Renard did to Tyson? It's enslavement. He's stealing that kid's ability, adding it to his own, and Tyson gets nothing from him but pain." Curtis looked up at the sky. "He's barely an adult. Some kids get their magic when they're *thirteen*. Who knows how long Renard has been leeching him like this? I keep thinking I'm going to stop learning about new kinds of horrible. What's the point of what we've gained if we don't try to stop the horrible stuff?"

"This world is full of bad things," Luc said. "Maybe we can find a way to help Tyson, but I don't think trying to depose Renard is a good plan. I'm not even sure I could dominate him. You remember the *séance*. We struggled to a standstill. Even if you're right and we can gain an edge by breaking his link to Tyson, in truth, I don't know if it would be enough."

"Got any other ideas?" Curtis sighed, pulling free from his grasp at last.

Luc shook his head. "We'll put our heads together."

Curtis glanced up, eyes bright. "What?"

"We'll think of a way to—"

"No. Put our heads together." Curtis tilted his head back and laughed out loud. "You are a freaking genius, Luc. We have all the skills right in front of us, we just need..." He frowned, looking back down. "Well, I have no idea what we need, but that hasn't stopped me before. It's what I do."

"Curtis?"

"I need to look some things up...And you need to go tell Eli he'll be helping us. I'm sure Anders won't mind *that*. Put our heads together. Damn right we will." He went back into the house without waiting to see if Luc was following.

Merde.

Chapter Eleven

They'd moved to the living room when Luc rejoined them. Anders was on the couch, Eli was in one of the plush chairs—he looked exhausted—and Curtis was pacing.

That couldn't be good.

"Do you think we can trust that kid?" Anders asked.

Obviously Curtis had filled the other two in.

"He seemed genuinely bound like Eli was, only all the more permanent. It was tattooed on his skin." Luc didn't bother to keep the disgust from his voice. What Renard had done to that youth was horrific.

Eli looked at him. "Tell me again why you don't think it's a good idea to put this asshole down?"

"Because I don't think we could," Luc said. His patience was worn thin, and the words came out sharper than he'd intended.

"Unless we knew where to find him," Curtis said.

"But we don't," Luc repeated. It wasn't like him to feel this angry, and he forced air into his lungs. Even all these years after dying, taking a deep breath helped settle his state.

Somewhat.

Curtis pointed at Eli. "He could do it."

Eli was shaking his head, but Curtis didn't let him speak. "Between all of us, we have what it takes. You can sense when a vampire's spirit comes or goes. We want to sense *where* Renard is when his spirit is coming and going. That's all we need."

Eli still shook his head. "It doesn't work like that. I can only feel it when I'm nearby. Maybe a block or two, on the outside. I told you."

Curtis nodded, slowly. Luc relaxed. Maybe he had a chance now to calm Curtis down and get him to see how dangerous this course would be.

"Sure," Curtis said, but now he was smiling. Luc tensed. "Ever heard of the law of constancy?"

Eli shook his head.

"In magic, there are tons of laws. They're a framework of how magic works. One of them is constancy. Constancy states all things that were once connected are always connected. I happen to have a little bottle of Renard's blood. That little bottle of blood was smeared all over your chest, and full of Renard's magic to bind you in place. That little bottle of blood is the magic equivalent of having him stand right beside you because he already did."

"I work with spirits," Eli said. "I can't do magic."

"But I can," Curtis said. He spoke faster. "On the full moon, the coteries gather. Three nights. Renard doesn't have a choice. On a full moon, vampires share blood and reinforce their ties to each other for another month. It's where the coterie is bound, where the seed of his dominance is grown, and where he'll be, *for sure*, for three nights."

Eli nodded. Luc thought he still didn't look convinced, but he was listening. Luc was listening, too, and growing all the more nervous as Curtis spoke. He was pretty sure he knew where Curtis was heading. He spared a glance for Anders. Anders was grinning. Given the smug look on the demon's face, Anders seemed to like the idea of tracking down Renard through the time he'd be spending with his coterie.

That settled it. If Anders liked the idea, it was absolutely the wrong thing to do.

"We have to renew our own bonds, too, Curtis," Luc said.

"We have two advantages," Curtis said. He held up a finger. "One, we bond in three different ways. We share blood the first night, soul the second, but on the third night, we use magic." He raised a second finger. "Two, you get up early."

"I get up early?" Luc blinked. His ability to rise before the sun had set wasn't particularly practical, though he did enjoy it.

"We have time to commute," Curtis said. "Though I guess if the sun was still up, you'd have to take the trip in the trunk."

"Awesome," Anders said. Luc glared at him.

"I'm still not following," Luc said. "Your ability with magic is brilliant. Eli's sense of the spirits is likewise impressive. But you said it yourself, you've never sensed a spirit, Curtis. You didn't even know Eli's gifts existed last week. And Eli doesn't use magic. That bottle of blood is of use to you, not him. I don't see how..." Luc trailed off.

Put our heads together, Curtis had said.

"Oh," Luc said.

Curtis nodded. "Exactly."

Anders looked between them. "What?"

Curtis didn't break his gaze from Luc's. "It works if we bring Eli into the triad."

Eli gaped at Curtis.

Anders chuckled. "I'm pretty sure my bed has room for four."

Eli looked at the demon. "What?"

Anders winked.

"Anders, don't be a dick," Curtis said.

"Eli's kind don't have covens, Curtis," Luc said. "They don't form groups at all, not the same way vampires or demons or wizards do. They're not a part of the Accords like the rest of us."

"It shouldn't matter," Curtis said.

"You don't know that," Luc said.

"Hey," Eli said. "Do I get a vote here?"

Luc looked at him. "Of course you do."

Curtis seemed about to say something more, but he nodded at Eli. "We can't force you."

Eli took a deep breath. "I'd like to help you. I really would. You know that. I don't know if what you're talking about could work—hell, I don't really know *what* you're talking about. But I want to go home. If I do this thing with you, I'd be bound to you. You guys have to do this every month. I know enough about bloodsuckers and weres and demons to know that much. Luc's right. We're different. We don't have that kind of set-up. Your kind brought those rules with you when you came across the ocean and decided you wanted to stay here. I'm not coming back here every month for the rest of my life. Even if it would mean getting that bastard. I'm sorry."

"I'm not asking you to sign on for life," Curtis said. "It would only be just this once. If it works how I think it'll work, next month, the triad would be back to just the three of us. It's possible with packs and coteries and covens, too. Any person can leave one group to join another. Or someone can just leave, though no one ever does that, since they'd be alone and vulnerable. Only if *you* leave, nothing changes from your status quo. You didn't have a coven in the first place. That's how you usually run. I'm guessing that wouldn't change just because it's me, Luc, and Anders you're leaving, rather than a typical coven or whatever."

Eli rubbed the back of his neck. "One month." He still sounded uncertain.

"Not even," Curtis said. "You could leave as soon as we've worked the spell, frankly. If we can work together to find Renard, then your part would be done." He snapped his fingers. "After that, you're good to go."

"I'm not leaving until Renard is done," Eli said.

Luc frowned. "But, Curtis, what happens to Eli? To all of us? Our bond has had an effect on all three of us. We're stronger than we were, and not in the way a traditional coterie or coven or pack would allow."

Curtis sighed. "I don't know. You're right. We got way stronger than we should have been by mixing it up. Adding spirits into the mix? I don't know. As long as I can make my magic work with his senses. That's all we need."

"And then we find Renard," Eli said.

Curtis nodded. "That's the plan."

"As plans go," Luc said, "it's missing a great deal of certainty. Finding Renard is only a first step. And we have no idea what it will do to us to add Eli into the mix. You don't even sound certain about what will happen to us once he's no longer a part of our group."

Anders laughed. "But it sure sounds like fun."

Curtis shrugged. "I'm open to better ideas."

Luc drew in a long, deep breath. "And if we find Renard? What then?"

"I break the Geas he's put on Tyson. Renard finds himself running without his pyromantic battery. We were pretty evenly matched at the *séance*. Take away a lot of his magic, and we can beat him."

"You think," Luc said.

Curtis nodded. "I think."

"Beat him?" Luc said.

Curtis swallowed. "Yeah."

Luc wasn't going to let him dodge the point. "You don't mean depose him. You mean kill him."

Curtis looked away. "If we have to."

"You have to," Eli said.

Luc ignored him and approached Curtis. He took the young man's shoulders, squeezing gently. "You're not a killer, Curtis."

"No, but Renard is. He's a murderer," Curtis said. "And he wants us dead. If it's him or us...?"

They looked at each other a long while, but Eli broke the silence. "I'm in," he said. "When do we start?"

Curtis relaxed his shoulders. Luc felt the relief like an echo down the bond they shared. He looked at Anders, and Anders raised his eyebrows, his typical cocky smirk in place. He'd already known the demon would want to go on the offensive.

"Four days," Luc said. Eli looked at him. "The next full moon begins in four days."

"Okay," Eli said. "What do I have to do?"

Curtis exhaled. "I need to figure that part out. But not tonight. Come on. You're wiped. You need to sleep. You and I will find a quiet place tomorrow, and you can give me a crash course in your spirit magic."

"It's not magic," Eli said, almost growling.

"Which is exactly the kind of stuff I need to know."

Luc watched them leave. "You're looking forward to this," Luc said to Anders, after they'd gone.

Anders shrugged. "I'm not big on letting people take potshots at me and not doing shit about it."

"So it's not just for the chance to *bond* with Eli?"

"That's just a bonus," Anders said, and winked. "A bonus with a really sweet ass."

"I don't think he's gay," Luc said.

Anders threw his arm around Luc's neck and tugged him in, rubbing his hand through Luc's hair with his free hand.

"But who can resist us?" Anders said. He let go, and Luc straightened. He resisted fixing his hair, knowing it would only encourage the demon.

"Fair enough," Luc said. "Okay. If this is the way we're going, then perhaps you should change before we go out for the evening." Luc eyed the demon's faded jeans and tight red T-shirt.

"Why?" Anders asked, looking down at his shirt. "Did I spill something?"

Of course. "Never mind," Luc said. He took the opportunity to tidy his hair on the sly while the demon wasn't looking. "Let's go."

"Same pub as before?" Anders sounded hopeful.

"No."

"Hey, you scored there just fine last time. That frou-frou guy in the suit." Anders slapped his shoulder.

"I settled for the least unappealing option."

"Po-tay-to, po-tah-to."

"No," Luc said. "Tonight, we are going somewhere more upscale."

"Whatever. But you're paying the cover."

"Of course, but how do you feel about crashing someone else's territory?"

Anders turned. "Say what?"

"If we're going on the offensive, it's time for some 'know thy enemy.' And, frankly, some misdirection and intimidation."

"I'm in." Anders grinned. They made their way to the front door. Luc pulled on what was now his only remaining black coat and handed Anders his leather jacket.

"And if you could call on the good detective, perhaps more to be learned there, too. Ask him tomorrow. He owes you for Curtis's help."

"Not sure he sees it that way."

"Then make him see it that way," Luc said.

Anders smiled. "This is a new look for you. Pissed-off vampire giving orders. I like it."

Luc tried not to rise to the bait. "Perhaps if you learn to obey, we'll make it through all this unscathed."

"If that's what it takes," Anders deadpanned, "we're doomed."

❖

"This is how the other half lives?" Anders asked.

Luc looked around the bar. It was clean and modern in design but tried too hard with too many shiny chrome and glossy black surfaces. The bar glowed with strips of LED lights that wanted to appear edgy but looked cheap. The crowd of twentysomethings in trendy outfits all eyed each other with a complete lack of subtlety, yet barely interacted beyond the glances.

Apparently, cocktails were half-price for women that evening, which explained why they outnumbered the men, and also, perhaps, why two separate bachelorette parties were under way. The two loud groups of women had screamed with delight upon encountering each other, hugging and trading phones to take photos of their groups.

From the outside, Luc had always assumed the interior of the bar would be classier. It was well-known among his kind as a place that vampires would frequent. He'd had to avoid it when he'd been alone, but since joining the triad, he'd never bothered to come here, thinking it would only underscore the difference of his group and ruffle the feathers of the more traditional coteries.

Also, at a gay bar, he was quite likely to find men with more style. Not to mention an appreciation for an evening of carnal activity.

And better music. Luc took advantage of the pause between two bass-heavy, unrecognizable strings of noise to answer.

"It's not quite what I expected," Luc admitted.

"It's fucking awful," Anders said, looking at the groups of people. One of the two bachelorette parties let out another round of ear-piercing screams as the bride-to-be, Luc assumed, was made to walk over to a particularly handsome man in a tank top and ask him to bite off a piece of candy from the candy necklace she wore. He tried to appear embarrassed and let his friends goad him into doing the thing he obviously didn't mind doing.

"Bet I could get that one," Anders said, watching the man tongue and nibble at the woman's neck while she cringed and blushed, and one of her friends ran over and held up her phone to capture the moment. Behind her, the rest of her group of friends shrieked again. It was a wonder they weren't all deaf.

"But why would you want him?" Luc asked.

Anders smiled. "I think he could use some time with a ball gag and handcuffs. Needs to learn his place."

Luc watched the man lick the woman's neck and then finally bite off a piece of the candy. He pulled away, crunching the small piece of sugar between his teeth, and winked at the bride-to-be. She looked like she'd rather be anywhere else, but her friends hooted and whistled.

"You may have a point," Luc said.

"Some people just need to be on their hands and knees," Anders said.

"Right on, bro!" A burly man wearing a backward baseball cap held up one fist in front of Anders. He wore a tight shirt that showed off a broad chest and thick arms, but his board shorts showed off a complete lack of legwork at the gym. He smelled like alcohol and cheap body spray, and he grinned at Anders. "Bitches, right?"

"Go away," Anders growled.

The man blinked, slow to process, then dropped his hand and muttered "douchebag" as he walked off.

Luc heard another chorus of shrieks. They both turned and saw the second group of women had sent their own bride to the same man in the tank top. He was trying to lick a lollipop she'd tucked down the front of her low-cut blouse and making a big show of missing. The woman wore a sash around her neck that said, "Buck a Suck!" One of her friends held a jar of loonies.

Anders exhaled. "Let's just burn the place to the ground."

"That's not why we're here."

"You said we were going to intimidate," Anders said. "Arson is intimidating."

Luc let it drop. He knew he'd get nowhere with the demon, but more important, three of his kind had just walked into the bar. He recognized only one of them—the woman who'd been with Renard and had helped Tyson carry Eli when Eli had been barely conscious. She wasn't wearing the casual suit this evening. Instead, she wore a loose-fitting sleeveless top with a low neckline. It revealed enough to tantalize, without being as trashy as what many of the women were wearing in the bar. Her skirt walked a similar line. In the bar, Luc thought she was easily the most elegant looking, but it was not a hard goal to achieve.

"There," Luc said. Anders followed his gaze.

The woman from Renard's coterie had arrived with two men—vampires, Luc assumed, though it wasn't easy to tell at this distance—but they stood together only a moment before separating into the crowd.

"Game on," Anders said and raised his bottle of beer to his mouth. He took a swallow, grimaced, and spat it back into the bottle. "Ugh.

Why would anyone mix grapefruit juice with beer? And why the fuck did I order this?"

"Because it's your habit to make poor choices," Luc said, watching as the woman moved through the crowd. She slid past a group of men, including the one in the tank top, who'd managed to retrieve the lollipop, given the white stick now protruding from his mouth. All eyes had turned to her. Luc could feel the cool brush of glamour even from across the room.

"Asshole," Anders said.

"Come on. Let's go ruin someone's night."

Luc saw the moment the woman felt his influence on the small crowd of men she spoke with. Her smile slipped a fraction, and she began to scan the crowd around her.

The three men, including the popular choice of brides-to-be in the tank top, turned to look at Luc as he came toward them. He'd always had a strong glamour. His sire had proclaimed the same, and though Luc tried never to think of his sire at all, let alone with any gratefulness, the talent had certainly been his best grace before he'd joined with Curtis and Luc.

After, it became a force to be reckoned with.

"Hello again," Luc said, smiling widely. He stepped right up to the woman and offered her cheek a kiss.

She accepted it stiffly, a tight smile forced into place at the last possible moment. "Luc," she said. On her lips, his name held all the warmth of an Iqaluit winter.

"I'm sorry," Luc said. "Your boss never bothered to tell me your name. I'm afraid he's terrible about his underlings." As he spoke, Luc let his glamour wash out over the three men without any attempt at subtlety. All three shivered, and Luc felt their attention shift to him.

She narrowed her smile. "Gabrielle." Luc felt her coolness spread as the men's attention returned to her.

"Gabrielle." Luc offered her the briefest, shallowest nod of his head. "It's hard to keep track. I know how quickly Renard moves through his people. The man is never satisfied, no?" Her glamour wasn't weak, but it had nothing on his. With only a modicum of effort, all three men were once again looking at him with a mix of admiration and interest in their eyes.

"I'm his second," Gabrielle said. It sounded like a warning. He could see her working now, concentrating. Her glamour was reaching its limit. The men shifted once again.

"I'm sure that's what the last guy said before you came along," Anders said. He didn't bother waiting for Gabrielle to reply, instead turning to the poor men who'd been snapping their heads back and forth like spectators at a tennis match.

"What are you drinking?" Anders asked. "I tried one of the microbrews, and it was shit."

The man in the tank top blinked a couple of times, struggling his way out of the layers of influence muffling his thoughts. "What?"

Anders looked at Gabrielle. "Oh, he's a winner."

The man's frown grew. "What?" he repeated.

"Problem, Gabrielle?"

Luc turned and saw the two vampires Gabrielle had arrived with had rallied to her side. No doubt they'd felt something through the link they shared with their blood-sister.

"Ah," Luc said, offering a large smile. "And you two weren't even worth third position. Hello. I'm Luc." He held out his hand. "I was just talking to Gabrielle about your boss, Renard, and his terrible habit of turnover."

The one who'd spoken took Luc's hand and shook it, though the gesture was perfunctory at best. His sandy hair was buzzed military short, and he was built strong, if not particularly tall. His Gatineau accent came through thickly when he spoke. "Stephane." He didn't seem to know what else to say and looked at Gabrielle.

Beside him, the third vampire from their little group, perhaps the most attractive of the three, if one enjoyed men who exemplified the metrosexual look, was peering into the small group of men. No doubt he could feel the conflicting influences that Luc and Gabrielle were still projecting into their midst.

Luc edged his glamour up another notch, and the men fell once again under his sway.

Gabrielle's grunt was almost too quiet for Luc to hear over the terrible music, but he had no difficultly feeling her break off her own attempts. "Perhaps your group should pick another place," Luc said. "Tonight. And maybe tomorrow."

"Or, y'know, from now on," Anders said.

Gabrielle tried to meet Luc's gaze, but her attempt faltered.

"Gabrielle?" Stephane said.

He sounded shaken. Good. Luc turned to him. "Bullies rarely do well when they meet those stronger than themselves."

Stephane found his voice. "Renard is stronger than us."

"Renard is the bully I'm speaking of," Luc said, looking the vampire up and down. "You? You're a…" He turned to Anders. "What's the word?"

"Flunky."

"*Le mot juste.* Flunky."

"You think you can beat Renard?" Gabrielle's confidence had returned. She sounded amused.

"Renard seems to think we're a threat. You three probably aren't important enough to know his plans, but he's been trying—rather feebly, I might add—to immolate us for days." Luc pushed another pulse of glamour out, and the three men audibly exhaled. The one in the tank top even took a small step toward Luc, as though he couldn't resist getting a little bit closer. Luc knew they'd barely be able to follow a word he was saying, so enraptured were they with looking at him.

"Trying to burn a demon," Anders added. "None too bright, your boss."

"It's clear he's afraid. He's trying to goad us into doing something foolish," Luc said. "And we are not foolish." Luc smiled and made sure Gabrielle saw a hint of fang.

"You have no idea what he can do," Gabrielle said, though the confidence she'd recovered earlier seemed once again to have faltered.

"You'd be surprised how irrelevant that is," Luc said. "You know enough of who I am to know I was alone before, yes?"

She nodded.

"Good. No matter how powerful a vampire might be, if that vampire is alone, he is nothing."

She frowned.

Stephane spoke. "Renard isn't alone."

Luc didn't turn to face him. "True. He has *flunkies*. Imagine, though, were they all…unavailable."

Gabrielle stared at him.

"Yes, you see my point. If Renard insists on pushing, we'll see how loyal his group is once its numbers start to falter. I'm sure Renard has many resources to draw upon, and he's never been shy to replace those he's found unworthy, so perhaps it wouldn't bother him." Luc smiled again. "But I wonder, dear Gabrielle, Stephane, and…whatever your name is…would it bother you?"

They stared. Gabrielle opened her mouth, but nothing came out.

Luc gathered will, feeling the near-painful pressure gathering behind his eyes, then released it at the three vampires with a single word.

"*Leave.*"

They all moved. Gabrielle was forced back only a single step, Stephane retreated three, and their third was halfway to the bar, fists clenched with the effort it took him to stop even that soon. They were young, then. Not completely without power, no. But young.

"Do I need to repeat myself?" Luc asked.

Gabrielle and Stephane left. Gabrielle grabbed the third vampire's arm as she passed him and all but pulled him out of the bar. Luc waited until the three had left the building before he released the glamour that held the three handsome men in sway.

They all blinked, shaking their heads. The one who'd been so popular with the bachelorette groups rubbed his forehead with the palm of one hand, nearly spilling the beer he held in the other.

"You okay, dude?" his friend asked.

Anders stepped closer to Luc as the three men shook off the glamour and headed back to the bar.

"We're going to try taking out his whole coterie one at a time?" The demon's skepticism was obvious. "Wouldn't the first one we attacked mean Renard got what he wanted? If we smack one of his, he could come at us with everything he has."

"Yes. So of course we won't, unless there's no other resort. But do you think Gabrielle believes Renard would consider the loss of one of his coterie worth that opportunity? Even if it was her we decided to destroy?"

Anders smiled. "I think he'd toss her to you himself if he knew you'd give him a reason to attack."

"Exactly. She must know that. And we just learned that Renard's second can't withstand my dominance. I didn't even have to draw on your help. Renard keeps his power to himself." Luc shook his head. "If he didn't have so damn much of it, I'm sure someone would have toppled him by now. He's a fool. Though it makes him no less dangerous."

"We knew he was strong already. But you're right. Those three were pretty pathetic. Does that make this a win?" Anders asked.

Luc nodded. "I think so. It's cold comfort, but now I'm sure Renard is the true and only significant threat from his coterie, which is not to say that fighting off a group of vampires would be easy, but still...And perhaps I've startled Gabrielle enough to put a crack in their loyalty. I daresay the word might spread of our 'plan' to winnow out Renard's coterie."

"That was beautiful." Behind them, someone applauded.

It surprised them both. They turned. Catharine and one of the women she'd been with at the *séance*—Anna, Luc remembered—stood just a few steps away from them. Catharine held up a single glass of red wine in a silent toast. Anna was smiling, her soft blue eyes full of amusement.

"Catharine," Luc said warmly. It was very unexpected. She seemed far too refined for a place like this. Even her outfit—a beautiful yellow silk blouse and a cream linen skirt—made her stand out. How could he have not noticed her? "I didn't realize you were here." He looked around the awful establishment. "Frankly, I'm surprised. It doesn't seem like the sort of place I'd expect to find you."

"No," she smiled demurely. "It is not. However, my Anna has a gift for sometimes knowing where interesting things might occur." She nodded to Anna, who returned the fond gaze. "And her...instinct... seems to have been very on target this evening."

"You have a knack for rare graces," Luc said, though kindly. He smiled at Anna. "Be they your own or otherwise." Prognostication? Visions? Or perhaps a gift for dowsing? He wondered which window to the future the pretty woman could open.

Catharine's grin was impish. "I believe in the charm of the unique. Your glamour, for instance." Her eyebrow rose, as though she were chastising him for not mentioning something she should know.

"Hardly unique. I've never met one of our kind without it," Luc said, though he knew full well what she meant. "At any rate, I am glad you enjoyed the show," he said, though he wasn't entirely sure that was true. Catharine had been an ally so far, yes, but he wasn't convinced it was a great idea to let her see the extent of his glamour, or how strong his will was against three members of Renard's coterie.

"We did."

Luc was torn. If this Anna could catch glimpses of the future, could she tell him anything of Renard's plans? Was it worth owing Catharine even more, just to ask?

If she was aware of the ambivalence he was struggling with, she didn't show it. "Well," she said, "we'll leave you to your evening. I would have words with that fellow, there." Catharine said, nodding. Luc followed her gaze; the popular handsome man in the tank top was once again preening for the benefit of the women around him.

"Have a good evening," Luc said.

Catharine and Anna crossed the floor to the bar. Luc watched her engage the man, while Anna seemed to draw the attention of the two others who were with him.

"Well damn," Anders said. "I was totally gonna put that guy in his place."

"Believe me," Luc said. "That's still where he'll be by the end of the night."

Luc took another look at the Lady Markham and her pretty blood-sister. He couldn't decide if he'd missed an opportunity, done the right thing, or if he'd outright blundered. Vampire politics. He shook his head. "Let's go. At this point, I'd rather be in that pub of yours than here."

"I knew it would grow on you."

"Much like mold."

CHAPTER TWELVE

It took Curtis three attempts to park the Mercedes. By the time he'd managed to parallel park, he was grinding his teeth. With a dark sense of triumph, he pulled the hand brake and exhaled. "I miss my car," he said. "It had a reversing camera."

He glanced at his passenger.

Eli didn't say a word. He hadn't said much of anything at all, really. Curtis knew Eli was less than pleased to be spending the morning with him. He tried not to take it personally. He had heard Eli arguing with his mother on the phone after breakfast and was pretty sure she didn't share his desire to help them take down Renard.

"Okay," Curtis said, trying for a more upbeat voice. "This is a great little church, which is neutral ground. I just need to pick up something, and after that you can start telling me what I need to know about your, uh…" He almost said *magic* again, but caught himself. "Gifts. I want to see if we can manage anything together as-is."

"I doubt we can," Eli said. "We have some wizards, too. It's a small coven, and they get shit on by your folk, but even they've never worked with those of us who speak to spirits."

Gosh, he's Mr. Positive. Curtis held his smile in place with an act of will. "Well, it's worth a try."

Eli undid his seat belt and got out of the car, closing the door with more force than he needed to. Curtis counted to five, then followed suit, the car shrieking at him because he forgot to pull out the keys.

I miss my car. The Mercedes was like stepping back in time to another era. A comfortable and opulent era, sure, but not the one Curtis was used to.

He supposed the car did suit Luc, though. It was sleek and classy and dark. It could roar and purr.

Curtis led Eli into the church. The last time he'd been there had been when the coven heads had called him out over some less-than-subtle magic he'd done. They'd forced him to speak while they used magic to balance a feather on its tip. The feather was enchanted to fall if an untruth was spoken. He'd explained that his sorcery had been self-defense, and the feather hadn't budged. Once again, they'd been forced to let him off the hook for a situation that they'd wanted to punish him for. When he'd asked them to return the favor and state they'd had nothing to do with the nine demons that had tried to suck his soul away, Malcolm Stirling himself had picked up the feather and said they were done.

Curtis exhaled. He could easily imagine the Families doing everything in their power to keep the Métis wizards out of anything important. Hell, from what he'd managed to read, most of the French covens had been forced back to France or been so integrated with the Families they had nothing left in common with their French traditions. Why would the Métis have been treated any better? He supposed some French wizards had to be left in Quebec, still using their magics through the lenses of saints and faith, but it was just one more item on his ever-growing list of things he didn't know and didn't have time to find out.

The interior of the church was cool and dimmer than the outside and had a natural hush. The wooden pews were empty at the moment, though Curtis knew Father Bryce would be around somewhere. It was a smallish community church, one of many dotted throughout Ottawa, but it had the benefit of a father who was well aware of the shadowy side of the world.

Eli looked around with interest. "It's nice," he said.

Curtis wanted to cheer. Finally, something that wasn't negative. "Thanks. I don't go to services anymore, but I like it here. It's quiet, and—like I said—neutral ground."

Eli turned his head. "There are quite a few spirits here, but they're all peaceful. This is a place of comfort."

Curtis couldn't quite help himself from peering around the room. He didn't see or feel anything. "So, are they ghosts of people who used to come here when they were alive?"

Eli shook his head. "Not exactly. The spirits of the dead can linger sometimes, and it's possible to call them and speak with them." His voice fell, and Curtis wondered if he was thinking of his cousin. "But these aren't former mortals. They're natural spirits—pieces of spirit that the prayer and kindness and compassion of this place freed from those who were here."

Curtis blinked. "Prayers make spirits?"

Eli shrugged. "They can. Anything can form a spirit—everything has a spirit."

"Sounds a little like mana. Or animism."

"That's fair," Eli said.

"So what can you do with a spirit like that?"

Eli's voice went flat. "That's a very magic thing to say."

"I'm a very magic kind of guy," Curtis said.

"It wasn't a compliment."

"Yeah, I don't find your subtlety much of a challenge, Eli."

Eli looked up, but he didn't seem angry. "Spirits aren't *tools*. It's not like what you do—you *impose*. I ask."

"If I *ask*," Curtis said, trying not to rise to the bait, "things can blow up. If don't impose, I won't be in control of what happens. For me, it's inside." He touched the center of his chest. "It's like a living thing, and it wants out. It wants to be used. If I give it an inch, it will take every mile it can manage." Curtis sighed. "I have to be careful every time I speak a word I don't use very often. I know you find the way magic works distasteful, I guess, but that's how it is."

Eli didn't speak for a few moments. "Lend strength for meditation, to calm the mind, or to ease pain, I think."

Curtis blinked. "Pardon?"

"The spirits here. That's what I could ask of them." He looked at Curtis. "But they could refuse. If I wasn't truly looking for something they wanted to associate with, they could just refuse to answer."

"So it's more like a partnership," Curtis said.

"Respectful friendship," Eli said.

"Huh," Curtis said, mulling that over. He remembered the fire that had been woven into Anders's jacket, and how Eli had said it was looking for another of its kind, like the spell was more or less conscious. It was funny. Curtis had always considered the source of his magic that way—like something inside him with wants and desires—but individual spells or enchantments? No. Those were things he did *with* the magic, not their own distinct beings in and of themselves.

He wondered if that was wrong.

"Is that you, Curtis?" The voice came from the front of the church, where a man in priest's vestments had entered. He smiled when we saw Curtis, and he approached with both hands out.

"Hold that thought," Curtis said to Eli. He walked down the aisle to meet the priest halfway. They shook, the priest taking Curtis's hand and then bringing him close for a hug. Curtis took in the faint scent of incense and soap and gave himself a moment to just enjoy the warmth of the hug.

"Father Bryce," Curtis said. "I'm glad you're in. Could I ask a favor?"

"Of course." The smile lines around Father Bryce's eyes always made Curtis feel safe. "And is this the boyfriend you never seem to tell me about? He's handsome."

Curtis turned pink.

They'd been sitting outside in the small park beside the church for nearly an hour and had gotten nowhere. Curtis lowered his hand and exhaled. "Okay, I swear I believe you that there are spirits all around us. But apparently, I'm spirit-blind."

Eli didn't say anything. Curtis looked at him. Eli sat on the bench with a faraway look in his dark eyes and a small line between his eyebrows. He clenched and unclenched his jaw. For the first time, Curtis noticed a small scar on the side of Eli's neck, just below the ear.

Curtis waited a few more seconds, biting his lip. Eli had made it perfectly clear he didn't like Curtis much, and though Curtis understood some of that, he was also pretty sure it wasn't helping them get in synch.

"Eli," Curtis said, and his voice came out a little weak. He cleared his throat. "Eli."

Eli blinked, coming back from wherever he'd been. He let out a small breath and turned to him. "Yes?"

"What's going on with you?" Curtis asked. He hoped he didn't sound patronizing.

Eli's expression remained grim. "What *does* your boyfriend think?"

Curtis blinked. "Pardon?"

"The priest. He wanted to know if I was your boyfriend. He said you never talked about your boyfriend. Does your boyfriend even know about your *thing* with Luc and Anders?" Curtis bristled at the heat in Eli's question.

"Okay, first there's no boyfriend," Curtis said. "Father Bryce thinks there is because he knows I let Luc and Anders move in. He assumed one of them was my roommate and the other is my boyfriend, and it was way easier letting him assume that than telling him the truth."

Eli frowned. "So you're single?"

"Well…" Curtis felt he was on shaky ground. "I don't know about that. Luc and Anders and I are…close."

"Close," Eli said.

"Yeah, close." Curtis could feel his skin burning and wished for the millionth time that he wasn't so easy a blush. "We have to renew the triad every month, and part of that is with Anders…and…I mean, I like them. Both of them, actually. Are we all boyfriends, though?" Curtis raised his hands. "I seriously have no idea. Anders literally can't do monogamy, not that what we're doing is monogamy anyway. Because there's three of us. And I'm never quite sure if Luc sees me as much more than the reason for his freedom, but they both do seem to like me. Luc takes me out to the opera and stuff, Anders is fun, and we have a good time…" He'd started out with a strong voice, but by the end, Curtis was almost muttering.

Eli was clenching his jaw again.

"Short answer? I think I'm more or less dating them both, but I don't think they'd say they're dating each other, and I don't think either of them would be happy if I were to date someone else." Curtis didn't even know where to begin to feel about all that. "But seriously, is the confusing state of my love life actually what's bothering you?"

Eli rolled his eyes. "This thing you want me to do. I have to… *bond*…with you guys."

"Yeah." Curtis blinked. The light went on. "Oh!" He leaned back on the bench. "Yeah, I could see how that might be awkward. What with the not being gay." Curtis winced, and then added, "Not that I should assume that you're not gay. Or that you're straight. Whatever."

"You assume correctly," Eli said. "Am I gonna have to…?" He didn't finish the sentence but looked at Curtis instead. Something like fear was in Eli's eyes, and for just a moment, it struck Curtis as a little bit funny. Eli was a big, strong guy. He was handsome, if you went for strong, quiet guys with chips on their shoulders. Sitting there, looking at how shaken and worried Eli was apparently feeling about "bonding," Curtis had to bite his lip to not burst out laughing. *Oh no! The gays!*

"Um," Curtis said, trying to find the right words. "No one would dream of forcing you to, uh, do anything you're not comfortable with. My part would be on the last night, and we'll be blending magic with your spirit sense, assuming we can get that to work. We'd be holding hands, that's it. The first night we share blood, which Luc handles. And, sure, he bites us in turn, and then usually bites his wrist for us to take a taste from—"

Eli's eyes widened, and Curtis rushed to calm him down.

"But it's okay. A vampire's bite actually feels pretty good, if they want it to. Luc can glamour it into a nice feeling. Don't worry. And it actually doesn't take very long. Or at least, it doesn't take much for us to renew the bonds, usually. I guess we might want a few sucks…No! I mean, swallows…No! I mean…You know what I mean."

"And with Anders?" Eli said. It was his turn to blush, and Curtis squirmed on the bench.

"So, Anders is an incubus," Curtis said. "Uh, as you know. I'm sure we can work something out that's pleasurable but not an…uh…" Curtis floundered, but the only word that seemed to want to come out of his mouth was "orgy." That probably wouldn't ease Eli's concerns.

"Not sex," Eli said.

"Yeah," Curtis said.

They stared at each other.

"You're sure?" Eli said.

"Yes," Curtis said. *Nope.* He needed to talk to Anders, stat.

Eli leaned back on the bench and exhaled. "Okay." Curtis saw the tension leave his shoulders, and the two stared at each other a little longer.

"I don't have anything against you guys for being gay," Eli said. And it was such an awkward straight-guy thing to say, Curtis wondered if he should just conjure up a rainstorm or something so they'd both have a reason to run away from this conversation.

"I get that," Curtis said.

"I have gay friends."

Curtis forced an over-bright smile. *He seriously just said that.* It was his turn to be silent.

Eli cleared his throat. "There was a guy when I was in grade school, and we maybe fooled around a bit. But I mean, all guys mess around. Y'know, when we're younger."

"Really?" Curtis said. "I never..." The look on Eli's face made Curtis falter. "Uh, but then, I mean, I was worried any guy I made a move on would freak out, so..."

There was a long, pregnant pause.

"Do you want to try again? I can call another spirit," Eli said.

"Yes," Curtis said, almost before Eli had finished asking the question.

They got back to work.

"Hi," Curtis said. He tossed Luc's car keys on the counter and walked up to Anders, leaning his forehead in the center of the demon's chest. Anders put down his coffee and wrapped his arms around him.

The wizard's voice was tired. "I'm now fairly certain I can make my magic work with Eli's spirits and pull this off. It only took three hours of tweaking until I could kind of sense the spirits he was calling, and I had to use my glasses and a piece of quartz. My head is pounding, my eyes are sore, and I'm beyond hungry. Also, an entire morning with Eli is like reliving grade nine gym class all over again, with even less fun and more dodgeball."

Anders gave the wizard a squeeze. "Where is Eli?"

"His Grumpy Majesty went upstairs for a shower. I want a bath, a nap, and an aspirin. Not in that order." Curtis pushed his forehead against Anders's chest, nuzzling him like he was a pillow. Another time that would have been a very welcome gesture, but...

"I'm glad you're home. We need to go out," Anders said. "I was almost ready to go without you."

Curtis groaned and gripped Anders's shirt in both hands, pushing his face into the demon's chest. "That's the opposite of a nap." He took a deep breath, then pushed off, looking up at him. "Why do we need to go out?"

"I need to check in with David. I told him we'd meet him for a coffee."

"Oh," Curtis said. "Okay then." He stretched, and Anders heard his neck pop.

That was too easy. "You don't mind?" Anders said.

"I can ask him about whether or not the coven heads are going to replace my car," Curtis said. "We've been emailing about it, and he's been really cool." Anders frowned. Curtis was blushing. "Let me write a note for Eli. He said he was going to sleep after his shower, too, so he might not even know we're gone."

Curtis wrote a brief note and put it on the fridge with a magnet. "Okay," Curtis said, taking a deep breath. "Can we take your car? I don't want to drive."

Anders nodded.

"Also, I want lunch after." Curtis paused. "Does your job pay enough to treat me to lunch, whatever your job is?"

Anders smirked. "Nice try."

"You're still paying."

"Fine."

They left the house, Curtis locking the door behind them. "So why are we meeting with David?"

"I'll fill you in on the ride there. Luc wants us to see if David knows anything about Renard."

"Won't that tip off Renard that we're asking questions? I'm pretty sure David will have to report back to the coven heads and maybe even Renard himself, given what he does."

"Luc said it was time for intimidation. I'll explain on the way."

"Fine by me. Renard's the whole reason I have a headache and had to withstand Mr. Grumpy-Butt all morning. Oh, and one other thing," Curtis said. "Eli would like to not have sex with you. Can we work with that?"

"What?" Anders said, stopping cold on the driveway.

"When we add him to the triad. He doesn't want to have sex with us. I said it wouldn't be a problem." Curtis was avoiding his gaze.

"Curtis," Anders said.

The young man looked up at him, sheepish. "It won't be a problem, will it? He's sort of...spooked."

Anders raised an eyebrow.

"He's straight," Curtis said. "He was all...'I experimented when I was a kid, but I don't want gay cooties.'" Curtis's attempt at Eli's deep voice was less than successful.

"I can work with that," Anders said, unlocking the car.

"Good," Curtis said, relieved. They got in the car. Curtis frowned. "Wait. What exactly does that mean?"

❖

Anders crossed his arms, wondering if David was late by accident or if this was a less-than-subtle message. Either way, it was annoying.

"Okay, he totally rocks that uniform," Curtis said.

Anders turned. David was approaching, and if he didn't looked pleased, it was still an impressive look. He wondered if the sunglasses were an extra touch just to add to the intimidation factor. Tall, wide, and blond, David cut an impressive figure to begin with. Adding in the cop outfit apparently checked off some boxes for Curtis.

"Don't get any ideas," Anders said, remembering how quickly Curtis had agreed to come back out again when he'd heard David's name.

"Believe me," Curtis said, "one demon is more than enough. Though, hello Officer."

Anders frowned, but Curtis just smiled at him.

"You're cute when you're jealous," Curtis said.

Anders grunted. They'd been waiting outside the coffee shop for ten minutes or so, and David didn't seem to be hurrying.

"Thanks for coming," Curtis said. "I didn't realize you'd be at work already. I thought you worked nights. Sorry if this is an imposition."

"I'm working early today. You're not an imposition," David said. Was it just Anders's imagination, or did David's tone seem a little too easygoing when he spoke with Curtis? "I'm sorry I haven't gotten back to you again about the car situation, but Stirling's people are on it.

They're clearing up any insurance fallout, and you should have a new car in a week or two. Stirling's man said they were going to give you this year's model."

"Wow," Curtis said. "I don't mind waiting for that. I can borrow Luc's car if I need it. That's...more than I expected. You were right. Thank you."

"Don't worry about it," David said, waving it off.

Anders watched them talk. No, it was definitely not his imagination. These two were being far too nice to each other.

"How's Ethan?" Curtis asked.

David pulled off his sunglasses and tucked them into the neck of his uniform shirt. "Much better. Is that what you two wanted to talk to me about?"

Curtis looked at Anders, and sighed. "Not really. How about I go get us all drinks, and we can walk. Coffee?" he asked David.

"Sure. Two milk," David said.

Curtis nodded and ducked into the shop.

"I'm glad Ethan's doing better," Anders said.

"This time," David said, and all the easy going "Officer Helpful" tone was gone. Of course.

"How were the Mormons?" Anders asked.

David's lip twitched just a little. "Helpful."

Anders grinned. "I'll bet."

David crossed his arms. "I'm tired of this."

Anders regarded him. It had seemed like a genuine enough confession, but David was a demon and a cop. Both gave him plenty of practice at spinning lies and putting on masks.

"Of what?" he asked.

David rolled his eyes. He pitched his voice low. "You know what. Being on our own. Doing everything the fucking Families want me to do, not to mention the bloodsuckers. And the goddamn werewolves get to order me around when they come to the city. Hell, the only ones who leave me alone are the demons, but these days even the demons seem to be doing their level best to make messes for me to clean up."

"Still bad out there, huh?" Anders said.

David just sighed. "It's not getting better, that's for damn sure. Everyone just seems pissed." He shook his head, and the look of exhaustion that had been there for just a moment was gone as fast as it had appeared. "And full moon in three days—it always gets worse those nights."

Anders nodded. He knew that. On the nights where the packs and wizards and bloodsuckers gathered to reinforce their bonds, the lone wolves were left confident enough to move out and about on their own. When he'd been on his own, he'd gorged himself for those three nights every month, trying to get enough to make it through to the next full moon without having to get out much and risk being spotted by a demon who had a pack and felt like kicking his ass just for the hell of it.

"Look," Anders said, surprised he was speaking even as the words left his mouth. "We've got something coming together. I think it'll make a difference."

David's gaze locked on his. "What are you doing?"

Anders shook his head. "No. I can't tell you."

"Jesus, Anders—"

"No," Anders said it again. "You're in no position to keep a secret if someone wants you to tell them. You just said it. You answer to way too many people." It came out harsher than he'd intended, and David's whole body tightened in response. "Sorry."

"Well, so long as you're sorry." David scowled. "Just remember exactly who put me in this position."

Anders glared right back. "You've got to be fucking kidding me. I taught you how to get by."

"Yeah, and I've been 'getting by' for years. And now Ethan is 'getting by.' Only you'll notice it took your wizard boy toy to keep him alive while he was 'getting by.' You know damned well we could be doing better than that, if you'd just help us. And you know it would be safer for you, too."

"That's not the first time you've passed along someone else's threat," Anders said.

"It's not easy getting a message through your thick skull."

"You know what, David? You're sexy when you're mad," Anders said.

"Oh, for fuck's sake." David took a step toward him, angry.

"See?" Anders said, and David stopped.

"See what?" His anger made his voice rough, but he was holding himself in check.

"You barely tolerate me. This invitation—it's not yours. I don't know why you keep asking me to join you and Ethan, but I do know you can't stand me. Even if I think you've got shit reasons for it, I know it."

David's voice was tight. "Chad—"

"Is dead. I know. And you loved him, and I fucked him, and we both know you couldn't have stayed with him when you were changing because you would have drained him dry." Anders held up his hand. "But that's not the point. Who the fuck is asking you to do this?"

David just shook his head. "No one."

"Right," Anders said.

"I'm serious. Fine. You're right. I don't really like you."

Anders snorted.

"But," David continued, "right now, you're the only other demon out there I know who's free to make a pack with Ethan and me."

"Wow, isn't that flattering?"

"No, it's not." David took a breath. "But someday I'm not going to be under the thumb of those bloodsuckers or the old bastards and their covens, and when that happens, *I know things.* Everything they've ever told me to do? The wizards, weres, vampires, fuck—even the other demons? All of that is currency. It's in the bank. But Ethan has to make it that far, or I'm no farther ahead than I was when I first changed and you came along. Without three, I can't cash out."

Anders regarded him. This, he was pretty sure, was really David. This was the cop who wanted to do the right thing, even if he didn't have a soul. David was going to make all the people who'd used him pay for it, and pay dearly. Justice might not be possible. In fact, given what Anders assumed David had been made to do time after time, he figured justice was no longer possible.

But he could get plenty of vengeance.

For the first time in decades, Anders really did find David hot.

"Renard," Anders said.

David leaned back. "What about him? What does he have to do with anything?"

Damn, Anders thought. If he'd hoped for a slip from David, he didn't get one. The man had a great poker face.

"Is it Renard pulling your strings?" Anders asked.

David glanced into the coffee shop. Anders turned and saw Curtis had made it to the front of the line.

"If he was," David said. "I'd warn you he's the only bloodsucker that makes Malcolm Stirling think twice."

"Fantastic," Anders groused. "So Renard wants me out of the triad."

David didn't agree or disagree, but after a moment, he added, "Anders, as far as I know, *everyone* wants your group to break up."

"Even you?"

David stared him down.

"Okay," Anders said, and the word made David grow very still.

"Okay?" David said. "Okay, what?"

"I'll help you."

"You'll join us?" David pitched his voice low.

"No." Anders shook his head. "But I'll help you. I don't know what that means right now. But…"

"But?"

Anders crossed his arms.

David sighed. "I guess that's all I get, huh?"

Anders cracked a small smile. "If everything falls to shit," he said. "I might be knocking on your door before you know it." *If Curtis's plan to use Eli craps out, if freeing Renard's sorcerer doesn't work, if Renard kicks our asses, if we can't stop him, if one of them dies…*

And if I survive.

"Wow. I'm plan B, huh? Isn't that flattering." David mimicked Anders.

"You'll live," Anders said.

"You owe us," David said.

Anders shook his head. "No. I don't. I got you both this far. You might think I owe you more, but that doesn't make it true."

David shook his head. "I'm trying to help you."

"You're trying to help *you*." When David looked at him with anger in his eyes, Anders held up a hand. "And Ethan. I get that."

"What are you planning?" David asked. "Because I'm not kidding, Renard's like the biggest and baddest vampire in the city, Anders. He's the damned Duke. People who get up in his face have a habit of vanishing. And he's not like other bloodsuckers. He only follows the rules when he has to."

"I know. I've had the pleasure of meeting him. Also, letter bombs and burning cars, remember?"

"I can't prove it's him," David said angrily. Whether he meant because there was no proof or because he wasn't being allowed to, Anders couldn't tell.

"I'm not surprised. Who wants you to find out my plans and report back?" Anders said.

They stared at each other. Neither blinked.

"Okay," Curtis said, coming out of the shop. He juggled three cups in his hands in a triangle. "Three drinks." His smile faltered when he saw David's scowl, and he gave Anders a pointed look. "Did I miss something?"

"Renard makes Malcolm Stirling twitchy," Anders said.

"Huh." Curtis held up the drinks awkwardly, and the two men took them from him. "Well, I suppose even Renard has to have some good qualities."

David laughed. He actually laughed. He bumped Curtis with his shoulder and said, "I like you, kid."

Curtis beamed. Anders scowled.

They walked through the Glebe together, avoiding Bank for the quieter side streets. Walking with a uniformed police officer was drawing a certain type of attention, but Anders noticed most people looked up and then looked away. Most of them even seemed a little guilty. He wondered if it was always like that. Did seeing a cop make you think of the bad things you've done?

He looked at David and figured that more likely, looking at David would make him think of bad things he wanted to do. But maybe that was just him.

"So. This tendency for people who piss off Renard to vanish," Anders said, coming back to the point. "What kind of 'vanish' are we talking about?"

David swallowed some of his coffee. "Things that can be written off as accidents, mostly. That's assuming we're talking about people who are visible in the first place. One of the demon packs had a pretty solid grip on downtown, and rumor was that Renard wanted them to bend the knee. They didn't, and now their grip on the downtown is a whole lot looser."

"But they didn't vanish?" Anders asked.

"About half of them did before their pack leader 'decided' to let Renard have more access." David looked at Anders. "That was one of the few times that Renard was open to negotiation. Usually, he's more of an obey-or-else sort of guy. The coven heads can't stand him, and they don't capitulate to what he wants, but at best that's a standoff. They give each other a wide berth. Renard's a warlock, which might have something to do with it—former wizard, and all that."

"Not as former as you'd like to think. Just ask my car," Curtis said. "I wonder why he wanted more access to downtown. The Château?"

Anders looked at David. David shrugged. "He didn't send out a memo."

"Were you involved at all with that so-called hit-and-run? Music student?" Anders asked.

"Her name was Chantale," Curtis added.

David looked down, his expression dark. "Yeah."

"That was Renard," Curtis said.

David's scowl deepened. "I'd assumed. I got my orders about her through his little boy-toy." He looked at Curtis. "I got a call. Kid said there was a body that needed to be 'written off as a hit-and-run.'"

"Tyson," Curtis said. "And he's on a very tight leash. He can barely speak without Renard's permission."

David scowled. "If you say so. He said it wouldn't be a big deal. Just another dead Indian. His exact words were, 'They go missing all the time.'"

Curtis turned away. "I hate this so much. Renard needs to go. All of this…"

"Curtis," Anders said.

Curtis shook his head. "I know. I know."

David put a hand on Curtis's shoulder and squeezed. It took effort for Anders not to knock his hand away. "He'll pay," David said. "Someday. They all will."

Curtis's nod was brief. "Hopefully very soon."

David regarded them both. "It's maybe not a good idea to tell me much more."

"We know," Anders said, and then he smiled. "But if you're asked, maybe passing along that we weren't worried in the slightest would be good."

David frowned. "You should be."

Curtis's eyebrows rose. "Oh, we are."

"Ah," David said. "I get it."

"And maybe mention how we were asking you about all the other members of Renard's coterie."

David frowned. "Renard's coterie? It's big—he's the Duke, after all. But he's never won any prizes for being a good leader among his own. He likes to find vampires who are good in a fight or have the same attitude as he does about the rules, but other than that, they're not really special. And he definitely isn't one to hold on to someone who pisses him off. He's released more members of his coterie than anyone I can think of." David shrugged. "And by 'released,' I mean they vanish. Or sometimes we find ashes and bone. They're all the same to him. I'd say he generally keeps his group up at a dozen."

"Make sure we sounded happy to learn all that," Anders said.

David frowned. "You're not dumb enough to try and take down his coterie."

"Aw, thanks," Anders said.

"He'd just replace them," David said.

"Still," Anders said. "It'd be inconvenient, no?"

David's frown grew, but he nodded. "Next time she calls, I'll say you were interested."

"Good boy," Anders said, nodding.

"He means thank you," Curtis said. He shoved Anders's shoulder, and the demon shrugged at him. David didn't seem surprised Anders wasn't being particularly polite.

"You ready for lunch?" Anders asked.

Curtis nodded. "Yeah. Thanks again, David."

"You're welcome," David said. "Like I said, they'll all pay eventually."

Curtis smiled.

"See you again," David said to Anders. "Soon."

Anders grunted. He didn't like how sure David sounded.

David left them, walking back toward Bank Street, and Curtis drained the last of his tea. "Tell me again why I needed to come with you for that?" Curtis said.

"David's nicer while you're around."

"He's a nice guy."

Anders snorted.

"Well, I like him."

Anders narrowed his eyes. "I could tell."

"Can we argue after lunch?" Curtis asked. "I find hypocrisy hard to handle on an empty stomach."

Anders frowned. "What? Hypocrisy?"

"If you're jealous of me flirting, it's hypocritical. Come on, there's a great Indian place near here. I want naan." Curtis started walking.

Jealous? Anders followed, tossing his empty coffee cup into a bin as he passed. He wasn't jealous. He'd already been through this with Curtis. It was one thing to play around in their little group. They needed to do that for maintaining their bond, and frankly, Anders liked what they had. He could even handle Curtis being with Luc. He knew they had to.

But Curtis with David? Or, really, anyone else? That made the hair on the back of his neck stand up and his stomach get tight in a very unpleasant way. No way.

"I don't like to share," Anders said, thinking out loud.

Curtis sighed. "Then order your own bread."

CHAPTER THIRTEEN

S haring blood was one thing, Luc thought, but this was going to be difficult.

The first night had gone smoother than Luc had expected. Eli had been a little reserved, so Curtis had gone first, offering his neck to Luc and making a bit of a show of how much he trusted Luc. The complete lack of fear on Curtis's part might have helped Eli's pride rise to the challenge, and Eli had followed suit with only a brief hesitation. Luc had been very careful to apply just enough glamour to make the bite feel pleasant, but not overwhelmingly so.

Licking his neck had been a bit less comfortable, but Eli managed that, too.

He had, however, struggled more when it came his turn to drink from Luc's wrist, something that even Curtis still couldn't quite find appealing. Still, the four of them had shared in each other's blood, and Luc had forced himself to lick the wounds on Curtis's and Anders's necks closed with less obvious pleasure than he usually showed.

He wouldn't be the one to spook Eli on the first night of their bonding.

Normally they would spend most of the evening together through the full moons. Often, the three of them would gather in Luc's bed, Curtis nestled between him and Anders, and they'd spend a few hours together. Luc usually slaked his thirst a few times between the three of them, though they'd learned early that the bare minimum of sharing a little blood was all that was truly required—another difference to their odd triad, which seemed to want to maintain itself.

Instead of the usual, they dealt with the sharing of blood in an almost businesslike manner. Although it felt a little cold to Luc, he understood. Eli might want revenge, but to pile up like puppies in a bed would perhaps have pushed him too far out of his comfort zone.

Instead, they'd ordered in takeout and shared blood before a large meal of Chinese food. Luc had some wine while they ate, and the four shared conversation while the blood tied them together.

Already, Luc felt *something*. Eli's blood had, of course, tasted different—all those with gifts had an extra spice to their blood. Eli's blood brought the sweetness of a dessert wine to Luc's mind, something he had no intention of sharing with Eli. He assumed the man would prefer to find out he tasted like beer.

But after, as they'd felt the bonds renewing, Luc felt a difference in the bond he shared with the others. Ephemeral, to be sure, but *something* was happening. Hope for their plan, however reckless and dangerous it was, began to grow in him.

And then he'd woken on the second night, and realized what was next.

The four of them gathered again, this time in Anders's room, and if Eli had looked hesitant the night before, now he looked positively frightened. At least Curtis had had the sense to suggest they all wear nightclothes. Luc noticed, though, that Anders had decided "nightclothes" meant a pair of black boxers and nothing else. He and Curtis were wearing white undershirts and cotton pyjama pants, as was the increasingly skittish Eli.

When Eli started to shake his head, Luc knew they were in danger of losing him. How in the world were they going to handle this?

"Eli," Luc said, keeping his voice as calming as he could manage. "Please relax."

"Right," Eli said. He stopped shaking his head, and he crossed his arms.

Merde.

"Now what?" Eli said.

"Look," Anders said. "We get it. You're straight. No one's gonna try and bend you over until you say it's okay—"

"Anders," Curtis said, when Eli took a step back from the demon.

"Seriously, guy," Anders chuckled. "Sorry. I couldn't resist. Here's the thing. All we need here is for everyone to feel good. Luc and I, we can help with that." The demon glanced at Luc, and Luc nodded. Eli watched them both with barely concealed skepticism.

"Let me ask you a question," Anders said.

"No sex," Eli said.

"No sex," Anders said. He almost didn't sound disappointed. "That wasn't what I was going to ask. Curtis told me you didn't want to go there."

"Okay." Eli's voice seemed calmer now. Luc wondered if he should maybe give the poor man a nudge of glamour, but decided against it for now.

"Be honest with me for a second, and understand we are the last people who are going to judge you, okay?"

Eli nodded.

"You ever look at a guy and think he's handsome? Wonder, maybe, what it'd be like to be him?" Anders's voice had lowered and softened. "I'm pretty sure every guy does."

Eli took in a deep breath. "Yeah, sure." It came out defensively, almost like a challenge.

"Think about that for me. Or imagine it. Look at me, and think about the kind of guy you wouldn't mind being for a while."

The changes were subtle at first and slow in coming. Anders didn't lose any bulk. If anything, Luc wondered if maybe the demon gained some mass, but he couldn't tell, as the demon's dark chest hair faded away and his musculature grew even more defined. Anders's usual wide chest and stocky frame became chiseled and almost statuesque.

Like Luc himself, Eli apparently thought that handsome men took more care in their grooming. Anders's scruff was now gone, and his hair shortened and tidied itself.

To Luc's surprise, in between blinks, Anders's eyes lightened to a cool gray, a shade he'd never seen the demon sport before. Anders's skin, on the other hand, darkened from its usual tan to something closer to Eli's own, and then a little darker. Luc shared a glance with Curtis, who raised his eyebrows in obvious approval. Anders was gorgeous this way.

"Come here," Anders said, still speaking softly.

Eli took a single, halting step, then seemed to gather himself and draw close to the demon.

"This is what you'd like to be?" Anders asked.

Luc was entranced. He had no idea Anders had this level of delicacy. Nor subtlety.

Eli's response was a curt nod. Luc could hear him breathing, a little faster than Luc would have expected. Was he aroused? Frightened? Both?

"Eli," Anders said. "I look at you, and I see this."

Eli's lip curled in a small smile. "Right."

"Not this exactly," Anders said. "But something like this. I wonder what it would be like to be you. You're handsome. You work hard at the gym, I can tell." Anders raised his hand and—incredibly gently—put his palm on Eli's chest.

Eli froze, and Luc wondered if Anders had gone too far, too fast. But as seconds passed and Anders just stood there, Eli pressed his own hand against the demon's chest.

"And this?" Anders smiled and slid his hand to Eli's shoulder, where the Métis tattoo was inked on his shoulder. "This is hot." Anders traced one finger along the symbol.

Eli swallowed.

"I know people look at you," Anders said. "They look, and they want to touch." He slid his hand slowly and gently across Eli's skin, stroking the length of Eli's arm, all the way back to Eli's hand. He pressed his own hand over it. "Can we look at you, Eli?" Anders asked.

Eli closed his eyes, but he didn't pull away. After what seemed to Luc like a very long time, Eli nodded. "Okay."

Anders took Eli's hand away from his chest and raised it into the air, then took his other hand and did the same. When he grasped the edge of Eli's borrowed white undershirt, Eli tensed, but he didn't stop Anders from lifting the shirt up and off.

"Look at me," Anders said once he'd dropped the shirt to the floor.

Eli opened his eyes as though it were an act of will. Luc imagined it was.

"You're hot," Anders said.

Eli let out a little puff of breath.

"We all think you're hot," Anders said.

Eli's frame tightened again and though his head turned just a little, he didn't look at Curtis or Luc.

"It's okay," Anders said, smiling. "You can just look at me if you want."

Eli nodded.

"I'd like to touch you again," Anders said. "Would you like that?"

"Okay." The word was barely a breath.

Anders moved closer to Eli, running his hands across Eli's bare chest and down his sides, resting his fingers low on Eli's hips. The tension between the two was palpable, and Luc caught a slight ripple in the air around the two.

It was working. Luc confirmed with a glance at Eli's pyjamas, he was becoming aroused.

"You can just look at me," Anders said. "Keep looking at me."

Eli was breathing faster but no longer seemed ready to bolt.

"We'd like to see the rest of you," Anders said.

Eli bit his lip, and the hesitancy returned.

"I can go first," Anders said. He took Eli's hands and brought them to his waist, sliding the man's fingertips along the edge of his black boxers.

Luc watched with fascination and arousal as Eli's hands steadied, then slid beneath the black fabric. When Eli pushed Anders's boxers down, Anders's dick was already hard. Freed from the boxers, it rose. Eli's hesitation was momentary, but Anders took his hand again to push the boxers until they fell to his ankles, and then he stepped out of them.

"Are you hard, Eli?" Anders asked, his voice taking on more of an edge now.

Eli's nod was barely a movement.

"Let's get off together, Eli. All of us. Just us guys." He hooked his fingers into Eli's pyjamas and no trace left of Eli's resistance was left. He stepped out of the fallen bottoms, naked now, and Anders smiled.

"Okay, you just look at me," Anders said to Eli. "We're gonna look at you. Because you're hot, Eli." As he spoke, Anders reached down and took a loose grip on his dick. Eli followed suit.

Anders broke eye contact with Eli for just long enough to nod at Curtis and Luc. They didn't come closer but soon all four were naked. They stroked themselves in a triangle around Eli, who looked at Anders while he worked himself. The scent of sweat found its way to Luc's nose, and he forced in a deep lungful to enjoy it. Eli was jerking himself harder now, and his breath was louder.

They were otherwise silent in the bedroom, but Luc found the play arousing in a way he'd never considered before. He wanted to touch, of course, but he enjoyed watching the muscles play across Eli's arms and chest and even his thighs as he stroked himself. Anders was right. Eli was handsome and masculine in a very appealing way. His fangs had grown sharp in his mouth.

When Anders reached forward and once again pressed his free hand to Eli's chest, Eli's breath hitched, and then he came. A rush of heat between the two men flared out among the rest, and Luc felt his own release come as he heard the telltale grunt from Anders and a softer, throatier noise from Curtis.

They stood, recovering, for a few moments. Eli had closed his eyes and was panting, his half-hard dick still in hand.

Anders dropped his hand from Eli's chest and looked at Curtis, one eyebrow raised. The silent question was obvious: *Was that enough?*

Curtis gave a little shrug but smiled. Luc agreed. He'd felt *something*, and it had definitely included Eli.

Eli opened his eyes, looking at Anders. "If we need to," he said, his voice even deeper than usual, "we can do that again."

Anders smiled. "Okay," he said. "Just to be safe."

❖

Luc woke.

When he came out of his basement bedroom, he saw Curtis, Anders, and Eli waiting for him. They were seated around the round wooden table Curtis used every month to lead him and Anders through a simple magical spell, a working of magic that bound them together for another month in the triad. It was always this way—first blood, then soul, then magic.

And tonight, spirit.

Wearing the pale gray robes of a wizard in moot suited Eli, Luc decided. The spirit-caller looked much recovered. After their previous evening, the fellow had been so visibly shaken at enjoying himself that he'd fallen into a near silence for the rest of the night until he'd excused himself to go to bed.

"Good evening," Luc said.

"Almost an hour and a half to sundown," Curtis said.

"Yes." This was the earliest yet he'd woken, and he had a feeling it had as much to do with Eli's participation in the last two evenings as anything else. He hoped this time would be enough for them to do what was needed and get to Renard before he'd have too much opportunity to prepare. Luc pulled out the fourth chair and sat. It seemed strange to be facing Anders, the table divided into quarters rather than thirds. Curtis's chalice, athame, pentacle, and wand were also on the table as usual, but he'd added a simple white candle in the middle.

"Okay," Curtis said. His voice shook, and he swallowed. "Here's the plan. I'm going to put us through a basic working first, calling the four elements like usual, and then Eli's going to bring in a spirit as well. If everything works as planned, we'll know right away if we pulled Eli into the triad or not. So far, it feels like we're on track, right?" He looked up.

"Yes," Luc said. From the moment they'd all shared blood, he'd felt *something* stirring inside.

"Fuck yes," Anders echoed. He was grinning. Eli looked at the demon, and Anders winked.

Slowly, Eli nodded. "I think so. I feel..." He paused, frowning. "Bigger? Fuller? It's hard to describe."

"That's probably me," Anders said. "I get that a lot."

"Anders," Curtis said, but Eli shrugged it off. Luc was happy to see the return of the demon's uncouth nature didn't seem to be bothering Eli as much. Luc supposed it would have been too much to hope Anders would retain the gentler, softer touch he'd had the night before.

"Just keep going," Eli said.

Curtis nodded and held out his hands. Luc took Curtis's in his right hand and Eli's in his left. Eli and Anders completed the circle. As Curtis began to speak, Luc felt the usual tremble of magic stirring in the center of his chest. It felt like a heartbeat—a curious sensation for him, to be sure—pulsing around the circle they'd formed.

"*Ignis, aqua, aer, terra.*" Every word was another pulse that spread through the four and circled back to Curtis. Luc felt warm, then cool; light, then heavy. Each pulse felt stronger than the last.

The athame rose off the table, tipping up and balancing on its point as though invisible fingers held it in place.

Another pulse.

The chalice filled with clear water that gathered from the air itself, filling the silver cup to the rim.

Another pulse.

The wand stood upright, the quartz crystal tied to the head of the wooden stick lighting up with a pale radiance that let out a palpable heat.

Another pulse.

The pentacle tipped up at one end and began to circle, like a coin spun on a tabletop. It started slowly and picked up speed. Soon it was spinning fast enough that it appeared to be a perfect metal sphere.

Curtis looked at Eli and nodded, still repeating the words of the simple invocation.

Luc felt Eli tighten his hand for a moment. Eli closed his eyes, took in a long, slow breath, and then opened his eyes again.

The candle lit, and the next pulse that came through the four of them was so strong it almost pushed them bodily away from the table. Luc managed to hold on to Eli and Curtis with some effort, and both young men gasped. Across from him, Anders threw his head back and laughed out loud.

"Fuck yes!" the demon crowed.

Curtis spoke quicker now. As he spoke in turn to each of the items on the table, they calmed down, and the surges racing between them grew more manageable. The pentacle slowed, then stopped and tipped over with a quiet clink. The wand dimmed, then fell to the table. The water in the chalice evaporated. The athame lay down.

Curtis looked at Eli again.

"Welcome," Eli said. It was obvious he wasn't talking to anyone seated at the table.

Curtis stared into the air between them. "Oh wow," he said. "I can feel that. Her? It feels like a her."

Eli smiled. "Definitely a her. Can you see her?"

Curtis shook his head. "No. But…Wait…" He frowned. "I'm not sure."

Eli's smile grew. He looked into the air between them. "Thank you for your help."

The candle snuffed out. Presumably, the spirit Eli had called to their gathering was now gone.

They let go of each other's hands.

"That was incredible," Curtis said. "That was a spirit, right? And I felt her. Did you guys feel her?" He looked back and forth at Anders and Luc.

"No," Anders said.

Luc shook his head. He felt strange. Refreshed in a way. But he couldn't be sure exactly what was different. Curtis was grinning and Anders frowning. Eli had put both hands on the table and was leaning against it, the faintest of smiles tugging at the corners of his mouth.

"Well, I'm pretty sure that worked," Curtis said. He turned his hands around, looking at the backs of them. "And I feel...Uh..." He frowned, hunting for words. "Awake?"

Luc nodded. That was it. He felt awake and aware and completely restored. "Yes. I know what you mean."

"Eli?" Curtis asked.

Eli took a few seconds, then nodded. "It's...it's different. I can feel the spirits, and you're right, I called one to the table and asked her if she'd help us join, and she did. And now..." He looked at each of them in turn. "Yeah. We...We definitely connected." He exhaled. "Wow. I can *really* feel you three. I think..." He closed his eyes. "I think I'm actually feeling your spirits. Not just that they're present, but actually *feeling* them." He opened his eyes again and laughed. "I'm even feeling spirits outside. Ones that are way too far away. I shouldn't be able to reach them from here, not to mention through your wards. This is intense."

"I think it's because they're my wards," Curtis said. "And you just got the same pass I worked into them for these two."

"I've never felt like this," Eli said. He was holding on to his chair like he might fly away at any moment.

"I just feel awesome," Anders said, shrugging. "Like I've slept for a week and had a whole damn pot of the best fucking coffee ever."

"You're all being shored up by spirits," Eli said, peering at them as if he could see something standing right beside them. Indeed, Luc supposed that was exactly what he was doing. "The first, basic thing we learn to do is ask the spirits for rest, health, and important dreams."

"Okay," Curtis said. "Let's find out just how connected we are." He rose and cleared off the table. He brought back a map of the city and unfolded it. He spread it out over the table and then put a small vial on the tabletop.

"That's Renard's blood?" Luc asked. He could already smell it, even with the cap sealed.

"Yes," Curtis said. "That blood was a part of Renard, and Renard used it to do magic on Eli, binding him in the Geas. The closer the sun gets to setting, the more Renard's spirit will gather until he wakes up."

"And Eli's gonna sniff it out," Anders said. He was still grinning.

"Fucking right I am," Eli said. They all looked at him. He blushed. They were all feeling a rush, and when Luc realized he was smiling, he knew he was just as affected as they were.

"Okay," Curtis said. He opened the small vial, put it in front of Eli, and then sat down again. "I'm trying a scrying with a divination, some geomancy, and a dash of augury." He smiled at Luc's amused stare. "And if that doesn't work, I've got a plan B and a plan C before I break out the big guns."

"What are the big guns?" Anders asked.

"I have no idea. I'm lying. This is my only plan. But blood and divination have long gone together, and given that it's vampire blood and was used to bind Eli, I'm giving this plan a big thumbs-up."

"Fantastic," Anders said, and he laughed again. "Okay, this spirit stuff is fucking sweet."

"Is this what you're like when you're drunk?" Curtis asked, but he was smiling.

"Better than drunk. This feels fucking awesome," Anders said.

"Gentlemen," Luc said, though he felt the same intoxication they did. "The spell?"

Curtis blushed. "Sorry."

"I just concentrate on the blood, right? And my sense of vampire spirits?" Eli said.

"Yeah," Curtis said. "If this works right, you'll get a bird's-eye view of the city, sort of. You'll be able to feel the spirits tied to vampires. You should be able to follow Renard's specific spirit through his blood because the magical connection to him will be the strongest. I'll be feeding you a way to see the magic, and you can already see the spirits. You'll get an idea of where that spirit is. And as it moves back to him, you should be able to see where he is. Which would be where we want to go. I'm also tying in some geomancy to mark the map for us."

Eli raised his eyebrows. "Right." He held out his hands. "As long as that makes sense to you."

Curtis nodded. "It does. Hands, everyone."

They formed the circle again. Almost immediately, Luc felt their connection form, a slow pulse that moved from one man to the next in their circle.

"If nothing happens, we'll wait ten minutes and try again," Curtis said. "I don't know how close we'll have to be to actual sundown to get a read on where Renard is, but it shouldn't matter. Even if we have to wait until sundown, Renard and his coterie will be sharing blood. They'll spend a good part of the early night together."

Luc nodded. He'd prefer to find Renard before the sun went down. If they could get to him before he woke, this could all be over at the speed of a blade or the press of a sharp wooden stake.

Curtis closed his eyes, took a breath, and began to speak.

The third attempt was the charm. Luc felt the magic move through the four of them each time Curtis chanted, but on the third time, half an hour from when they'd first tried, something changed. Sunset would be in about twenty minutes, and maybe that was the difference. But whatever it was, the magic flowing from Curtis, through Luc and Anders, and into Eli surged with a palpable difference.

Luc turned to watch Eli. He inhaled sharply, surprised, then opened his eyes.

"Oh..." he said. He looked around, but his eyes weren't focused on what was directly in front of him. Luc glanced at Curtis, but Curtis had his eyes closed and was speaking with an even, steady cadence. Whatever he was doing—scrying, augury, divination—it was taking effort.

"Luc," Anders said, looking down at the table.

Renard's blood was rising out of the small glass bottle, drop by drop. It gathered in the air in front of Eli like a small red cloud. Eli looked right through it without seeming to see. The blood separated into finer and finer drops, a red mist that hovered over the table in front of the Métis. Eli bit his bottom lip.

"No," he said, almost to himself. A single pinprick of blood moved from in front of him and landed on the map with a barely audible impact. "No," he said again. "No." Every word sent another fine trace of the mist on a curve down to the map.

Luc watched, fascinated, as the blood hit the map one speck after another, slowly forming small groups of deep red bloodstains across the paper city streets.

"Oh, hey," Eli said, laughing. "Hi, Luc."

At his name, Luc turned, but then saw a single point of blood strike the map precisely where they were now, at Curtis's house. It dawned on him then what he was seeing, and he looked at Anders.

Anders nodded. "All of them," Anders said, voice low.

All the vampires in Ottawa are being marked on this map. That was far beyond what they'd hoped to attain, and a deeply useful piece of knowledge to have. Luc looked at Curtis, who continued his chant, eyes closed. Was there no limit to what Curtis could do?

The drops were hitting the paper like rain now. Luc watched as it fell into four major groups, which made sense. The Lady Markham's coterie, Denis's coterie, Étienne's coterie, and—of course—Renard's. But which was which? One group was close enough to Sandy Hill that he assumed it belonged to Catharine. He watched the map forming and shook his head in awe.

He was less than surprised to see how few single drops of blood were scattered through the city. Lone vampires, eking out their survival without a coterie. Less than a dozen so far. More than enough to form a whole new coterie, if they could only find each other.

Or trust each other.

He looked just in time to see a drop of blood land at Victoria Island, where Lavoie was forced to stay.

"Got you," Eli said, his voice a mix of satisfaction and anger. Luc saw the thin cloud of blood quiver in front of Eli's unseeing gaze. Eli twitched, and all but one of the single drops of blood rained down onto the map with an audible wet patter. The last, single drop of blood, hovered in front of Eli's face.

"There," Eli said, and the drop struck the map.

Luc looked down.

Renard.

Now they knew where he was.

Chapter Fourteen

The moment Luc felt the sun dip below the horizon, he joined the others. They were idling in Anders's SUV. To Luc's surprise, Eli was behind the wheel. He climbed in behind him.

"I didn't think you were coming with us," Luc said, trying to hide his disapproval.

"I can drive you there," Eli said. He pulled out onto the road and made a left.

"He promised to stay in the car," Curtis said.

"I'm not stupid," Eli said with annoyance in his voice. "Even with whatever the hell we just did, I'm no match for an angry vampire, let alone a whole bunch of them. Don't worry, I'll stay put. But I'll be nearby."

"Next left," Anders said, and Eli made the turn.

"The three of us are stronger when we're closer to each other," Curtis said. "I figured it would be the same with what Eli's bringing to the triad. Quad. Whatever."

Luc couldn't fault the logic. "Fair enough. But if someone comes after you, Eli, floor it. Get out of there. And don't leave the car."

"Yes, Dad."

Luc raised his eyebrows, but when he met Eli's gaze in the rearview, the young man gave him a small smile. Luc settled back in the car. Beside him, Curtis was muttering to himself, practicing what he intended to do, Luc assumed. He reached out and touched Curtis's forearm, and the wizard relaxed.

"This will work," Luc said, forcing a confidence he didn't feel into his tone.

"I'm feeling a little linchpinny," Curtis said.

"I'll buy you the time you need."

Curtis smiled and went back to his mutterings.

"*This* is where the highest muckity-muck bloodsucker lives?" Anders's voice was disbelieving. "It's kind of a dump."

Luc wouldn't go that far, but their drive west had taken them almost to Kanata before they skirted north past suburbs and big-box stores. They'd left behind the clustered city blocks of tightly packed houses and had now pulled up to a long gravel driveway leading to what looked more like a vacation cottage than a home. It was not, however, the kind of building a *Duc* deserved. Surely those above him in the *lignage* had offered him something better than this? Renard might not follow tradition to the letter in his dress or manner, but this was by far too humble a place for him to live.

"I wouldn't say *dump*," Curtis said. "But it's not what I was expecting."

"This isn't his home," Luc said, quite sure of it. "I would guess that Renard doesn't bring his coterie back to his own home during the full moon, but goes elsewhere. Perhaps this belongs to one of his coterie. Either way, if he doesn't invite his blood-brothers and blood-sisters to his own space, it is to our benefit." It spoke even more of a leader who didn't trust his own lieutenants, and that both pleased and worried Luc. Everything they learned about Renard seemed to add to the same conclusion: He was powerful, he didn't trust anyone, and he took risks.

It was not a good combination.

"If you say so," Anders groused.

"It means he's not on his own turf, with his own considerable abilities bent toward protection," Luc said. "Let's go."

Curtis and Anders got out of the car. Luc leaned forward and put his hand on Eli's shoulder. Eli still had both hands on the steering wheel. "Stay in the car. And at the first sign of trouble, drive."

"I know," Eli said. Luc wasn't sure he believed him, but he couldn't do anything about it now.

Luc climbed out and joined the other two. They walked as quietly as they could toward the small building. The only approach was the long curved driveway, and Luc could feel the tension of the others through their bond. He also felt Eli, falling behind them, like an anchor of calmer emotions. At the top of the driveway, the large yard lay open all the way to the cottage.

"Wait," Curtis whispered.

Luc paused, sharing a glance with Anders. The demon's frown told him Anders didn't know why Curtis was stopping them either, though they could both no doubt feel the sudden alertness running through Curtis.

"*Lapin?*" Luc asked. Like Curtis, he kept his voice as low as he could. He hoped Renard and his coterie wouldn't hear them at this distance. They hadn't had an hour yet of time to bond, so he hoped they'd begun but hadn't finished.

"I can feel something…" Curtis peered ahead into the yard. "Or at least I think I can." Luc followed Curtis's gaze but saw nothing. Renard's cottage—if this indeed was his cottage—was dark. It appeared unguarded, though he doubted that. He felt exposed, standing there. Luc knew wherever Renard and his coterie were, they were already awake.

Curtis crouched, lowering himself to one knee as he looked across the grass surrounding the cabin. He tapped one finger against his leg.

"Curtis?" Anders asked. His voice was barely audible.

"There's something here," Curtis whispered. He raised a hand and flicked his wrist. A sudden breeze kicked up, and the grass bent over in a wave that moved across the yard—

—and caught fire in three places.

Luc stepped back. The three spots of fire had erupted from nothing and were a bright yellow-white in the darkening evening. They twisted and writhed like snakes, and to Luc's keen hearing, they made an almost painful mewling.

Balefire.

The three blazes were already dying down, their flames hissing and snapping but finding no fuel. The grass lay untouched. What was it Curtis had said? They only burned flesh and bone? One by one, with soft cries, the three spots dimmed, flickered, and died. The night was dark again.

"As far as minefields go, those would be pretty effective," Curtis said.

"He sure likes his fire," Anders said.

"It was his chosen element in life," Luc said. "And with the sorcerer bound to him, he wields more than enough power to play with fire as much as he'd like."

"Not for long," Curtis said.

"So. Does that mean they know we're here?" Anders asked.

They all shared a glance, waiting. Nothing happened.

"Are there more mines?" Anders asked.

Curtis frowned. "Not nearby, but I don't think I'm getting a clear sense of the whole yard." He squinted into the darkness. It was much darker now than when they'd left their car, parked at the side of the road. "I'm not sure if that's everything he's done right up to the front door, either. If it were me, I'd have a lot more defensive spells and wards in place."

"So we're not gonna knock on the front door, then," Anders said.

"Bad idea anyway. Luc can't enter without an invitation. If we go in, we'll be at a severe disadvantage," Curtis said. "I can't imagine this place not belonging to Renard or one of his coterie. They wouldn't meet somewhere where residency wasn't on their side."

Luc had to agree. This was why their plan hadn't involved any strategies of invasion. It was also the weakest link. What Curtis needed was time—something the speed of a vampire could easily negate—and the element of surprise. That, at least, Luc hoped they had.

"So, when do we do this?" Anders asked.

"You're ready?" Luc asked Curtis.

Curtis bit his bottom lip. "One more thing." He took a couple of steps back from them and pulled a flask out of his backpack. He unscrewed the cap, then held his hand over the opened canister. Raising the hand, he spoke soft words of magic and gestured around himself, making a circle.

Water rose from the open flask and fanned out around him, hovering in the air at about the height of his waist, forming a circle that surrounded Curtis. He turned his hand once more, and the water flowed, an endless stream of water moving around him. Running water, bolstered by magic, Luc assumed. It wasn't a perfect protection, but it would slow a vampire down.

"Okay," Curtis said. "I'm set. But remember, what I need most is time. I'm going to do this as fast as I can, but if Renard catches on to what I'm doing, he's going to be pissed."

"And if Tyson isn't here?" Luc asked.

"Then what I'm trying to do gets much, much harder." Curtis smiled grimly. "But I think we're okay. The minefield says Tyson's here. That kid's got some amazing ability with fire for Renard to use him like that, but the Geas is a bit like us—the closer we are to each other, the stronger we are. My fire magic is best when Anders is near me. There's no way Renard wouldn't keep Tyson close by."

"I have an idea," Anders said.

Luc turned to look at him.

"We get the fuck on with it?" Anders raised both hands, scowling.

Curtis nodded at Luc.

Luc positioned himself, mindful of the ring of water surging around Curtis. Anders stepped up beside him, leaving Curtis behind and between them in the safest position they could place him. Luc put his hands down to his sides and turned his head to look at Curtis.

"Go ahead."

Curtis raised one hand toward the cottage and spoke more magic. His words were even and strong, and Luc felt a brief breeze pull in around them, then rush away. A moment later, an ear-splitting crack of thunder erupted across the yard and echoed through the night air.

"Knock, knock," Curtis said.

"I want you. Right here, right now," Anders said.

"Focus," Luc chided, eyes on the door.

They didn't have to wait long.

And it was Tyson who opened the door.

❖

The Geas-bound sorcerer regarded them for a few long seconds of silence.

"Why are you here?" he asked. His voice was strained, and he reached to the front of his shirt, as though the inked lines of the Geas were holding back his very breath. As far as Luc knew, they very well could be.

Or perhaps Curtis was already trying to work on them.

"I'd like to speak with Renard," Luc said. He didn't spare a glance behind him at Curtis, but he could feel the wizard's interest and attention on the young man standing at the front door of the cabin. "I know this is unusual, and I ask your forgiveness for the intrusion. If you would fetch him and return with him, we would appreciate it."

"It's a full moon," Tyson said. His voice was a little stronger now, and he frowned at Luc. "They're all..." He paused, biting off whatever he'd intended to say. "I'll try."

He turned and went back inside, closing the door behind him. Luc risked a look at Curtis. The ring of water still surrounded him and was moving in a circle, but now Curtis also held his athame in one hand, lowered and at his side. He shifted his stance, holding the blade beside his thigh, as unobtrusive as he could make it.

Luc raised an eyebrow in silent question. Curtis gave a slight shake of his head in return. Luc was unsurprised. Tyson was still bound. If Curtis could have freed him in a few seconds, it would likely have been apparent.

He turned back to face the door just in time to see it open again. Tyson had returned, and Renard was with him, as were perhaps a dozen other vampires. Renard stepped out onto the small front porch, and Tyson slipped out from beside him. Luc couldn't help but notice Tyson had gone as far as he could from Renard.

Renard was handsomely dressed in a pair of black dress pants and a white collared shirt that was stained with blood on the collar and at the wrists. The others in his coterie were similarly attired and had similar stains.

That answered why they hadn't come racing to investigate when the balefire "mines" had been tripped. They hadn't even taken a moment to lick all the wounds to heal the flesh, Luc thought. They had probably rushed through sharing blood with each other. He saw wounds on the necks of two of the other vampires who stood farther back—one of which was the familiar blond from nearly a year ago, the one he and Curtis and Anders had bumped into in the bar on that first night of their freedom.

It occurred to Luc he still didn't know the blond's name. For some reason, that made him smile. He looked and saw Gabrielle, standing close to Renard, as well as the other one from the bar—Stephane.

"Luc," Renard said. "This is not a night for discussions. This is a night for renewing bonds. Perhaps you forgot, what with your… unusual group, but maybe you should go home and do whatever it is you do to keep your silly little group together?"

"We already have," Luc said, enjoying the slightest widening of Renard's eyes. He and his coterie may have hurriedly shared each other's blood, but it was only the barest version of the bond needed to maintain a coterie. It took time. Renard knew that, and he was no doubt confused that Luc had already somehow managed to renew their bond and get there so soon after the sunset.

Luc spread his hands. "I understand it is a bit of an intrusion for us to come by on this night. But we needed to speak with you." He was speaking formally and slowly.

Buying time.

"And you felt it had to be tonight?" Renard said. His voice left no doubt of his skepticism. His smile was barely more than a smirk. "And you had to come here—and who told you where I was this evening, exactly?"

The question was spoken casually, but Luc knew it was anything but.

"We asked one of your bloodsuckers," Anders said from beside him. Luc fought hard not to grin. Trust the demon to take an opportunity to make Renard doubt his own people. There were advantages, Luc had to admit, to having someone around who always thought the worst of people.

Renard's features hardened. It struck Luc again that while Renard was handsome in a classic sense, his baseness somehow shone through, rendering him a sort of ugly that no amount of grooming or style could erase. This was a man who'd decided his existence and power were more important than any other number of lives and freedoms. He was vile. "What do you want?" Renard asked. The thin pretense of amiability was gone.

"We have a request," Luc said. The longer he could draw this out, the better. He could feel Curtis's concentration like an ongoing hum along the odd bond of the triad. Indeed, having included Eli, the feeling was stronger than usual.

It would also be helpful if Luc could get Renard off the front porch, where the residency would start to weaken. Every step away from the cabin door would be of benefit.

"So spit it out," Renard snapped. He showed no signs of moving.

"We come to ask an end to your hostilities," Luc said.

Renard laughed. "*My* hostilities? Luc, I have no idea what you're talking about. From where I stand, you three are the ones being hostile to me. This is the third night of the full moon, when we gather and we bond—and here you are on my doorstep with your demon and your wizard, who is holding an athame and standing in a protective circle of water." The last he added in a near sneer. Renard left little doubt how worried he was about the barrier of running water.

"My wizard is tired of escaping severe burns," Luc said.

"Burns?" Renard's eyebrows rose, the picture of innocence. "I admit I have some leftover talent for magic, but severe burns would be beyond the ability of a once-wizard who is now a vampire."

"Says the guy with little fireballs planted all over his yard," Anders said.

"I would rather your demon not speak to me." Renard scowled.

Luc shrugged. "I hear that request a lot."

"Enough," Renard said. "I've told you I have not attacked you. Unless you have some sort of definite proof, it's time for you to leave."

Luc opened his mouth to speak again, but Renard held up his hand, cutting him off. "Leave," Renard repeated.

That was it. Staying would be offense enough, Luc knew. Renard would be well within his right to attack them now.

"Curtis?" Luc asked.

"Yep," Curtis said.

Renard frowned. Luc saw the *Duc* look past him again, to where Curtis stood, and Luc heard Curtis speaking the even, controlled words the young man used when working magic. He didn't dare turn his head, instead watching Renard.

It didn't take Renard long. The smile on his face told Luc Renard had gotten exactly what he'd wanted. "Alex, kill the wizard," Renard said. "Gabrielle, Stephane, if Luc or the demon so much as twitch, kill them all."

Three of Renard's vampires stepped down off the balcony of the small cabin, moving past Renard. The blond one—Alex, Renard had called him—glared past Luc with utter contempt and then seemed to blur into motion.

Luc fueled his own speed when the blond was already halfway

across the yard. The world around them slowed to a crawl. The moment Luc stepped forward to meet the blond, Gabrielle and Stephane launched from the balcony. They ran at him and Anders, and Luc braced himself as the blond grew closer. Luc lashed out at him, but Alex ducked and twisted. Luc's blow didn't connect, but it moved him closer to Anders. Anders tripped the blond vampire with a kick, and Alex went down onto the grass between them.

A second later, Gabrielle and Stephane were upon them. Luc saw the white-gold flame of Anders's hellfire ignite on his fingertips and swipe through the air in arching lashes while Stephane moved just fast enough to escape contact. Gabrielle was more aggressive, forcing Luc back a step with an assault that blurred even to Luc's blood fueled senses.

The fight was on.

Curtis maintained the chant—*so damn close!*—and held the athame at his side. He desperately wanted to look at Tyson on the front porch but didn't want to give away his game. He didn't think Renard was likely to translate what he was doing, assuming Renard knew enough Latin or Icelandic to make out what Curtis was even saying.

He flinched as three vampires vanished in a blur, but he managed to maintain his concentration. He ignored Renard, ignored the sound of bodies impacting each other just a few steps in front of him, and drew power up into his core, through his skin, down his arm, and into the blade of the athame. The magic built and flowed, eager and willing. The blade grew cool in his hand, and small sparks of static flicked from the tip. The athame was an extension of his will.

The first vampire, the one Renard had so casually instructed to kill him, had crashed to the ground between Luc and Anders, a blur that resolved itself into a tumble of limbs.

As the last words left his lips, Curtis saw the blond vampire rise to his feet, dusting off the front of his pants and smiling at him from the other side of the circle of water that hovered between them.

"You do know I'm strong enough to cross water and tear you in half, right?" the blond said, fangs extended.

"I wouldn't suggest it," Curtis said. The magic flowed down his arm, through his palm, and into the blade. The athame sparked and crackled. He needed a clear shot, but he didn't dare take his eyes off the vampire in front of him.

The vampire laughed at him and took a slow, mocking step forward. The water struck the vampire across his chest, spreading across the white cotton shirt and splashing onto his arms. "See?" the vampire laughed, "I—"

The water hissed and smoked, and the shirt turned red where it was wet. The vampire shrieked and stumbled back.

Curtis gestured with his free hand, and the entire circle of water rushed at the blond. It surrounded him like a second skin and was almost instantly red with blood.

"Holy water," Curtis said. Then he looked up at the cabin, found where Tyson stood in the far corner of the balcony, and raised the athame. "Tyson!" he yelled.

Renard pushed himself over the porch railing and landed in the front yard. The sorcerer turned, looking at him, and then at Curtis.

Renard's eyes widened.

Curtis had no time to be gentle. The holy water would be fouled by the vampire's blood, and though Curtis was fairly sure the blond wouldn't recover, there were more where he came from—not the least of whom was Renard himself.

Curtis pointed the blade across the yard at Tyson, sent a brief prayer to all the goddesses he could think of, and flicked the blade up in the air, releasing the magic.

"No!" Renard's voice was high.

Luc managed to throw Gabrielle to the ground, hard. She scrambled back from him, crawling, and Luc risked a glance to the front of the cottage.

With the blood fueling his graces, it all stretched out slowly. First, a burst of black liquid erupted from Tyson's chest, through his shirt. The young man fell, crying out in pain, the sound distorted and lengthened. The ink spread up in the air in a single arc, then landed in drops all across the yard. Blood began to weep through the front of Tyson's shirt.

The Geas, Luc assumed, had been broken. Whatever benefit Renard had garnered from the young sorcerer would be gone in a moment. Luc looked at the young man, who raised his gaze at his former master.

Tyson's eyes were a solid black with no trace of color or white. They were not the eyes of a sorcerer.

They were the eyes of a demon.

Blue-white fire flared down Tyson's arms, pooling in his hands. He raised his arms, turned, and expelled two streams of hellfire at the small cottage. The porch ignited under the blast, and the flames spread with an alarming speed, even to Luc's enhanced senses.

Renard and the remainder of his coterie fled the porch, Renard spitting words Luc couldn't catch. Tyson tipped over backward and slammed into the ground. The flames around his arms snuffed out, but the damage was done. The cottage blazed.

There would be no residency to fall back on.

Hesitating, Luc tried to catch up on what he was seeing. Tyson was no sorcerer, but a demon. Renard had bound a demon to him, to use the demon's abilities with fire—Curtis had said that much was possible, but why had Tyson let them believe he was a sorcerer?

Renard took a step toward the prone demon. Tyson didn't struggle. Instead, he turned his head to face Luc. Tyson's eyes once again turned an inky black.

A rage unlike any he'd ever felt slammed into Luc's skull. Luc curled his hands into fists, and the world itself seemed to slow even more as his vampire graces burned with renewed purpose.

Beside him, Anders bellowed. Anders had grown claws from his fingertips, and each burned with a brilliant golden white fire as he slashed them through the air at the vampire facing him. His eyes were twin suns, they burned so brightly. The demon's features distorted, becoming more base and frightening than Luc had ever seen before.

Gabrielle had recovered, climbing back onto her feet. The rest of Renard's coterie were rushing them now, fleeing the burning building as much as attacking, and Renard himself was approaching behind them, yelling.

Luc was furious. *Renard. His coterie. They will all die.*

Behind him, Luc heard Curtis's voice, pitched loud and full of rage. The haze of hate and anger was almost too much to bear, but even this far gone, Luc felt some small corner of his thoughts telling him to protect Curtis. Curtis was powerful and capable of defending himself, but he could be far too slow against the speed of vampires.

Luc swung as he leapt and crushed Gabrielle's rib cage with one closed fist, snarling incoherently, fangs fully extended. Depths of strength he'd never attempted to touch rose willingly in this unrelenting rage. Luc needed these vampires to die, needed them to be out of his way, and he needed to get to Renard and destroy him. Gabrielle landed on her side, blood spraying from her mouth. She curled into a fetal position.

Luc stood near Curtis, spreading his arms and bracing himself against the approach of most of Renard's coterie.

Beside him, Curtis was chanting, but two of Renard's vampires had circled far around where Luc and Anders stood and were almost on the wizard. Curtis raised his hand and opened his mouth, but the first vampire collided with Curtis and sent the wizard stumbling back.

Luc twisted, tore the vampire from Curtis, and swung him bodily into the second, who had tried to flank them. The sound of bones breaking beneath flesh was beyond satisfying.

Luc turned back, and then Renard was upon him. The warlock was snarling now, and Luc could feel the man's will battering his mind, demanding he retreat—but Renard's will was weaker now. Even though it was still strong, Luc found the will to resist the urge to step away, barely hesitating. Luc moved in front of Curtis and tried to keep between him and Renard. His chest ached, and he dimly realized he was burning through the blood he'd taken over the last days at an alarming rate.

Most of him didn't care. Most of him wanted to tear Renard limb from limb, but that small part of him managed to think through the fury. A voice told him he needed to fight the anger and keep himself focused. He didn't dare overextend himself, not yet. Not when a half dozen of Renard's coterie still circled them with only him and Anders to hold them at bay. Curtis still needed protection.

He let his grace ebb, and the world returned closer to normal speed.

Renard leapt for him, bright twists of fire trailing from his fingertips, and Luc had no choice but to dodge back and left. Renard swiped again, and Luc stepped to the side with barely a breath between them. Renard was herding him, breaking him away from Curtis and Anders, and Luc could do nothing about it. He had little doubt the damage Renard's touch could inflict, even without the power he'd once drawn from the Geas.

"Necto!" Curtis said, in a voice that Luc had never heard him use before. It burst from him with a righteous anger. From the corner of his eye, Luc saw one of the vampires fighting Anders drop to the ground, pulled down so violently that once again Luc heard the sharp wet noise of breaking bones. Anders grabbed the second and spun with him, throwing the vampire into one of the others circling them.

Luc barely recognized the demon. Anders bore twin curved horns smeared with blood from where they had erupted from his temples and split his skin. The raging Anders leapt forward, both arms alight with his golden white fire, and tackled the two vampires closest to Curtis, knocking them aside. The scent of charred flesh joined the thick smoke from the burning cottage.

A flare of light made Luc turn just in time. Renard's hands shot past Luc's face, the fire on his fingertips dazzling Luc's eyes, and Luc snarled, leaping back.

They sparred, exchanging blurs of fists and teeth and kicks that Luc could only spot on an instinctive level. Renard's warlock blood gave him an advantage over Luc. Luc didn't want Renard to make even a brief contact with him, not with that flickering radiance sending flames from his fingertips. He struggled to remember Lavoie's other warnings, but the rage he felt was unrelenting.

He needed to think, but he barely had time to match Renard blow for blow, and every instinct he had was telling him to rend, and tear, and destroy.

To his left, Anders raked his flaming claws along the belly of one of the remaining foes, and the vampire fell, spilling innards onto the lawn. The other launched a high kick and caught Anders across the cheek. He fell back under her assault.

"Tenebrae!" Curtis snapped. Her next strike missed and she yelped in confusion, blinking her eyes. Anders shoved his claws into her chest, and she screamed as she fell, flames pouring down the arms of the demon and setting her alight. *"Necto! Tenebrae!"* Curtis's voice

was nearly hoarse behind him. Luc had lost his mental tally of the foes still remaining. He couldn't concentrate on anything but avoiding Renard's blows.

Anders's fire blazed somewhere to his left. Curtis cried out once, then twice. There were more sounds of bones snapping, the scent of burning flesh, the sting of ozone in the air. The roar of the cottage was louder still, and the light it cast across the yard was almost blinding to Luc's predator sight.

Renard and Luc spun, punching and biting. Luc's shoulder was burned and torn—the pain was incredible. Renard's forehead was bloodied from a well-timed feint, but Luc knew he hadn't done as much damage as Renard was doing to him. Luc connected a lucky strike to Renard's chin, and the vampire tumbled backward, but at the last moment pushed off with his legs. Fueled by his graces, what should have been a fall was instead a backflip. Renard landed on his feet a few paces away. The warlock glared at Luc.

Around him, Renard's coterie was breaking. Gabrielle lay still, the two he had swung together were only now barely regaining their feet, one fighting for balance on a broken leg. The one Anders had gutted was beginning to rot, too wounded to recover, and the vampire he had pierced through the chest was already nothing more than ashes, bones, and dust. Anders stomped brutally on one still held by Curtis's binding. More lay in a small tangle just beyond Curtis, who was standing holding his side. Blood seeped through his fingers. Shadows moved beyond that, but Curtis and Anders were more than holding their own. They were making Renard's coterie pay with their lives.

And the remaining members of his coterie were starting to hesitate.

Luc didn't care. Hatred pulsed between his temples. Renard needed to die. Nothing else mattered. Some small instinct made him look past Renard just for a moment, and he saw Tyson had reclaimed his feet. The young demon stood with his arms wide, the air around him distorted as though it radiated with heat.

Luc didn't know it was possible to feel this level of hate. The soft voice that had been cautioning him was growing lost in his thirst to destroy Renard and everyone and anything in the way. Between the burning cottage and the oncoming roar of his own anger, Luc could bear it no longer.

Luc tensed to leap, willing to die if need be, so long as it gave him the chance to tear Renard's head from his body.

Anders's SUV tore through the front yard and slammed into Tyson. The demon rolled up and over the hood, flying sideways and tumbling out of view. The SUV ground to a halt, digging thick ruts into the grass of the yard.

The red rage in Luc's head vanished. He shook his head, feeling like he'd just woken from some sort of nightmare. He saw Curtis and Anders doing the same... He turned his attention back to Renard and saw the *Duc* recovering, too.

"Tyson is a demon?" Curtis's voice was shaken and weak.

"What have you done, you ignorant *orphelin?*" Renard thundered, and Luc barely turned in time to see him break apart into a thick mist. What small wounds he had delivered, Luc realized, would be no hindrance to the warlock now. Before Luc could yell a warning to the others, the mist had rolled over him. He felt the warlock's gaseous form trying to force its way into his body, tearing and ripping at his flesh. Luc fell to his knees, clawing uselessly at the very air around him as Renard's essence poured into his ears and eyes and nose. The mist forced its way into his mouth and down his throat, the pain driving him to his knees.

"Tempestas."

The gas retreated. Clean air rushed past him, and the heavy pressure of Renard's assault was gone. Luc watched the mist pull away and collect itself into a tight sphere of whirling mist a few feet away from him. He saw Curtis, his eyes red with burst blood vessels and bleeding from his nose and left ear, one hand held out in front of him. Near him, Anders was on his hands and knees, coughing and spitting a thick wad of blood onto the grass.

Tyson stood behind Curtis, a single hand on the wizard's shoulder. Tyson's eyes were an inky black, his skin pale and bruised, his shirt torn and bloody, his other arm hanging loose and at an impossible angle— dislocated at the very least, if not outright broken. The hatred on the demon's face was chilling. The air rippled.

"What part of 'I have a facility with air' was unclear?" Curtis spat each word, raising his other hand. A trail of blood dangled from his bottom lip. Luc looked at the sphere of mist that was Renard, and realized the warlock hadn't retreated. Not willingly. Curtis had forced him back.

One of Renard's remaining coterie took a single hesitant step toward Curtis. Tyson inclined his head, and Curtis glared at the vampire.

"*Necto.*"

The vampire slammed into the ground with a crunch.

"Curtis—" Luc tried to say more, but a bubble of blood popped in his throat. He staggered to his feet and tried to get to Curtis. Curtis curled his fingers into his open palms, and the air filled with static.

Luc felt a pull deep inside, and he lost his balance again, sliding down onto one knee. Curtis was drawing on their bond, tearing power from him. It was an agony.

Anders cried out.

"*Boreas. Zephyrus. Notos. Eurus.*" Each word Curtis spoke made the air itself tremble. Cold and hot gusts of wind were lashing across the field now, fogs forming and breaking, sparks of static electricity dancing like a cloud of dragonflies. Luc watched him, barely able to keep himself upright. Each word pulled at him with a white flare of pain that seemed to be shredding him from the inside out.

Curtis's magic would kill him. "Curtis…" He said, but it was lost in the tumult of the air itself.

The gales of wind buffeted at Renard's misty sphere, lashing at it and tugging at it in turn, twisting and pulling at the tightly balled sphere.

"Go to hell," Curtis said, and he snatched his hands apart. The winds tore at the sphere of mist. Renard's gaseous form was stretched in all directions and pulled wider and wider apart. It strained to hold itself together.

It failed.

The air filled with a fine red mist.

Luc tasted blood.

"Asshole," Curtis said, and then he fell backward. Tyson caught him with his one good arm before he hit the ground. Tyson blinked, looking up at Anders and Luc, his eyes returning to their regular hue. Blood continued to drip from his nose. His ruined shirt fell open, his lean chest covered in weeping welts—the remains of the Geas, Luc assumed. Luc rose to get to Curtis's side, but Anders beat him there, crouching over him and looking at Tyson warily.

The demon regarded them with a bland expression.

"If anything happens to him—" Anders began, but Tyson raised a hand. Anders's voice was raw and filled with an exhaustion Luc well understood. He felt emptied. Ruined. Whatever Curtis had done, it had driven them all to the edge of self-destruction.

At Tyson's behest.

"I stopped influencing him. I'm free now." Tyson looked at them. He no longer sounded young or afraid. "I have to say, I'm impressed. I was pretty sure your wizard could handle breaking the Geas, but I didn't expect the entire coterie to be destroyed." He glanced over at the two remaining upright vampires, who crouched, clutching themselves and staring low to the ground in fear. "More or less."

"He nearly killed us," Luc said. That, more than anything, would be hardest for Curtis to bear. Even if it was Tyson's fault. To the best of Luc's knowledge, Curtis had never harmed someone he cared about with his magic before.

"Tell him it was my fault." Tyson shrugged. "Explain it to him. He's young. He'll rationalize." He straightened, albeit shakily, and he winced as he shifted his mangled arm. "And thank him for me. Renard asked me to make your wizard angry enough to make a mistake, so he'd have a reason to put you all down. After seeing Curtis react to the offering at the *séance*, I knew the thing that would make him angriest was my forced servitude." Tyson looked at the prone wizard. "He is very compassionate."

It wasn't said as a compliment.

"Never show your face to him again," Anders growled. His eyes lit with a golden light. The horns were gone, Luc noticed with a dull vagueness creeping into his thoughts, though the wounds on either temple remained.

Tyson seemed startled and took a step back. "I wanted only to free myself. And that's done." He looked up. The fog and clouds that Curtis's rage-fueled magic had conjured were fading, and the moon had risen enough to cast shadows. Tyson stepped back again, moving into the darkness.

"I am in debt to you all," Tyson said, but Luc discerned no pleasure in his words. He bowed and vanished into a shadow-walk.

"He was no incubus," Luc said.

"He's a fury. They're usually women. It's a different clan of demon," Anders said, gently wrapping his arms under Curtis and lifting him. The wizard groaned. "We feed on lust. Their kind use wrath." He looked at Luc. "We need to get Curtis home. And we need to get out of here in case someone sees the fire and calls for help." The cottage was still blazing.

Luc nodded. He glanced at the defeated vampires. The two who were still upright and mobile kept their eyes averted, unsure if the other prone figures around them would still contribute to a coterie. If not, Luc could dominate them into doing whatever he wanted. He wanted to take satisfaction, but he felt only exhaustion. If none of Renard's other vampires survived, the two remaining vampires would be in grave danger.

They would be alone.

"Go," Luc said. Even wounded, the two vampires moved as quickly as they could, leaving in a blur. Luc wasn't sure where his mercy had come from, but was too tired to care.

He looked at those remaining. The one that had tried to hurt Curtis—the one Luc had crushed—moved only feebly. Gabrielle was still. If they didn't recover before sunrise, they would die in an agony of flame. The others that Curtis and Anders had dealt with seemed no better off, and some were already rotting. They might survive if they made it to shelter.

Luc turned away. His mercy had limits. "Eli?" he called.

The SUV had dug deep furrows into the yard in front of the cottage, but looked like it had survived its impact with Tyson unscathed beyond a dent in the hood. The driver's side was facing away from Luc, but the passenger side window lowered.

"All clear?" Eli's voice was raw.

"Yes," Luc managed.

Eli got out of the SUV and came over to help them. Between the two, Eli and Anders managed to lift Curtis. The wizard was still unconscious and very pale. Anders was covered in bruises and open cuts. Luc himself was burned and bloodied.

Anders chuckled.

"What?" Eli asked.

"You drove right into him." The demon seemed to find it funny. He laughed again, nearly dropping Curtis in the process. "Wham."

"I could feel what he was doing to you three. I was trying to fight back. It wasn't affecting me. I don't think he knew I was there. But you guys were already pissed, and he was making it worse. I had to do something. So I ran him over." Eli's own laugh was more nervous than amused. "Besides, you guys said I had to stay in the car."

CHAPTER FIFTEEN

W hen Mackenzie opened the door, her face said it all.
"I look that bad, huh?" Curtis said.

Mackenzie shook it off. "No! I mean, well, yes. But...Are you okay?"

Curtis waved a hand. "I've got some healing stuff going on. Ask me again in a couple of days. I don't remember the whole speech, but I'd love to come in for a bit, if you're not busy."

"Of course." She offered him the formal invitation, and he managed to reply without mangling the words too badly. The force of the ward, which had been pressing against him since he'd started up the walk, vanished. He sagged in visible relief.

"Do you want a coffee?" Mackenzie asked, taking his jacket. "Or, like, a shot of something?"

Curtis laughed. "No. I had a tea before I left."

"Come on through. My mother's out, so we're on our own."

"Good," Curtis said. Though Mackenzie gave him a quick glance, she didn't say anything more.

They ended up in the same parlor where he'd been before. Curtis sank into one of the chairs and sighed deeply. He rubbed his eyes, wincing at the pain flaring behind them. Mackenzie sat across from him.

"Can I ask what happened?" she said.

Curtis let his hand drop. "I'm sure you'll find out anyway." He exhaled. "Long story short? We went toe-to-toe with the warlock, and we won." He tried to smile, but he was pretty sure it failed, given the worried look on Mackenzie's face.

"Won?" she asked.

"It's a euphemism for 'destroyed.' My head is still ringing from the sorcery."

"Your eyes?" she said.

"That wasn't sorcery." Curtis closed them. He knew they were still gross—burst blood vessels were not a good look for anyone—though they already looked a lot better than the night before. Healing magic wasn't his forté, but things had picked up speed with a little help from Eli. "No, that was from when the warlock turned into mist and tried to smother us through every available orifice."

"Oh my God."

"Yeah," Curtis said, and he surprised himself by chuckling. "That was pretty much the sentiment."

"Are you okay?" she asked.

"I will be. I've got healing spirits on the job, as well as some magic."

"Spirits?"

"Long story." Curtis exhaled. "I just needed to talk with someone…" He let the words trail off. What was he going to say, really? He needed to hang out with someone who still had a soul? According to Eli, Anders and Luc had a soul—they were sharing his. He opened his eyes. Mackenzie was watching him, and everything about her body language said she was genuinely concerned for him.

He wondered if it was true.

"Ever since I found out about magic, I've been figuring it out as I go along," Curtis said. "Mostly I've just wanted to be left alone— which, it turns out, is the most impossible thing in the world."

Mackenzie smiled. "Tell me about it."

He sighed. "I barely know what I'm doing. I didn't want to be with the people who killed my parents. I didn't want to be a part of something that foul." He winced. "I'm sorry, I'm tired. I don't mean you…"

She shook her head. "I have no illusions about how the Families run, Curtis. I'd love things to be different. I hope they can be, but…" She puffed out a breath. "But."

"But," Curtis agreed.

"You sure you don't want anything? Another tea?"

"You know what? I'd love one." Maybe it was a delaying tactic, but he was too tired to care. If he was about to learn something about Mackenzie he'd regret, then he'd like to hold on to this version of their relationship a little longer.

She got up. "I'll be right back."

She left him there, and he looked around the parlor. It was pretty, he thought. Classy without being stuffy. It appeared so normal unless you knew what you were looking for. Casual pieces of sculpture artfully arranged on the corner table were actually bind runes—tall pieces of wood with intricate patterns carved into them. Small crystals hung from the braided ropes that tied back the curtains. More protection, he thought, or maybe alarms or obfuscations. Even the floor, hardwood and polished to a sheen, had what had to be hand-carved designs around the entire border of the room.

Magic was everywhere if you looked closely enough.

Mackenzie came back with two cups of tea. She handed him one, and he brought it to his lips. It was hot and had a lovely spicy scent to it. He took a sip. Jasmine? Cinnamon? He wasn't sure.

"This is incredible. Thank you," he said.

"My mother's creation," she said. "She's a big tea nut. It's an earth thing." She sat down and drank some of her tea. "You were saying you didn't want to be a part of the Families."

Curtis nodded. "Right. So I came up with the triad. Me, and Luc, and Anders. I thought it was a great solution. We had our freedom, and so long as we stayed out of everyone's way, everyone would leave us alone. But again, no offense, I had a run-in with Malcolm Stirling that blew those illusions out of the water."

"They're not all like him," she said, and then she shrugged at his expression. "Okay, they're mostly like him. But it's changing. A little. I hope."

Curtis took another sip. "Point being, I think I'm starting to learn. When I got the letter bomb and when those demons attacked and…" He put his cup down again and rubbed his eyes. "And all the other stuff, I knew I needed help. And there you were."

Mackenzie smiled.

"Right where you wanted to be," Curtis said.

Her smile faded. "What?"

Curtis sighed. "I like you. And I really want to trust you. You helped me so much, you have no idea how screwed I would have been if you hadn't been around in the library, and we hadn't figured out how to break a Geas. I'm really, really grateful for your help."

"Okay," she said. She sounded wary.

"But I'm going to ask you two questions, and I hope—I really hope—you'll be honest with me."

Mackenzie put down her cup. "I don't have a dove feather handy, but if you want a truth spell, I'm sure we could come up with something." Her voice was much colder than before, and Curtis couldn't help but feel scolded.

"I don't need a truth spell," Curtis said. "I want to believe you."

She exhaled. "Okay."

Curtis held his cup in both hands, feeling the warmth spread through his fingers. "How long had you been following me on campus? Because the more I think about how we met, the more I'm surprised I didn't notice you coming up to the top floor of the library with me, and the less I can believe that you just happened to be there when some demons decided to jump me."

Mackenzie bit her lip. "It's not what you think. I had nothing to do with those demons, Curtis. I promise."

"I know," Curtis said. "If I thought you'd been tied up with that warlock, I wouldn't have come."

Mackenzie seemed to relax, just a fraction. "Okay."

He waited for her.

"About three weeks?" she said, looking up at the ceiling. "Maybe a month? I knew who you were. I'd heard about you from my mother," Mackenzie said. "And I wanted to meet you, but I didn't think you'd be open to a handshake and a 'by the way, I'm the daughter of one of the people in charge who had your parents killed.'"

"Fair enough." Curtis had to give her that.

"It really isn't what you think," Mackenzie leaned forward. "You've pulled off some *incredible* magic, Curtis, and you've had *no one helping you.*"

"Okay," Curtis said. It was his turn to be wary.

"We learn magic," Mackenzie said, and as she warmed to her discussion, she spoke faster. "But we learn the magic that our parents learned from our grandparents and so on and so on." She waved a hand in the air. "But you've done things we didn't even know it was possible to do."

"We?"

"The Craft Night group. We…experiment. We try to push the boundaries. But it never occurred to us to try to bind a wizard and a demon and a vampire together into a coven, let alone that it could work." She shrugged. "It might sound dumb, but that's why I wanted to meet you. Only until those demons showed up, I wasn't sure how to break the ice. You were kind of standoffish in the library, even if we did finally have a topic in common thanks to the runes. It was a way to start talking to you, and I took it. You have a reputation for doing things differently, and it's true—the glasses you mentioned, as a way to see if someone was a wizard or a vampire or whatever? None of us would've ever thought to try that sort of thing."

Curtis blinked. "Why not?" They were getting off-topic a bit, but he wanted to know.

Mackenzie smiled. "Because it's considered an attack to use divinations on someone else."

Curtis blanched. "But it doesn't use divination. I swear it's not an attack. The enchantment is on the glasses, and I use it to see the flow of energy *around* someone…I know you don't just throw magic at someone standing in front of you, I swear."

Mackenzie nodded. "Exactly." She smiled. "You walk right up to the edge of breaking traditions, and then you sidestep the rules without breaking them. That's what worries them."

Well, crap. Curtis held his cup, enjoying the heat and the scent of the tea. She seemed honest. In a way, it made their reasons for getting to know each other identical: because they wanted access to magical know-now. He wanted to know someone who'd been taught how to do things properly from a young age. She wanted someone who made it all up on the fly. It sounded just simple enough to be the truth. And he wanted to believe her, which was the problem.

"Number two," she said, interrupting his thoughts.

"Sorry?" he said.

"You said two questions. What's the second?"

"Oh," he said, and he took a deep breath. Well, this would definitely let him know if he could trust her. He was in her house, under her wards, and he knew damned well he wouldn't be able to defend himself if she decided what he knew was something he shouldn't.

She helped you with the Geas, he thought. *If she'd wanted you hurt, she never would have done that.* But it was more than that, Curtis knew. Killing Renard had changed things. It didn't matter that Tyson had manipulated him. It didn't matter that Renard wanted them all dead. What mattered was Curtis was very tired of being afraid and in the dark. He needed help. He needed people who knew more about magic than he did.

He needed friends.

"Okay," Curtis said, and he braced himself. "Second question."

Mackenzie raised her eyebrows.

Curtis pulled out the map from his pocket and unfolded it. He leaned forward, showing it to her, and he put his finger near a single drop of dried blood. "Why do you have a vampire in your basement?"

❖

Ethan looked completely better, of course. Demons never took long to heal, and Anders imagined David made sure there were enough willing visitors for Ethan to stay in top shape. All traces of the cuts and bruises were gone, Ethan's skin once again smooth and handsome—in a pretty, young way.

His scowl, on the other hand...

"What are you doing here?"

Anders leaned against the side of the house. "Hi, Ethan. Good to see you, too."

"Fuck off."

"Aw." Anders put a hand over his heart. "You wound me."

Ethan snorted. When Anders didn't go anywhere, Ethan slumped his shoulders and sighed. "You want to speak with David?"

"Out back," Anders said and nodded. "Both of you. That way you don't have to invite me in."

"You're never invited," Ethan said, and Anders decided not to point out how recently he'd been inside their home. *Curtis would be proud of my restraint.* He smiled as Ethan closed the door and made his way down the steps and toward the gate that led into the fenced back yard.

He didn't have to wait long. David came through the sliding glass door a few moments later, Ethan right behind him.

"What do you want?" David said.

As far as openings went, it wasn't the most friendly, but he supposed he couldn't blame them.

"You know how Renard was trying to get you two to take me in? Don't worry about that anymore. It's been dealt with."

The stunned look on both of their faces was going to give Anders satisfaction for years to come. "Pardon?" David recovered first, but it didn't ring true.

Anders just let one eyebrow rise.

"Fine," David said. "But it wasn't all self-serving. That vampire was right. You and your friends aren't going to be safe. The flicks, the bloodsuckers—nobody is happy with you three. You're too different. Too out of control. Too—"

"Powerful," Anders said, cutting him off.

David exhaled. They regarded each other for a few long seconds.

"So now what?" David asked. "You're just here to brag, or...?"

"No. I'm here to help."

"Right," Ethan snorted. "Like you give a shit about either one of us."

Anders looked at the kid and shrugged. David hadn't told him, he supposed. Fair enough. Ethan probably wouldn't have been willing if he'd known where some of his meals had come from. "You don't have to believe me. But you do have to listen to me."

"Like hell," David said, and he turned to go. Ethan followed suit.

"I found you a third."

They froze.

"What?" David's voice was barely a whisper.

Anders stepped back and turned to face the tall birch that grew in David's backyard. He could feel the shadow there, and with a great deal more finesse than he'd ever managed before—*probably Eli's influence*, he thought—Anders *pulled*.

David and Ethan watched, tense. No doubt they could feel him doing something with the shadow, something they'd never seen done before. If he was honest with himself, Anders wasn't sure he could do what it was he was trying to do, but why would he start being honest with himself now? Strength drained from the flood of power he aimed into the darkness, and he was just beginning to think he might have overestimated himself when he felt a connection take hold. It struggled for a moment in his grasp, but now that he had the satisfaction of having found what he wanted, Anders wasn't about to let go. He redoubled his efforts, and after what might have been a full minute, the resistance abruptly stopped. The shadows parted, and a demon stepped out.

Tyson's gaze was, if anything, even less friendly than Ethan's had been. He didn't look anywhere near as tidy, either, though his arm wasn't hanging limply by his side anymore. Anders figured Tyson was still on the run and still trying to figure out his next move.

Perfect.

"One of these days, someone is going to be happy to see me," Anders said.

No one laughed.

"Okay, not today, then." He turned back to David. "Here's your third."

David blanched.

"Him?" Ethan sputtered. "But he's the one who threatened us! He's probably the one who had me beaten!"

"Those were Renard's orders, actually. This guy," Anders jerked his thumb over his shoulder at Tyson, "was under Renard's control. Until recently. Now, don't get me wrong, he's a conniving little shit who also tried to get me to vacate my spot on the triad so he could have it for himself."

David looked startled, and Ethan stared openly. Tyson's scowl only grew.

"What? You think I'm too dumb to figure that out? You wanted me out of the picture, but you also wanted Curtis to figure out how to get you free. Those two things don't line up very well. Curtis needs a third if he wants to stay a free agent, right?"

Tyson swallowed, then nodded.

Anders enjoyed watching him squirm. "Well, sorry, kiddo, but the position is taken. However, these two fine gentlemen would be much obliged—"

"Hold on," David raised his hand. "Why would we take *him* in? He nearly had Ethan killed just to get you to join us. He worked for that fucking Duke. What kind of demon works for a vampire?"

"You work for them all the fucking time, and the wizards, and anyone else who decides you're useful." At David's glare, Anders laughed and started ticking off points on his fingers. "Let me lay it out for you. One, you'd finally have some fucking autonomy. Two, this guy might look like a fucking boy band lead singer, but he's also a fury. A wrath demon, David. You know how many of those there are around these parts? Let alone how many male ones? Not many."

"Yeah, but—"

"Wasn't done." Anders held up his hand. "Three, and this is the most important one, so pay attention: *because I fucking said so.* You three all fucked with me and mine, and I get it—you didn't want to. But you all had to because you were vulnerable to other people giving you orders. You three work together, and that ends today."

They all stared at him.

"Well, fine, it ends in a month. Next full moon. Close enough." He glanced at Tyson. "Given that you were planning on taking my place, I assume you don't mind sucking dick, do you?"

Tyson blinked.

"Perfect." Anders turned to go. "Just keep your noses clean for the next four weeks and form a proper pack." He snapped his fingers. "And that's that."

"Why would you help me?" Tyson asked. It was not the confident, careless voice he'd had the last time they'd spoken. The confusion seemed honest, though Anders knew better than to assume it really was.

"I'd say 'enemy of my enemy,'" Anders said, "but the truth is, I just want you somewhere I know. These two?" He gestured to David and Ethan. "They know the game. Better than that, they don't want to play it. I want you benched." He shook his head. "Scratch that. You already owe me for what you did to Curtis. I want you benched and owing me twice." He smiled. "There. That honest enough?"

Tyson nodded.

"A month, guys," Anders said, heading for the tree. "Keep your heads down, and you'll make it."

"Anders." It was David.

Anders paused, turning.

"Thank you," David said. Anders could only imagine what it had cost David to say that.

Anders grinned. "Hey, it's time to cash out."

David's smile would have sent chills down Anders's spine, had he any secrets he'd entrusted to David. As it was, he found himself smiling right back. The Families, the bloodsuckers…Their lives were going to erupt into some serious chaos about a month from now, all thanks to the pairing of sex and wrath.

My work here is done.

Anders stepped into the shadow and vanished.

Luc looked down at the small white invitation and tapped his finger against it. At least they'd had three nights' respite before it had shown up. Curtis had only left the house once in that time and hadn't spoken to any of them when he'd come back, except for Eli. When Luc asked, Eli said Curtis had only asked him for help with healing.

He hadn't even gone for a run yet.

"How is he?" Anders asked.

Luc opened his mouth to answer, but Curtis's voice came from the stairwell.

"I'm fine."

They both turned.

If he allowed himself the pride, Luc had to admit he'd done another fine job. The suit Curtis wore was black this time, though he'd ordered a shirt the same color of gray as a wizard's robes in moot to go with it. It had a far more modern cut than the last, showing off both his shoulders and his trim waist, and the black tie was held in place with a simple golden pin. The heirloom cufflinks were in place. Curtis had bathed, and he looked fresh and replenished. His eyes had even healed over the last four days due to a combination of Curtis's own magic and Eli's healing spirits. Curtis looked calm, collected, and handsome.

And beneath it all, Luc could feel the trembling uncertainty and emotional turmoil through their bond.

"You're sure you wish to come?" Luc asked again.

Curtis laughed. "If I remember the rules from last time, it takes three."

Luc smiled. "It does."

"I suppose Eli could go?" Curtis said.

"I don't think we want anyone to know Eli had anything to do with any of this," Luc said.

"Where is he?" Curtis asked.

"He's in his room. He said he needed to work on something."

"Almost ready," Anders said. Luc looked at him and watched as the demon's rough edges began to smooth into the classier, more elegant form. Luc stopped him, putting a hand on his arm.

"Don't," he said.

Anders blinked in surprise, but the changes undid themselves. His hair curled again. The five o'clock shadow returned.

"This time," Luc said. "We come as we are."

"Shiny," Curtis said. "Let's be bad guys."

They both stared at him.

"That's it. No more kisses until we have a marathon session with my DVDs." Curtis shook his head. "I'm serious."

Luc exchanged a glance with Anders, who shrugged.

"Can I change into jeans, then, if we're all about being ourselves?" Anders asked. The demon wore a suit similar to Curtis's and Luc's, though Anders's shirt was a rich orange to Luc's wine red.

"Not that much," Luc said.

Anders rolled his eyes.

"If it's all the same to you," Curtis said, "after this one, how about we don't go to another *séance* for, oh, let's say…ever?"

Luc straightened Curtis's collar a fraction, then met his gaze. "I can't promise that. And I'm sorry this is happening so soon. But I can certainly make it wait a good long time. There are some benefits to vampire politics. We rarely rush."

"I'll take it," Curtis said. He sounded tired.

Luc stepped back. "We should go."

"The sooner we get there, the sooner we can leave," Anders said.

"That's the spirit," Curtis said.

Luc couldn't help but agree.

Most of the faces were the same, though, of course, there were now only the three other coteries apart from Luc's own. From the nine vampires gathered, he saw Denis first, then Étienne, and, finally, the Lady Markham. Catharine approached him and bowed. It was a deep, respectful bow, and Luc returned it in kind, matching the depth and time. It was more than he owed her, strictly speaking. He saw she noticed, and though she gave him a bemused smile, she said nothing.

"You remember Anna," Catharine said, nodding to the woman on her right. Anna bowed, deeper than Catharine had done, as was fitting. Luc's bow in return was shallower, not much more than a tilt of his head, but he made sure to hold it a few seconds longer than was strictly necessary. If Anna was surprised by the extra courtesy, she didn't let it show.

"And may I also present Jennifer," Catharine said. "She will be new to my coterie. This is her first *séance*."

Luc was surprised. For a *séance*, a vampire brought the two next strongest members of the coterie, or the most levelheaded, or some other combination that would lend itself to the ever-shifting game of vampire politics, but a vampire not yet bound to a coterie? Even if this Jennifer was spoken for and protected by Catharine, it was unheard of to bring her to a *séance*. He regarded the second woman, intrigued. Her long chestnut hair was pulled back in a simple braid that was elegant, if understated. She had hazel eyes and a simple prettiness. Her dress was a very pale pink, which she had accented with gold for the most part, though around her neck she wore a beautiful antique cameo with the profile of a cat instead of a face.

She bowed. "It is such a pleasure to meet you."

Luc froze. Between the cat pendant and her voice, he figured it out. It took all his effort not to react. Her voice was different now that she'd healed. Luc assumed that process had taken more blood than he could imagine, given how damaged the woman had sounded. The blurred gurgle was gone, and her skin was unblemished. He met her gaze once she rose from her bow, and he saw she understood he recognized her.

Lavoie. With Renard gone, his control over her would have ended. Catharine must have wasted no time in going to Lavoie, and now she would have a warlock in her coterie.

He wondered how many "brutes" had gone missing in recent days.

Vampire politics, he thought. But he had to admire Catharine's swiftness. She did indeed like to gather the unique.

"It is lovely to meet you, too," Luc said. He took Lavoie's hand and brought it to his lips. He introduced her to Curtis and Anders. Both men bowed in turn.

Luc moved through the paces of greeting Denis and Étienne—
they had brought the same companions as before—and then, when all
the niceties had been seen to, it was Catharine who raised her hand.

The room fell silent.

"We are here, tonight, to welcome our new *Duc*," she said. "And it
is tradition for us to pay our respect to the former *Duc*, Mathieu Renard.
The latter, I would suggest, might not take long at all."

Denis cracked a small smile. Étienne actually laughed out loud.

Catharine tapped her lips with one perfect finger. "Perhaps the
less said, the better." She turned to Luc. "We welcome you, *Duc* Luc
Lévesque. I have been given permission to place you in the *lignage*
by the court in Quebec, in the name of the *Reine* of France, as he who
defeated the previous *Duc* in fair combat as none here contest. May
your rule last the nights eternal, and may we all know a peace we have
not seen in a great deal of time."

Luc nodded. "I hope so. It is also tradition that I offer all those
who wish to challenge my position a chance to do so, I believe."

No one spoke.

"Well," Luc said. "Frankly, I shall do my best to leave you all be.
I am not one who desires more than I have. As long as you all maintain
your positions and your coteries, I pledge not to interfere. I have only
one request."

Denis and Étienne eyed him warily, but Catharine simply waited.

"Lone vampires, those without a coterie of their own. I would
prefer they not be abused. I have a hope to find a solution to their
problem that doesn't involve more destruction."

Denis blinked but didn't seem unwelcome to the idea. Catharine
actively smiled. But Étienne looked discomforted.

Well, Luc thought. *It didn't take too long for me to upset someone,
did it?*

"And feeding?" Étienne asked. Luc knew what he meant, of
course. There could be only one interpretation of the question.

"I would not interfere where I am not needed. I will say senseless
death is to be avoided," Luc said, and he felt a surge of relief come
from Curtis. He resisted the urge to look at him, knowing full well what
the other vampires referred to as "senseless" would not line up with
Curtis's interpretations. Here was another case where he did not intend

to disabuse Curtis of his illusions. Instead, Luc regarded each of the other vampires in turn.

"As always, we seek to cause none to look for us. I would also ask that you make no trouble with those who make no trouble for us. Leave the werewolves alone, and also those who can speak with the spirits. Understand, I don't speak of delivering justice, of course," he said this as he met Catharine's gaze, and she dipped her head slightly in understanding. "But I put it to you all to counsel your own coteries. Keep your own peace, and I won't have to do it for you."

He didn't think he could say it plainer than that.

"Now," Luc said. "Shall we relax and enjoy an evening of each other's company?"

"Ignis," Curtis said. All heads turned as the candles throughout the room lit as one.

Luc looked at him. Curtis gave a little shrug. "It's tradition," he said.

Luc smiled.

The groups began to mingle. To his surprise, Luc saw Curtis head over to speak with Catharine. Once again he was impressed with the young man's bearing and comportment. In another time, Luc had no doubt Curtis could have been an aristocrat.

"So." Anders's voice pulled him out of the reverie. "Can we talk about the rhyme?"

Luc turned to him, confused. "Pardon?"

"Seriously? You're the *Duc* now." Anders was grinning.

"Yes," Luc said.

"*Duc* Luc." Anders's grin grew. "That's…awesome."

"Anders."

"*Duc* Luc." Anders snorted. "Luc the *Duc*."

"Anders."

"Oh, even better: Lucky Ducky."

"I *can* have you killed."

"Sure thing, Mr. Quack."

EPILOGUE

W ell?" Curtis asked.
Luc shared a glance with Anders. The vampire wasn't sure what to say. Curtis had come to both of them shortly after Luc had woken, Eli in tow, and had told them he had a surprise to show them. The four of them had climbed into Curtis's new car, a hybrid that had apparently shown up that day, courtesy of the Families.

"It's a nice car," Luc said.

"What? Oh, no. That's not the surprise." Curtis's smile was infectious.

"I don't like surprises," Anders groused from the backseat.

"I think you'll like this one," Eli said. Anders grunted, and Luc could tell the demon was even less pleased Eli was in on the surprise. Eli and Curtis had been thick as thieves for days, even though Eli was planning to leave soon. Luc had been as surprised as Anders, given how Eli and Curtis hadn't seen eye to eye on almost anything, but he wasn't going to complain. Curtis was almost like his usual self again.

They drove from their home in Riverside to a different part of the river. When Curtis pulled the car to a halt and parked, he grinned at both of them and then climbed out, walking out onto the sloping grass.

Luc followed.

Curtis raised his arms and asked them what they thought.

"I'm not sure what I'm looking at," Luc admitted. Curtis's surprise didn't appear to be anything more than a big field beside the river.

"It's grass," Anders said. He pointed.

"Yes, I can see that," Luc said.

"Well, you seemed confused, ducky."

Luc bristled.

"It's not just grass," Curtis said, interrupting. "It's a lot. And it's going to be our lot."

Luc and Anders turned to look at Curtis.

"Our lot," Luc repeated.

"For our new house," Curtis said.

Anders opened his mouth, then closed it.

Eli nudged Curtis's shoulder. "Speechless demon. Well done."

"New house?" Luc said.

"Not just a house, a chantry," Curtis said, speaking faster. He was grinning. Luc shook his head, unsure of what that meant. Curtis added, "That's a magic house that's been handed down for generations."

"You're building a house that's been handed down for generations?" Anders said, frowning.

"What?" Curtis blinked. "No. What I mean is, I'm going to work on it every step of the way. I've told the contractors that I want to inspect everything at every step, and that my uncle is an ultra-orthodox type, so he wants to bless the house a lot." He waited, but Luc could see Curtis was still waiting for him to get the point. "Guys, I can protect this house from the inside out."

Luc started to see why he was so excited. "No more letter bombs."

Curtis nodded. "No more letter bombs. No more demon attacks. I can work wards into every brick, every beam, every freaking *tile* if I want to. It'll take time. I'll have to sell the Riverside house when we're done, but that'll pay off this place completely, and I'll be more or less back where I started financially." He grinned. "And you'll have more room in a basement if it's designed for you from step one."

Luc smiled. "That's kind of you. You did all this yourself?"

Curtis smiled. "Eli helped me pick the lot. Apparently, there are some friendly spirits who don't mind us moving in."

"It's only polite to ask," Eli said.

Anders was smiling. "I get a bigger bedroom?"

Curtis laughed. "I've got the blueprints back home. I'll show you both. It was a good design to begin with, but I tweaked it for us."

"When did you start all this?" Luc asked.

Curtis exhaled. "After my car blew up. Or a little before, actually. Mackenzie's house is a chantry, and it's basically a magical fortress." He paused a few seconds, obviously thinking about something, then shook his head and continued. "I'm tired of feeling vulnerable in my own house. It's not designed to protect us. I can only do so much with wards, and I'm only one person."

"It was your parents' home," Luc said. He reached out and took Curtis's hand, squeezing.

Curtis squeezed back. "I know. And I did think about that. But... they're gone. What they'd want for me..." He paused again and swallowed. "They'd want me to be safe." He shrugged. "Look, I'm lucky. They left me a lot of money and no mortgage. The house we live in is free and clear, and it's in an expensive part of the city. I can sell up. This isn't as high class as Riverside, so that means more space, more privacy for each of us, and I can magic this place up like nobody's business." Curtis was grinning. "And after all, a *Duc* needs his palace."

"Walk me through it," Anders said. The demon was smiling, and it was obvious he'd caught Curtis's infectious excitement.

"Sure," Curtis said, and he started walking and pointing. The two only took a few steps before Curtis pointed out the row of trees, tall enough to cast impressive natural shadows, even on cloudier days. Anders grunted in agreement.

"What do you think?' Eli asked, coming to stand beside Luc.

"It's a beautiful spot," Luc said. "We're still in the city, but it's definitely more private. It's a good choice."

Eli nodded. "And you're relieved that Curtis doesn't feel like he's walking away from his childhood."

Luc regarded him. "That's true."

Eli smiled. "Curtis is excited to have a place of his own. And I think Anders is considering bringing someone here to...uh...break the place in before the concrete is even poured." Eli rubbed his temples. "No offense, but I'm really looking forward to switching off this pipeline into your heads. Doesn't it drive you crazy?"

"It's not like that for us," Luc said. "I can sense how they feel sometimes, but that's it. It's probably your own gift with spirit and communication, bolstered by the triad—or quad, I suppose—that's causing your insight."

Eli exhaled. "Ah."

They stood quietly for a moment, listening to the distant chatter of Curtis and Anders. Curtis was gesturing to the river. Anders threw one arm around the younger man's shoulders.

"When do you leave?" Luc asked.

Eli gave him a sideways glance. "I thought you couldn't read my mind?"

Luc smiled. "I don't have to."

"Tomorrow," Eli admitted. "First light. Not that I'm not grateful, but it's time to go. My brothers are worried, and my mother. I'll need to explain all this to them..." He gestured to the field in front of him, though Luc knew what he meant.

"If you have any trouble with any vampires in your area, let me know," Luc said. "You have my number. And my protection."

Eli chuckled. "See, now that's going to be very hard to explain to my mother."

"I have already told the others." Luc smiled, showing a hint of fang. "A more formal declaration will come. Maybe you could explain it to your mother as a treaty."

Eli laughed. "That *really* wouldn't help."

"I suppose not."

They stood quietly for a moment. Luc could hear Curtis's voice from farther in the field, excitedly explaining his plan to build a small greenhouse for growing some of the plants that he'd learned were useful in earth magics.

It was, on the whole of it, a good plan, Luc thought.

He turned back to Eli, who surprised him by holding out his hand. After a second, Luc took it. They shook.

"Thank you," they said, at the same time. Luc's eyebrows rose. Eli laughed.

"For killing Renard," Eli said. "You didn't have to help me."

"Ah," Luc said. "I was about to say much the same thing."

"You're a pretty good guy," Eli said. "For a vampire."

"We all have our flaws." Luc's smile grew. "But I'm sure we'll overcome them."

Curtis and Anders returned.

"Ready to go?" Curtis asked.

"Ready to move in," Luc said.

Curtis's smile was wide. "Well, it's going to take time."

Luc looked at the piece of land and imagined a home there. He smiled again, his fangs extending just a little. He realized he was very much looking forward to this. Before he could stop himself, he spoke.

"Pardon?" Curtis said. The other three had already started for the car. The young man paused, looking back at him.

"Freedom," Luc repeated.

Curtis nodded. Anders smiled. Even Eli looked relaxed. Luc had no illusions about their safety being absolute now that Renard was gone. There would always be enemies. He looked at Eli again and considered for the first time that he might also find allies.

Or even friends.

"Freedom," Luc said again, forcing a deep breath of air into his lungs.

It smelled wonderful.

About the Author

'Nathan Burgoine grew up a reader and studied literature in university while making a living as a bookseller. His first published short story was "Heart" in the collection *Fool for Love: New Gay Fiction*. Since then, he has had dozens of short stories published, including Bold Strokes titles *Men in Love*, *Boys of Summer*, and *Night Shadows*, as well as *This Is How You Die* (the second Machine of Death anthology). There are more stories with the characters from *Triad Blood* included in the Bold Strokes Books erotica anthologies *Blood Sacraments*, *Wings*, *Erotica Exotica*, and *Raising Hell*. 'Nathan's standalone erotic short fiction can also be found in *Threesome: Him, Him and Me*, *The Biggest Lover*, and the Lambda Literary finalist *Tented*. His nonfiction pieces have appeared in A *Family By Any Other Name*, *I Like It Like That*, and *5x5 Literary Magazine*.

'Nathan's first novel, *Light*, was a finalist for a Lambda Literary Award.

A cat lover, 'Nathan managed to fall in love and marry Daniel, who is a confirmed dog person. Their ongoing "cat or dog" détente ended with the rescue of a six-year-old husky named Coach. They live in Ottawa, Canada, where they mostly play video games, board games, and tabletop RPGs like the geeky nerds they are.

Books Available From Bold Strokes Books

Triad Blood by 'Nathan Burgoine. Cheating tradition, Luc, Anders, and Curtis—vampire, demon, and wizard—form a bond to gain their freedom, but will surviving those they cheated be beyond their combined power? (978-1-62639-587-9)

Death Comes Darkly by David S. Pederson. Can dashing detective Heath Barrington solve the murder of an eccentric millionaire and find love with policeman Alan Keyes, who, despite his lust, harbors feelings of guilt and shame? (978-1-62639-625-8)

Men in Love: M/M Romance, edited by Jerry L. Wheeler. Love stories between men, from first blush to wedding bells and beyond. (978-1-62639-7361)

Slaves of Greenworld by David Holly. On the planet Greenworld, the amnesiac Dove must cope with intrigues, alien monsters, and a growing slave revolt, while reveling in homoerotic sexual intimacy with his own slave Raret. (978-1-62639-623-4)

Final Departure by Steve Pickens. What do you do when an unexpected body interrupts the worst day of your life? (978-1-62639-536-7)

Love on the Jersey Shore by Richard Natale. Two working-class cousins help one another navigate the choppy waters of sexual chemistry and true love. (978-1-62639-550-3)

Night Sweats by Tom Cardamone. These stories are as gripping as the hand on your throat. (978-1-62639-572-5)

Soul's Blood by Stephen Graham King. After receiving a summons from a love long past, Keene and his associates, Lexa-Blue and the sentient ship Maverick Heart, are plunged into turmoil on a planet poised for war. (978-1-62639-508-4)

Corpus Calvin by David Swatling. Cloverkist Inn may be haunted, but a ghost materializes from Jason Dekker's past, and Calvin's canine instinct kicks in to protect a young boy from mortal danger. (978-1-62639-428-5)

Brothers by Ralph Josiah Bardsley. Blood is thicker than water, but you can drown in either. Jamus Cork and Sean Malloy struggle against tradition to find love in the Irish enclave of South Boston. (978-1-62639-538-1)

Every Unworthy Thing by Jon Wilson. Gang wars, racial tensions, a kidnapped girl, and a lone PI! What could go wrong? (978-1-62639-514-5)

Puppet Boy by Christian Baines. Budding filmmaker Eric can't stop thinking about the handsome young actor that's transferred to his class. Could Julien be his muse? Even his first boyfriend? Or something far more sinister? (978-1-62639-510-7)

The Prophecy by Jerry Rabushka. Religion and revolution threaten to bring an ancient civilization to its knees…unless love does it first. (978-1-62639-440-7)

Heart of the Liliko'i by Dena Hankins. Secrets, sabotage, and grisly human remains stall construction on an ancient Hawaiian burial ground, but the sexual connection between Kerala and Ravi keeps building toward a volcanic explosion. (978-1-62639-556-5)

Lethal Elements by Joel Gomez-Dossi. When geologist Tom Burrell is hired to perform mineral studies in the Adirondack Mountains, he finds himself lost in the wilderness and being chased by a hired gun. (978-1-62639-368-4)

The Heart's Eternal Desire by David Holly. Sinister conspiracies threaten Seaton French and his lover, Dusty Marley, and only by tracking the source of the conspiracy can Seaton and Dusty hold true to the heart's eternal desire. (978-1-62639-412-4)

The Orion Mask by Greg Herren. After his father's death, Heath comes to Louisiana to meet his mother's family and learn the truth about her death—but some secrets can prove deadly. (978-1-62639-355-4)

CPSIA information can be obtained
at www.ICGtesting.com
Printed in the USA
LVOW11s1549250717
542590LV00001B/231/P